D0566330

Just What Kind of Mother Are You?

Just What Kind of Mother Are You?

Paula Daly

Grove Press
New York

First published in Great Britain in 2013 by Bantam Press an imprint of Transworld Publishers

Printed in the United States of America

ISBN: 978-0-8021-2162-2

Grove Press
an imprint of Grove/Atlantic, Inc.
154 West 14th Street
New York, NY 10011

For Jimmy

He arrives with time to spare. Reverse-parking, he gets out and the cold hits him. Slapping him hard in the face and stinging his skin. He smells good. Expensive.

He's parked a few hundred yards from the school at the viewing point. On a clear day there's an uninterrupted vista across the lake, over to the mountains beyond. In better weather there'd be an ice-cream van, Japanese tourists taking photographs. Not today, though. Not with the clouds so low in the sky, and not with the autumn darkness fast approaching.

The lake water reflects the trees. It's a muddy, coffee-coloured brown – soon to be slate-grey – and the air is still.

Maybe he should get a dog, he ponders briefly. Something friendly – a spaniel perhaps, or one of those white, fluffy things. Kids love dogs, don't they? It might just be worth a go.

He checks for signs of life but for the moment he's still alone. It's just him, watching. Sizing up the scene, weighing up the risks.

Risk assessment is part of his job. Mostly he just makes stuff up, putting down on paper whatever the fire-safety officer wants to read. Along with a few extras, though, enough to give the impression that he actually gives a shit.

This is different. This, he really does need to look at carefully. Because he knows he can be rash. He knows he can be lacking in the necessary thoroughness and can end up paying for it later. He can't afford for that to happen now. Not with this.

He checks his watch. Tons of time before he's expected elsewhere. That's the great thing about his job, it leaves plenty of time for this other . . . interest.

That's how he's thinking of it at the moment, just an interest. Nothing serious. He's figuring things out, seeing if he likes it. Kind of the way one might do with evening classes.

'Come along for a couple of sessions of calligraphy before you pay in full.'

'Conversational French might not be for you, after all.'

He knows his interest can wane quickly, but that's what makes him successful, because, don't all successful people have a low boredom threshold?

As a child he'd been told he couldn't stick at anything, couldn't sit still and focus on one thing at a time. He can still be like that so he needs to check before committing. He wants to be sure. He wants to be certain he's going to follow it through before taking the first step.

He checks his watch. Three forty. They'll be here soon – the first few making their way home.

He gets back inside his car and waits.

His plan is to gauge his reaction. See if what he thinks will happen does happen. Then he'll know. Then he'll know for sure.

When he spots them his pulse flickers. Each is coatless, hatless, wearing shoes inappropriate for the season. The first to pass in front of the car are a couple of girls. Dyed hair, sulky expressions, big, shapeless legs.

No, he thinks, that's not it. That's not what he wants at all.

Next are two groups of boys. Fourteen- or fifteen-year-olds. Slapping each other across the backs of heads, laughing at nothing. One of them glances his way before sticking two fingers up. This makes him laugh. Harmless enough, he thinks.

That's when he sees her.

She's alone. Walking purposefully. Spine erect, with short, neat steps. She's around twelve – though she could be older. She might just be young-looking for her age.

She passes in front of the car and again his pulse quickens. He feels a shiver of pleasure flash through him as, momentarily, she slows. She's hanging back from the group of boys, unsure of what to do. He watches rapt as her face changes, watches as it takes on a determined expression, and at once she makes the bold decision to overtake.

Half skipping, half running, she flits off the pavement and picks up her pace. She's fawn-like! he thinks, totally delighted by her. Her slim ankles are moving quickly as she pulls away from the group.

He glances down and sees that his palms are wet. And it's then that he knows for sure. Smiling, he realizes he had not been wrong to come here.

He drops down the sun visor and checks his reflection. He looks exactly the same as he did ten minutes ago, but marvels at how different he feels. It's as if all the pieces have clicked together, and he understands, perhaps for the first time, what people mean when they say, 'It just feels right.'

Turning the ignition, he flicks on the heated seat and, still smiling, heads towards Windermere.

DAY ONE

Tuesday

1

I WAKE UP MORE tired than when I went to sleep. I've had five and a half hours and, after hitting the snooze button for the third time, I lift my head.

It's the kind of tired I'm beyond finding reasons for. You know the sort, you first notice it and you think: What is *wrong* with me? I must have some crazy blood disorder. Or, worse, I must have contracted something really awful because no one can feel this tired. Can they?

But I've had the checks. The blood tests came back normal. My GP – a wily old guy who I'm guessing has had more than his fair share of women in complaining of being exhausted all the time – broke the news to me with a wry smile. 'Sorry, Lisa,' he said, 'but this thing you're suffering from . . . it's just life.'

Often I feel like I'm in a giant social experiment. As if some bright spark decided to get all the women of the western world together as part of one big study: Let's educate them! Let's give them good, meaningful work to do! Then let's see what happens when they procreate. Let's watch it *blow*!

You think I'm moaning.

I think I'm moaning.

That's the worst part. I can't even complain without feeling guilty, because I've got everything. Everything a person could possibly want. Should want. And I do. I want all of it.

Where did I go to? I think, looking in the bathroom mirror as

I brush my teeth. I used to be so nice. I used to have time for people. Now I'm in a state of constant tired irritation and I hate it.

I'm overwhelmed. That's the only word I can use to describe myself. That's what it will say on my headstone.

Lisa Kallisto: she was just so overwhelmed.

I'm the first up. Sometimes my eldest gets downstairs before me if her hair is going through an unruly patch, if she needs to devote extra attention to it. But, usually, at six forty, it's just me.

'Get up an hour earlier,' the magazines say. Embrace the quiet time, the time before the frenzy starts. Plan your day, make your tick list, drink your hot water with a slice of lemon in it. Detox and you *will* feel the benefits.

I get the coffee going and start scooping kibble into bowls. We have three dogs, all Staffordshire Bull Terrier crosses – not what I'd pick if I had the choice, but they're good dogs. Clean, good-natured, good with the kids, and as I let them out of the utility room where they sleep, they fire past me in a rush of giddiness, sit by their bowls, expectant. 'Go ahead,' I say, and they dive in.

Walking them in the morning is generally my husband's job, because Joe often works late. You're imagining him in an office, tie pulled loose, hair ruffled, deadline looming? I do it myself sometimes. Never thought I'd marry a taxi driver. Especially one with 'Joe le Taxi' painted on the side of his people carrier in great big silver letters.

Joe did an airport run down to Heathrow last night. Some Arabs offered him double the usual fare if he acted as their personal driver for the time they were here in the Lakes. They wanted the usual: trips to Wordsworth's house, Beatrix Potter's farm, boat rides on Ullswater, Kendal Mint Cake. I heard him roll into bed around four, round about the time I'd woken up panicking that I'd forgotten to post a

Congratulations on Your New Baby card out to one of my kennel girls.

'Get a good tip?' I mumbled, my face pushed hard into the pillow, as Joe wriggled in next to me, smelling of beer.

He always keeps a couple of cans in the car if he's on a late. Then, he says, he can get straight off to sleep the minute he climbs into bed. I'm sick of telling him it is not good – taxi driver swigging away at the wheel – but he's beyond stubborn.

'Tipped me a hundred quid,' he answered, giving my buttock a quick squeeze, '. . . and I'm planning on spending the lot on new underwear for you.'

'You mean for you.' I yawned. 'I need a new exhaust.'

For the past eight years I've bought new underwear for Joe's birthday – underwear for me. Every year I question him – 'What do you want?' – and every year he stares at me, like, *Do you really need to ask?*

Once he said he wanted to shop for it himself. But we did away with that arrangement when he came home with *red* everything. Including red fishnets. 'Best if I get it from now on, Joe,' I'd said to him, and he'd said, 'Okay,' kind of crestfallen. Though I think he knew deep down I was never going to go for that trashy get-up.

The dogs finish eating and trot to the back door as a pack. My favourite is Ruthie. She's a Staffy crossed with either a Red Setter or a Hungarian Vizsla. She's got the brindle coat of a Staffy, but instead of the usual chocolate, autumn browns, she's had her colour turned up in a mad show of russet and henna, copper and bronze. And she has these long, long legs, which make her look as if she's swapped bodies with another dog.

Ruthie came to the shelter five years ago in a batch of unwanted puppies. A bitch kept for breeding got loose for the day and had a litter of seven. Ruthie was the one we couldn't home, so, as is often the way, she ended up at ours.

Luckily, Joe is kind of a natural. He's got that calm authority dogs seem to gravitate towards. He understands dogs in the same way some people understand numbers, or circuit boards. Even if we have a problem case and I bring it home, Joe's zen effect usually means the dog is settled in by bedtime.

I open up the back door and the dogs rush out, just as the cold and the cats rush in. Winter's here early. Snow had been predicted and there's been a heavy fall overnight. The chill seeps into my bones in an instant. I hear the cry of an animal carry across the valley on the thin air and shut the door quickly.

The coffee's ready and I pour myself what the coffee houses call an Americano – espresso topped up with hot water; my cup holds almost a pint. I hear movement coming from upstairs, small feet on floorboards, the toilet flushing, a nose blowing, and I rally myself. I read somewhere that children measure their self-worth directly from the look on your face and was horrified to realize I'd been greeting my children looking kind of vague. This is because I have a hundred and one things going through my head at any given moment – but they don't know that. I'm sure they must have spent the first few years of their lives wondering if I actually recognized them at all. I feel dreadful about it now, so often I go a bit too much the other way. My youngest son laps up the attention. But my older two, particularly Sally, who's thirteen, have taken to eyeing me suspiciously.

She sits at the kitchen table now, full lips swollen from sleep, hair pulled up high in a ponytail to be dealt with later. Next to her is her iPod Touch.

She spoons Rice Krispies into her mouth while at the same time shooing a cat away with her elbow. I watch her from over by the kettle. She's dark like Joe. They all are. Ask Joe where he's from and he'll tell you Ambleside. Most people assume he's Italian. He's not. Kallisto is a South American name – Brazilian

– though we reckon Joe's of Argentinian descent. He has dark hair, dark eyes and dark skin. As do the kids. Their hair is shiny-black and straight, and they have Joe's absurdly long eyelashes. Naturally, Sally thinks she's ugly. She thinks all her friends are beautiful and she is not. This is something we're working on, but of course she distrusts everything I say, because I'm her mother. And what the hell would I know about anything?

'PE today?' I ask.

'No. Tech.'

'What are you making?'

I'm never really sure what Tech is. It seems to encompass woodwork, sewing, design, pretty much everything—

Sally puts her spoon down. Looks at me as if to say, *You are joking?*

'We're doing food tech,' she says, keeping her eyes fixed on mine. '*Food* tech, as in cooking. Don't say you forgot to get the ingredients. The list,' she says, pointing towards the fridge, 'is right there.'

'Shit,' I reply quietly. 'I completely forgot. What do you need?'

Sally gets up, scrapes her chair across the flagstone floor. All the while I'm thinking, *Please be flapjacks, please be flapjacks.* I have oats and can cobble together the rest. Or crumble. Fruit crumble would be good. She can use those apples up, throw in a bit of something else from the bottom of the fruit bowl. It'll be fine.

Sally grabs the piece of paper. 'Pizza.'

'No,' I reply, gutted. 'Really?'

'We need ready-made tomato sauce, mozzarella, something for the base, like a baguette or pitta bread, and our own choice of toppings. I thought I'd have spicy chicken and green pepper. But I don't mind having tuna, if that's all we've got.'

We have none of those ingredients. Not one.

I close my eyes. 'Why didn't you remind me about this? I

specifically told you to remind me. Why didn't you remind me when I told—'

'I did.'

'When?'

'After school on Friday,' she says. 'You were on the laptop.'

That's right, I remember. I was trying to order a delivery of logs and the website wouldn't accept my credit-card details. And I lost my temper.

Sally's face now changes from the satisfaction of being in the right to that of mild panic. 'Tech is third period,' she says, her voice rising. 'How am I supposed to get the stuff by third period?'

'Can you tell the teacher your mother forgot?'

'I told her that last time, and she said, "No more chances." She said it was just as much my responsibility. She said I could go to the shop myself for the ingredients if I needed to.'

'Did you explain to her that we live in Troutbeck?'

'No, because that would have been argumentative.'

We stand there looking at one another, me hoping an answer will magic itself into my head and Sally wishing that I was better at all of this.

'Leave it with me. I'll sort it,' I say.

I'm thinking about the day ahead, pouring apple juice into glasses, as the two boys sit down at the kitchen table. We've got fourteen dogs in the shelter at present and eleven cats. The dogs I've got space for, but one of my most dependable cat fosterers is going in for a hysterectomy tomorrow, so I need to take delivery of an extra four cats this morning. And there are two dogs arriving from Northern Ireland as well that I'd clean forgotten about.

The boys are arguing over who is having the last of the Rice Krispies because neither of them wants the stale Fruit & Fibre that's been at the back of the cupboard since summer. James is eleven and Sam is seven. They're both skinny with big brown eyes and no common sense. They're the type of boys Italian mothers slap across the head a lot. Kind boys, but silly, and I love them fiercely.

I'm resigning myself to the fact that I'll have to wake up Joe and send him out for the pizza ingredients when the phone rings. It's seven twenty, so whoever it is does not have good news. Nobody rings me at seven twenty with good news.

'Lisa, it's Kate.'

'Kate,' I say. 'What's happened? Is something wrong?'

'Yes – no – well, sort of. Listen, sorry to ring so early but I wanted to catch you while you still had the boys at home.'

Kate Riverty is my friend of around five years. She has two children, who are similar in age to both Sally, my eldest, and Sam, my youngest.

'It's nothing major. I just thought you'd want to know so that you can address it before it gets out of hand.' I stay silent, let her go on. 'It's just that Fergus came home last week saying that he would need money for school, and I didn't really think much of it at the time. You know how it is . . . they always need money for something. So I gave it to him, and it was only when I was chatting to Guy about it last night and he said that Fergus had asked *him* for money also that we thought to question him.'

I have no idea where this is going, but that's not unusual when speaking to Kate, so I try to sound interested. 'So what do you think he wants it for?'

I'm guessing she's going to tell me the teachers have set up a tuck shop. Something she's not in agreement with. Something she's against *on principle.*

'It's Sam,' Kate says bluntly. 'He's been charging children to play with him.'

'He's what?'

'Children are paying him money to play with him. I'm not sure exactly how much because . . . he seems to have a type of sliding scale in operation. Fergus is a little upset about the whole thing, actually. He's found out he's been paying substantially more than some of the other boys.'

I turn around and look at Sam. He is wearing Mario Kart pyjamas and is feeding milk directly from his cereal spoon to our old ginger tom.

I exhale.

'You're not cross that I rang, are you, Lisa?'

I wince. Kate's trying to sound nice, but her voice has taken on a shrill quality.

'Not at all,' I say. 'I'm glad you did.'

'It's just that if it were me . . . if it were one of *mine* doing this – well, I'd want to know.'

'Absolutely,' I tell her. Then I give her my standard line, the line that I seem to be giving out to anyone and everyone regardless of the situation I'm faced with: 'Leave it with me,' I say firmly. 'I'll sort it.'

Just before she hangs up I hear Kate say, 'The girls okay?', and I reply, 'What? Yes, fine,' because I'm flustered, and I'm embarrassed, and I'm not really thinking straight. I'm wondering how I'm going to tackle the problem of Sam's new enterprise.

But when I put the phone down, I think, *Girls?* What does she mean by that? Then I dismiss it, because Kate often gets me on the back foot. Confuses me with what she's really trying to say. It's something I've had to get used to.

2

WE LIVE IN A draughty rented house in Troutbeck.

Troutbeck sits to the east of Lake Windermere and is the kind of place you find in books entitled 'Quaint English Villages'. There are supposed to be two hundred and sixty houses in Troutbeck, but I don't know where all those people are hiding because I hardly see any of them.

Of course, a lot are holiday lets. And many of the cottages are home to people who've retired here – so they're not always part of the usual day-to-day goings-on, I suppose because they don't have children living in the village. Or grandchildren they pick up from school a couple of days a week. Or take to swimming lessons, or to the park.

I used to think it bordered on tragedy the way families lose touch, the way people sever ties, putting a pretty place to live above being together. But now I realize that's just how people like it. They don't always want to be together.

My mother has a flat in Windermere village. She and my father never married – we were his second family, his *other* family – and because of something shitty that happened when I was a kid, something that we don't ever talk about, we never see him. I'd ring my mother to pick up the ingredients Sally needs for cookery, but she doesn't drive, so I've asked Joe to do it. Poor thing, he's exhausted. He's only had a few hours' sleep, too.

I back the car out with Sam in the front seat next to me and wave to the older two as they wait for the minibus.

I don't know if this is a national thing, or if it's just local to Cumbria, but if you live more than three miles away from the nearest school, or if there's not a suitable pavement to walk upon, your kids are eligible for free transport. And since no proper buses run up here in Troutbeck, this takes the form of a taxi – well, a minibus. (Not Joe. Joe's a one-man band. He generally just carts old ladies to hospital appointments, or garden centres, or to bridge club.)

I could send Sam in a taxi as well if I wanted to, but I have this fear that a rogue driver would steal him away, be on a ferry bound for Zeebrugge before I realized he hadn't made it into school (I've enquired, and the drivers are not CRB-checked). So I drop Sam on my way to the shelter, and it's useful because it's one of the only moments during a normal working day that we get some time together.

We discuss all sorts. Sam's still of an age when he believes in Father Christmas and he thinks of Jesus as having superhero status. To Sam, Jesus has quite obviously got superhero powers, because 'How else could he do all that stuff?'

Sam went through a big Jesus phase last year and kept banging on and on about him. Which I didn't see the harm in. But then I had Joe at the dinner table, hopping mad, slamming his fork down, saying, 'That school is *corrupting* him.'

I negotiate our way down the lane. It's a narrow, badly potholed stretch of track with no passing places. I have to time my departure just right or else I meet the minibus coming the other way. And it's always me that has to reverse, because the driver has a bad neck and can only use his mirrors. In fairness, his vehicle is a lot wider than mine.

Sam has his hat on and his hood pulled up over it because of the car's frigid interior, so he can't hear a word I'm saying. And my exhaust is blowing. It needed replacing a month ago and is getting worse by the day. I sound like a boy racer every time I press on the gas. I ask Sam about school and if there's anything he wants to tell me.

'What?' he says.

'"Pardon,"' I correct.

'Pardon? What?'

'Is there anything going on at school you want to tell me about?'

He shrugs. Looks out the window. Then he turns and tells me excitedly about a child who brought in a lava lamp for Show and Tell. And one, when can we get a lava lamp?, and two, why can he never bring anything in for Show and Tell?

Inwardly, I'm cursing this mother, whoever she is, for giving me something else to do. Show and Tell. Brilliant.

'Show and Tell,' I explain patiently, 'is an American thing. It's like Trick or Treat. English people just don't really do it.'

'Everybody does Trick or Treat except us.'

'No they don't.'

'Yes they do.'

'Anyway,' I say quickly, 'what's this I hear about you making people pay to play with you?'

He doesn't answer. I can't see his face hidden behind the fur of his hood, and now I've got to concentrate because I'm on the main road and it's not been gritted particularly well. A rush job.

I have a momentary flash of panic as I imagine the taxi driver in charge of the kids' minibus, taking a bend too fast and sailing off the edge of the road, down to the valley floor below.

I picture the vehicle as it rolls and rolls, coming to a stop by a John Deere hay baler. The windows of the bus are blown out, and my kids sit there motionless like limp crash-test dummies.

I shiver.

Sam says, in answer to my question about pay for play: 'Pardon?'

'You heard me.'

Reluctantly, he explains, 'I don't make *everyone* pay,' and I can tell he's more disappointed than sorry. Probably thought he could go through life making money in this way, and he can sense by my tone that his venture has come to a premature end.

I turn to him. 'What I don't get is why these kids are willing to pay you. Why are they giving *you* money when they could just as easily play on their own or with somebody else?'

'Dunno,' he says innocently, but then shoots me a mischievous look. One that says, *I know. Are they, like, idiots, or what?*

Five minutes later and we pull up outside school. I look to see if Kate's car is in its usual place by the gate, but she isn't here yet. I do like her, but it does annoy me how she insists on going into school each day. Because really, there is no reason for it.

Her son, Fergus, is almost eight. He's more than capable of removing his coat and shoes, changing into his indoor pumps and finding his way to the classroom. The school has only eighty kids. He's not going to get lost. But Kate's one of those mothers who enjoys chatting with the teacher. She likes to watch Fergus slowly taking off his shoes, rolling her eyes at the other mothers while clapping her hands together, saying, 'Come on, chop chop! Quicksticks! Pass Mummy your boots!' Kate doesn't have a proper job. She and her husband get a steady stream of income from renting holiday cottages. So all Kate has to do when she gets home is put her washing machine on and write thank-you notes to people she doesn't really like.

I'm jealous of Kate's life.

There, I've said it.

It's taken me a while to get to this point. Before, I couldn't admit it. I used to complain to Joe. Blame him in a roundabout way for my having to work full-time, blame him for the fact I had to face every day exhausted, and—

My phone is ringing.

I pull it out of my pocket and see that it's Sally. Perhaps the minibus has not turned up. Maybe the driver's not been able to start the engine in the cold weather.

'Hi, Sal, what's up?'

Sally is crying. Big, choking sobs. She can't get her words out.

'Mum?' I can hear noise in the background, more crying . . . the sounds of traffic. 'Mum . . . something really bad has happened.'

3

DETECTIVE CONSTABLE Joanne Aspinall is almost at the station when she gets the call about the missing girl. Thirteen years old. And not a worldly-wise thirteen either. Joanne wonders if there even is such a thing. I mean, what difference would it make if she were an astute girl? What if *she was* used to being out and about on her own? Would that change anything? Did it make it any less urgent?

Missing's missing. There shouldn't be a difference.

But when Joanne sees the photograph, she shudders. It has to be said, this girl *does* look young for her age. Astonishingly young, in fact. And Joanne has to admit, even if it's only to herself, that the thirteen-year-olds who go gadding about in Wonderbras and tall boots tend to turn up eventually. Usually returning home sorry and sheepish, sad and scared, wishing they'd not put their parents through that anguish. Because all they wanted to do was prove a point.

Joanne had been no different when she was young. Leaving the house, screaming at her mother that she was old enough to take care of herself, desperate to be taken seriously as a grown-up. When really, *grown up* was the last thing she was.

Joanne thinks about the strange confidence that seems to come to girls at this age, and decides that this confidence, this intrepidity, comes later in boys. Round about the sixteen mark. That's when their cockiness is heightened and she starts seeing boys who've never been involved in any kind of trouble before suddenly start making nuisances of themselves.

They'd had a memo in the office just last week. The army was on the lookout for kids whose life could be 'turned around with the right sort of guidance'.

It said: 'They could have a lot to offer the British Army,' and Joanne thought, Yes, I bet they could. The self-preservation instinct is woefully lacking in young lads; they'll happily walk into battle, happily regard themselves infallible, indestructible. No wonder the bloody army wanted them.

After the quick brief on the missing girl, Joanne makes her way to the address. She knows the house. Years ago it used to be the old vicarage, before the church sold it off. Too big and expensive for the clergy to heat.

The family aren't known to the police; not many residents of Troutbeck are. It's not *that* sort of place.

Joanne deals with very few serious criminal offences from within the boundaries of the National Park. It's one of the safest areas to live in Britain. You see the same people every day, so it's hard to hide if you do screw up, if you do shaft someone or do something illegal.

People move here wanting a better life, wanting a better life for their children. So generally they keep their heads down. They do their best not to antagonize their neighbours. They feel privileged to live here and they try their hardest to make sure it remains that way.

But it's not always easy *to* stay here.

House prices are off the scale, and industry is non-existent. So those who move here had better have a good way to earn a living, or else they won't last. Those who come thinking they'll open up a twee coffee shop, florist's or artist's studio get a rude awakening when they can't make the mortgage payments.

Joanne's noticed how newcomers will proudly announce that

they're 'local' after living here for perhaps just a couple of years. As if it's a badge of honour. Joanne can never quite make sense of that. She is a local. Lived here all her life. She's not sure it's something to go on about, though.

Her mother and Auntie Jackie moved to the Lakes from Lancashire back when they were teenagers, to work as chambermaids, and Jackie scoffs at the idea of being accepted as a 'local'.

'Local?' she'll say derisively. 'What do I want to be classed as one of them for? No sense of humour . . .'

Joanne slows the car as she approaches the Rivertys' driveway.

Their daughter is not the type of girl to disappear. Joanne knows that now. No, Lucinda Riverty is not that type at all.

Joanne adjusts her bra and climbs out, thinking that when she was back in uniform, at least she got the clothes for free. Now, trying to find suitable work clothes took up almost as much time as the paperwork. And since her bra size is a cruel 38GG, it's hard to find tops that don't make her look like a barrel.

She zips up her parka, then makes her way up the path, thinking that at least she can ring the doorbell now without being worried about being mistaken for a strippergram.

Not that that was likely to happen here today.

'Mrs Riverty?'

The woman shakes her head. 'I'm her sister, Alexa. Come in, they're all in there.'

Joanne flashes her warrant card, but the woman doesn't look at it. She doesn't ask who Joanne is, because nobody bothers at times like this. They get you in quickly, don't want to lose any time.

They're already beating themselves up for the minutes they've wasted so far. When they knew something was off, something was wrong, when the universe was whispering to them there was trouble.

The woman gestures for Joanne to go along the hallway and to the right. Joanne steps into the vestibule and wipes her feet. She glances ahead of her: muted Farrow & Ball paint colours, seagrass matting on the stairs, a dotting of tasteful black-and-white photos of the kids. Joanne spots a girl of around five dressed as a ballerina holding some tulips and a Dorothy bag, and thinks that this must be Lucinda.

The room is already busy with people, which also happens at times like this. Everyone comes straight over. Every family member, every friend. People turning up to be together, to wait.

Joanne's used to it. She's used to the faces – expectant but confused. Who is this woman in the black parka? What is she here for?

'I'm Detective Constable Aspinall,' Joanne says.

Always best to give her full title instead of using the 'DC'. Women, particularly, don't really know what DC means anyway. Give a member of the public a policewoman in plain clothes and they don't really know what to do with her.

Is she here to console the family? Make tea? Family liaison – is that it? Is she even a real police officer?

They're not sure. Best to tell them who she is and what she's here for right from the get-go.

All eyes move from Joanne to a broken-looking blonde woman sitting in the middle of a sagging, taupe sofa.

This room's for the kids. It houses the old furniture, the stuff that doesn't matter any more, the stuff nobody gets cross about if it's ruined with spilt drinks, with felt-tip pens.

A four-year-old TV is in the corner, and beneath it a stack of game boxes: PlayStation, Wii, Xbox. Joanne knows the names of these things even if she can't correctly distinguish one from the other, not having any kids of her own.

The blonde goes to stand, but Joanne says, 'Please, don't get up. 'Are you Mrs Riverty?', and the woman nods her head, just slightly, spilling the mug of tea she's holding in the process. She hands her tea to the man seated next to her.

Joanne looks to him: 'Mr Riverty?', and he says, 'Guy,' attempting to smile, but he can't make his face work in that way today.

He stands. His eyes are anguished, his face so full of grief. 'Have you come to help us?' he asks, and Joanne says, 'Yes.'

Yes, that's what she's come for. Joanne has come to help.

This is the second missing girl. That's why Joanne was sent straight here. If Lucinda had been the first, these early stages would be covered by a couple of uniforms. But Joanne's department are working with Lancashire on this one, and after a series of screwed-up abduction cases in the south, everyone's on high alert.

Two weeks ago, a young girl had gone missing from Silverdale, just over the border from Cumbria into Lancashire.

Molly Rigg. Another one who looked younger than she was. Another girl who *shouldn't have gone missing*, her boss said.

Molly Rigg turned up at teatime, twenty miles from her home, when she walked into the travel agents in Bowness-on-Windermere.

The November rain was lashing and the place was jam-packed to bursting with people wanting to escape the gloom – perhaps on an all-inclusive to the Dominican Republic. Joanne had seen it advertised in the front window: £355 per person (branded drinks extra).

Molly had been stripped bare from the waist up, and didn't know where she was. No clue as to what town she was in. She'd chosen the travel agents because she thought the staff in there would be 'nice'.

They were.

The manager removed everyone from the shop with the minimum of fuss, while the two Dolly Daydreams manning the front desk got Molly covered up in an assortment of their own clothes. By the time Joanne got there they were clinging on to Molly so fiercely, so protectively, that it was hard for Joanne to get them to let go.

One of the two, Danielle Knox, had told of how she'd glanced up from her flight schedules and seen Molly, standing silently, rainwater pouring down her bare shoulders and young chest, her arms crossed around herself, shivering.

She told of how her mouth fell open as Molly asked her quietly and politely, 'Please can you phone my mum? I need you to get me my mum.'

Molly later said that she had been taken to a bedsit and raped more than once by a man who spoke like the people from *The Darling Buds of May*. Molly's mum was a fan of the series and watched the reruns on ITV3 on Sunday afternoons while Molly did her homework in front of the fire.

Joanne wonders just how much Kate and Guy Riverty know about the case. Or even how much attention they'd paid to poor Molly before they found themselves in this, the very worst of similar situations, with their now-missing daughter, Lucinda.

Kate Riverty asks Joanne if she thinks it could be the same man responsible for both, and Joanne answers with, 'Let's not think that way right now. There's nothing to suggest it's the same person at this stage.'

Which of course she doesn't mean. But Joanne knows that, regardless of the solid performance Mrs Riverty is putting on, no mother is ready to hear such things.

Joanne is also careful not to speculate on whether Lucinda has actually been abducted *or not.*

A child does not return home? Parents assume abduction.

Forget the statistics. Forget the runaways. You go suggesting that their child has not been abducted and you get a meltdown.

Joanne looks around at the frantic faces in the room. She does not want a meltdown.

4

I'VE BEEN SITTING here with my head in my hands for ten minutes? Half an hour? I don't know how long when there's a knock on my car window.

'You okay?' Jessica's mum mouths. I don't know her name, she probably doesn't know mine, but she's the mumsy type that will always stop if she sees someone in distress.

I nod my head at her.

'You're sure?' she persists. Her face is clouded with concern. I must look a real mess.

I nod again, more firmly this time, because I cannot share this with anyone. Not right now, not yet.

She leaves, but not before taking another glance at me, to check that I'm okay – because that's what mothers do. They check. They make doubly sure. They confirm that all is well.

And I had not.

I'd been so caught up in . . . *what* exactly? What had I been doing? Because as I think back to yesterday, I can't come up with anything. Nothing at all.

I look around. Kate's car is still not here. Of course it's not. She won't be coming to school today. She won't be dropping Fergus off, she won't be chatting with the school secretary about a collection she's organized for the teaching assistant, who's leaving at Christmas. She won't be sorting through the lost property, handing out school sweatshirts to their rightful owners. She won't be telling Fergus to *Hurry up! Chop chop, get your boots off, sunshine.*

I put my hands on the steering wheel. I need to move from here, from right outside the school gate. People are beginning to stare.

No one knows yet.

No one knows what I've done.

I start to cry. I need Joe. I need him in that way you need your mother when you're small and despairing. When the sky is falling in. I need him, but I'm scared to hear his voice.

Finally I dial his mobile. He answers on the eighth ring, he coughs a couple of times, then shouts, 'I'm up! I'm up! I'm on my way to Booths now, don't worry, I haven't forgotten.'

'Joe?'

Instantly, he realizes I've not rung to berate him about the pizza ingredients. 'What is it, baby? What's happened?'

'It's Lucinda,' I say, straining to keep my voice level. 'Kate's daughter, Lucinda. She's gone missing.'

'Aw, Jesus, Lise. When? Where was she? Have you spoken to Kate? Has she gone to the police?'

'Joe, it's worse than that,' I say, choking on the words. 'It's worse than that, because it's my fault. It's my fault she's gone.'

'How can it be your fault?' he says. 'That doesn't make any sense.'

This is Joe. He leaps to my defence even if he's not in possession of all the facts. It doesn't matter what I've done. Doesn't matter whether I'm guilty or not. Joe will launch a counter-attack on whoever is attacking me even if I'm in the wrong.

But today it's worthless.

'Lucinda was supposed to be staying at ours last night,' I say. 'She was supposed to come home with Sally after school and work on a project. I don't know what it was for, geography maybe, I can't remember. But Sally didn't' – I struggle with the words – 'Sally didn't—'

'Sally didn't go into school yesterday,' he finishes for me.

'That's right,' I say quietly. 'She didn't. She said she felt sick and I didn't have time to argue, so I let her stay at home. When Sally got on the minibus this morning and Lucinda didn't, she started panicking about the project and rang Lucinda's mobile. When Lucinda didn't answer, she rang Kate—'

'And Kate said, "Isn't she with you?" '

'Yes.'

The horror of what we're facing slaps me in the face for the second time as it dawns on Joe. I can picture him, sitting on the edge of the bed, not up as he'd pretended to be, but in his underwear, his head hanging low.

'So, she's been missing since – when?' he asks. 'Since yesterday afternoon?'

I don't speak.

'Shit,' he says, realizing. 'Has she been gone since yesterday morning?'

'We don't know yet,' I say, 'but it's overnight, Joe. She's been gone overnight and she's only thirteen. Thirteen! She's only thirteen.' I am sobbing fully now. 'What's happened to her? Jesus, Joe, it feels like it's happening to us, only it's worse because it's not our daughter I've lost, it's not *our* daughter . . . it's Kate's.'

Joe sighs then says as softly as he can, 'Lise, why didn't you tell them Sally was ill?'

'I told Sally to text Lucinda and tell her she wasn't coming in, but I should've done it myself, I should've rung Kate—'

'*Kate*,' he says emphatically. 'Dear God, *Kate*,' he says again.

I imagine his expression.

'Joe,' I say carefully, 'are you meaning that this would be easier if this was somebody else's child? Not Kate's? Is that what you're saying?'

'No,' he answers firmly, but then admits: 'You know what I mean, though . . . don't you?'

I do, but I don't let myself think that way. I close my eyes. I feel as if I've been shot in the stomach. I can't move.

'Help me, Joe,' I cry to him. 'Help me. I don't know what to do.'

'I will, baby,' he shushes gently. 'I will. Where are you? I'll come and get you. Don't drive. I'll come.'

Like us, Kate and Guy Riverty live in Troutbeck, but their house is on the other side of the valley. We leave my car outside Sam's school and Joe drives us up there in the taxi.

Sam jumped out of my car and got himself into school when I was receiving the awful news from Sally. I don't think I even said goodbye to him. Sally was not in good state. I have no idea what to do about her. Whether to bring her home or leave her at school. She said the police were at school taking statements, and she wasn't sure if she's even allowed to come home until she's spoken with them.

My mind is blank and my body leaden. I look at Joe. 'I don't know what to say to Kate and Guy – what the hell am I going to say to them?'

'Tell them you're sorry. Say that. Kate'll need to hear it.'

He's right, of course. It's just that I'm so scared.

'What if she screams at me? What if she throws me out?'

'Then you'll have to take it. You have no choice.' He looks at me, his face woeful. 'I won't let her hurt you, if that's what you're worried about. I'll stay with you.'

I turn away, sickened at myself. 'Listen to me – scared of facing her, when her only daughter is *gone*. How fucked up is that? I should be thinking of ways to support her.'

Joe reaches across and puts his hand on top of my tightly clasped palms. 'It's not your fault, Lise,' he says.

I don't respond. We're almost at Kate and Guy's and if I say what I want to say, if I scream, 'Of course it's my fault! You *know* it's my fault,' and allow the hysteria I'm holding inside to surface, I won't be able to get out of the car.

I close my eyes and steady my breath. Instead I say, 'Thanks for coming to get me, Joe.'

He looks across at me, his eyes sad. 'Always,' he says simply.

5

DC JOANNE ASPINALL gets behind the wheel of the grey Mondeo. She'd been given the choice of Midnight Sky or Lunar Sky. Grey, basically. But Joanne wasn't bothered about the colour; for her, it was all about engine capacity.

In recent years they'd lowered the spec for the plain clothes, the thinking behind it that detectives don't find themselves in many car chases, it mostly being traffic who deal with the druggies on the run, the stolen vehicles. Which was a shame, because Joanne liked a good chase.

At the station they said Joanne had two speeds: stop, and gone.

Sometimes she wondered if she'd made a mistake joining CID. Slow cars. And she'd certainly be making more money by now as a uniform; she'd be a sergeant. It was harder to rise up through the ranks as detective. That's why the force was short of them. It put the younger officers off, especially if they had families to support.

Joanne glances back up to the house and considers the scene she's just left. Naturally, her first instinct is to suspect the family. The statistics don't lie. Children are almost always abducted by someone they know.

It's one of the trickiest approaches to pull off as a detective – gathering the necessary information from the family, simultaneously keeping a demeanour of total empathy and clocking the parents for anything out of the ordinary.

Of course Joanne's been trained never to make assumptions. Not in this job: it wastes time. It clouds judgement and leaves avenues unexplored. The words of Joanne's old chemistry teacher pop into her mind each time she thinks of this: 'Never assume,' he used to say, during experiments, 'because to *assume* makes an ASS out of U and ME.'

Joanne smiles briefly as she takes out her notepad. She observes the list in front of her and, without really understanding why, she underlines the name Guy Riverty. The missing girl's father. She sees she's already written it bolder than the others. Already gone over the 'G' a few times without realizing, when she was questioning the couple.

What was it about him? There was no previous; he was all very above board and proper. But even so something didn't sit quite right with her. Joanne looks around at the snow-covered valley as she thinks. Guy Riverty had an awkward, uncomfortable air about him. Babbling, but not really saying anything. Richard Madeley sprang to mind.

Babbling per se was fine with Joanne. After an incident, particularly something unsettling, people tend either to talk continuously or to go silent; there was no in between. They either needed to tell Joanne *absolutely everything*, beginning at the moment they were born and leading up to whatever had put them in the particular time and place of the incident, or else they said nothing, they became mute.

Joanne was good with the mutes. Especially the guilty ones. She didn't use tricks. No good cop, bad cop. No 'Trust in Me' routine, like Kaa, the hypnotic snake from *The Jungle Book* who had frightened Joanne to death when she was a kid. No, Joanne was methodical and conscientious. She started at the beginning and worked her way through to the end until she got what she needed.

If this made her boring, she didn't care. If it got up her colleagues' noses, she didn't care about that either. She worked this way because it was the only way *to* work. You get cavalier-cocky during an investigation and there's only one outcome: you end up looking like a complete tosser. And Joanne had worked with enough fools over the past few years to know that swinging your dick about didn't guarantee results. Quite the contrary.

Joanne taps her pen on the steering wheel and thinks about the missing girl.

Lucinda Riverty.

Thirteen years old, slight, small, with her mousy-brown hair cut just below her chin. She likes school, she's doing grade-five piano, she's not keen on sport, not what you'd call outgoing. But neither would you say she was introverted. Just an ordinary girl.

But, to her parents, an *extraordinary girl.* An extraordinary girl who's now gone.

'Who took this one?' Joanne wonders out loud.

6

ALWAYS, SAYS JOE.

Me and Joe together, always.

It's what he said to me when I pushed his babies out. What he says when I'm vomiting hard over the toilet after too much wine. Or when there's a beautiful woman in the pub and my face falls, and when I check to see if Joe's looking at her, and he's not, he's looking at me, and he's smiling at my insecurity. *Always*, he says, and I'm okay again. It fixes me.

If I screw up, it doesn't matter. Because, to Joe, nothing I do is ever really a screw-up anyway.

Don't get me wrong, he's as bad-tempered and as hot-headed and irritating as the next man. And we've definitely had our moments. But they were just moments. No different to any other couple faced with kids, faced with having to *be* better, having to *do* better, than we ever thought possible. Day after day after day after day.

Kate's house suddenly comes into view and I see there is a ton of cars parked outside already. All at once I lose the breath from my lungs. 'Oh, Christ, Joe, I don't think I can go in there. Pull over, will you?'

He does as I say and cuts the engine.

We're in a passing place about fifty yards from Kate's. The house looks so imposing. More than it has ever done before. It's a grand house, built entirely from lead-grey Lakeland stone.

Today it's bleak and exposed. There's a Christmas tree in the front bay, but its lights are off.

'What do you want to do?' Joe asks me.

'I know I've got to go in. But I just want to go home and crawl into bed. I want to bury my head and hide.' I turn to him, and my voice cracks. 'I don't want to see what I've *done* to her, Joe.'

He nods, understanding. 'You have no choice, though. It would be worse if you didn't show up. They'll be expecting you.'

'I know.'

For a minute we sit in silence. Me working through what I need to say, and Joe letting me have some space. There's a foul, putrid taste in my mouth. I keep swallowing to shift it, but it's no use, my mouth is dry.

When Joe senses I'm maybe starting to get a grip on things, he speaks. 'What do you reckon Kate and Guy will be thinking right now? Will they be considering . . . you know, the worst?'

'What, that she's already dead?'

Joe flinches.

'Well, there is *that* possibility,' he says, 'but I was thinking more along the lines of the young girl who turned up in Bowness. Remember? The one who was raped?'

I put my hands to my face. I'd forgotten all about that poor girl. Discarded on the street, no idea where she was.

When I'd read about her I'd immediately thought of Sally. About how self-conscious Sally can be. So much so that she turns away from me when undressing. If we're out shopping, she has this way of trying on shirts, a way of covering herself so I don't see the front of her bra. When I'd read the story of the girl, an image of Sally had flashed into my mind: Sally naked from the waist up. Sally walking into that busy travel agent's asking for help after her hellish ordeal, quietly dying inside.

'Please, no,' I whimper to Joe. 'Please don't let that be Lucinda. She's so young.'

Joe scratches the area of skin under his chin. He hasn't shaved yet and the re-growth is starting to itch.

'Is there any chance she could have meant to do this?' he speculates.

'How do you mean?'

'You know the girl better than I do, Lise. I don't take that much notice of Sally's friends . . . I try to stay out of the way.'

I look at him sharply, surprised by his words. 'Yes, but *you do know* Lucinda, Joe. She's not just one of Sally's friends, is she? She's been in and out of our house constantly for the past few years. How can you say you don't know her, when—'

'It would be *weird* for me to take an intense interest in her is what I'm trying to say,' he cuts in. '*You* know Lucinda. You know what's going on with her. You see Kate often enough – how much do you talk about the girls?'

'The norm, I suppose. She's not said she's worried about her – not that I remember, anyway.'

'And Sally's not said if Lucinda's unhappy? Or if she's got a boyfriend? Or if Kate pisses her off to the extent that she'd run away from home?'

'Do you think Kate pisses her off?' I ask.

'Don't all mothers piss their teenage daughters off?'

'I suppose, but—' I stop myself. 'Christ, Joe, we shouldn't be discussing this. We really shouldn't. Kate is falling apart in there and we're here debating if her daughter has got the hump about something.'

'But it is possible,' he says.

'Yes. And it's also possible *our* daughter would run away, but do you honestly think she would?'

He doesn't answer. Just looks up at the house and unclicks his seat belt, signalling that we'd better move before someone sees us.

We leave the taxi in the layby and walk towards Kate's, our

breath making soft clouds as it hits the raw air. As we start up the front path the door opens and a uniformed police officer comes out. He's carrying two laptops, and the sight of this makes my blood run cold. I feel like I'm watching the news, watching events unfold in someone else's life. Not Kate's. The PC's young and fresh-faced and he nods to us as we stand aside to let him pass. Then he does a double take as he sees Joe.

'All right, Joe,' he acknowledges.

'Rob,' Joe replies. But that's it, that's all they say. I don't ask how Joe knows him because I'm almost at the house and my stomach is heaving. The postbox-red, highly glossed front door has been left ajar. I don't press the doorbell. It would seem too much of an assault to hear its loud, shrill tone right now. Instead I knock lightly and go straight in – something I've never done before in all the time I've known Kate.

I hear the low murmur of voices and pause there in the hallway, gathering myself. Joe has come in behind me, and I feel his touch on my shoulder. *Go on,* he urges silently. *Go on, move forwards, you'll be okay.* But I'm not okay.

The door to my right, the drawing room – or lounge, as it's known in our house – is shut tight. They're all in the den.

I walk in. The room is filled with bodies. I don't see Kate's face at first, as she's sitting down. My view of her is blocked by a couple of farmers from up the valley who are telling Guy where they'll begin their search. But I know she's there, and I freeze, unable to advance any further.

Kate's sister, Alexa, is a few feet away and when she sees me her jaw tightens. Her husband, Adam, is with her and for a moment I think he will approach. But then I sense he's been told not to. Embarrassed, he looks away.

The two farmers in front of Kate part and, suddenly, there she is.

She takes one look at me and crumples. Like she's been

deboned. Spatchcocked like a chicken. She can't speak for crying.

I crouch down in front of her and take her hands in mine. Her skin is ice-cold. 'Kate, I'm so sorry . . .' I say. 'I'm so sorry I've done this to you. I'm so sorry I let this happen.'

She's nodding and crying, because she knows. She knows I am not a bad person. Knows that I'm not lax and uncaring and sloppy.

She knows that, even though I can never be the mother she is, I try my best.

I cup her hands in mine, but there's a tremor coming from deep within her that's spreading out to the ends of her limbs. I feel as if I'm holding a small, trapped bird in there, and my instinct is to drop my head, lift her fingers to my lips.

I had been so scared she'd blame me publicly. So frightened of her reaction. Now I realize she's too damned terrified and heartbroken to start shouting. It's all she can do just to stay sitting upright.

'What can I do, Kate?' I say to her. 'Tell me what to do to help you? I have to do something—'

There are footsteps behind me. 'Don't you think you've done enough?'

It's Alexa.

I close my eyes briefly, knowing what is to come.

Kate goes to speak: 'Alexa . . . don't.'

'Don't what? Don't say what everybody's thinking?'

'Don't make this any worse than it already is.' Kate takes her hands out from within mine.

'It can't *be* any worse. How can it be any worse?'

The room has fallen silent. Whereas before there'd been hushed voices, arrangements being made, plans for the best course of action, now there is nothing.

I stand from my crouched position and turn to face Alexa.

She's rigid with anger. Both hands are glued to her sides as if she doesn't quite trust herself not to go for me. A giant vertical vein has risen up on her forehead.

There is nowhere to go. I must face this. I almost want this. I need to take some punishment, or else the guilt I will dump on myself later will swamp me.

I look into Alexa's steely eyes and say, as steadily as I can, 'This *is* my fault. You are right to shout. You are right to blame me. I deserve your anger.'

She slaps me hard.

I stumble backwards.

'You stupid, stupid bitch!' she screams. 'You think that because you come around here admitting it was your fault that it's all okay?'

'No,' I say, my hand reaching for the stinging skin of my cheek, 'no, that's not what I meant.'

'Kate's daughter is gone! Do you understand that? Do you understand what your incompetence has done to this family?'

I'm crying. 'Yes, yes, of course I do. But I don't know what to say, I don't know what to do. I can't make this better whatever I do and—'

Guy is striding across the room now, and I back away, shrinking from the onslaught which is sure to come from him as well.

Where is Joe? I scan the room quickly, but he is not here. I need him. Where is he?

'Alexa, that's enough,' Guy says firmly. 'Look at Kate.'

We turn our eyes down towards Kate on the sofa and see that she's collapsed sideways. Her whole body is jerking in a series of slow convulsions. Her eyes are open and her mouth is contorted into a kind of silent scream.

I move towards her.

'Get away,' commands Alexa. 'Just get the hell away from her.' And I stand there, helpless.

'I'll ring for an ambulance,' Guy says.

As I look around I see the eyes of the room are upon me. Without knowing what else to do, I cover my face with my hands because I can't stand it. I can't stand their condemnation.

The strength has gone out of my legs and I know I'm falling. Suddenly, Joe is at my side and I feel his arms around me. 'Come on, baby, let's go,' he whispers, and I sob into his chest. 'Come on,' he says again.

'Yes, Joe,' Alexa snaps. 'Get her out of here.'

Joe guides me out, but as I reach the door I can't help turning around to look at Kate one last time. She seems to have stopped convulsing but she remains on her side, her eyes perfectly rounded and staring in my direction.

'Kate,' I whisper to her, my face pleading.

And she gives me just the faintest nod in response. 'Find her,' she mouths.

7

WE'RE BACK INSIDE the car and I'm screaming at Joe, 'Where the hell were you in there? How could you leave me to face that on my own?'

He looks at me, stunned. 'I went to find Guy,' he says tersely. 'Where did you think I was? Fucking off out the way so they could have a go at you?' He shakes his head. 'I didn't know Alexa was going to rip into you like that, did I?'

I'm crying so hard I can hardly breathe.

'I thought the right thing to do would be to speak to Guy,' he says. 'Tell him how bad you felt, let him know that we'd do anything we could . . . I couldn't find him in the kitchen so I went to talk to Kev Bell. He's getting a few men together to start a search.' Joe shakes his head again like he can't believe I'm accusing him of deserting me.

'Isn't it a bit soon for a search?' I say. 'What if Lucinda turns up?'

'What if she doesn't?'

'Did you hear what Alexa said to me?'

'Not all of it.'

I fumble in my pockets for a tissue, can't find one and have to make do with a rag Joe uses for cleaning the mist off his windscreen. 'She said my incompetence destroyed the family.'

'Not mincing her words then.'

He's not looking at me. He's staring straight ahead.

'Joe . . . ?' I whimper.

'What?' he replies, his voice still strained.

He turns the ignition and puts his hand on the gear stick. I see it's trembling wildly, which, even under these circumstances is not the reaction you expect from Joe. When he notices it himself, he snatches it away.

'Lise, they're upset,' he says finally, sighing. 'They're feeling desperate . . . it's bound to happen . . . blaming you, blaming somebody. It's human nature. What did you expect?'

I know he's right, but it hurts to hear this. What I need now is the Joe of old, the one who backs me up no matter what.

I try to imagine how I would be if this were happening to me. If the shoe was on the other foot. Would I direct the blame so readily on to another person?

I turn to him. 'Joe, I know we're talking about this like I am responsible, and I know that I *am* responsible, but do you really think it's all my fault? Or am I being . . .'

I don't finish the sentence. I feel so pounded by Alexa's attack I'm not sure what I'm thinking.

Joe starts fiddling with the heater, directing the heat from our feet up towards the screen. When he realizes I really do want an answer, he stops. Turns around in his seat to face me. 'Honestly?' he asks. 'You want me to be totally honest with you?'

'Yes,' I say firmly, but the fear in my eyes tells him to tread carefully.

'You should have rung them to say there was no sleepover.'

I screw my eyes tightly shut.

'But don't you think Kate should have checked, or something?' I press. 'Don't you think it was partly Kate's fault that she went through all of yesterday, and overnight, and into this morning, without checking on Lucinda? Not even once?'

Joe's expression doesn't change. 'Not if she thought Lucinda was with you. No, I don't.'

I can't speak. Because as Joe is giving me his assessment of things, I remember that Kate did check, didn't she? She checked this morning when she rang me about Sam. 'The girls okay?' she'd asked, and I'd said yes.

Joe's face now softens into sadness. 'You ready to go?' he asks, and I nod.

He sets off along the road. He's about to take a right and head down the valley towards home, but just as he's slowing he crunches the gears. The car jolts wildly. Kangaroos twice and stalls outside the post office.

'Jesus, Joe!' I yell, startled. 'What the fuck's the matter with you?'

We drive the rest of the way in silence.

When we get home I crawl into bed. I pull the covers over my face and lift my knees so I'm in the foetal position. And this is when the really bad thoughts come. This new situation of wretchedness mixes in with the old self-hatred. With the other guilt-laden mistake of my past that I haven't yet shaken loose. It happened four years ago.

The thing is, he thinks, as he sits outside the three and a half million pound house with lake access, it really is just a matter of perspective.

For example, Spain's age of consent is thirteen years old. Not that he's using that to justify his actions. He just thinks it's an interesting fact that a developed country, not so far from the UK, can have such a different approach. Along with Japan. Their age of consent is thirteen as well. To find that kind of freedom in England, you'd have to go back – what? – about two hundred years, when girls could legally marry at twelve.

Not that he'd want to marry a girl of twelve – that would be absurd – he's simply saying that, if he'd wanted to, he could have done it back then, that's all.

He checks his watch. The estate agent is six minutes late. Why do they have to be so inept? He taps his fingers on the steering wheel, and then, as has become his habit lately, he rubs away the fingerprints with the sleeve of his jacket.

To kill time he focuses on the view through the windscreen and begins smiling. It's the smile he's been practising in front of the mirror for the past few weeks. His natural smile can border on smarmy, shows a few too many teeth, so he takes the trouble to get it right. Makes sure his eyes take on that shiny quality women love.

Smile at a woman like you're noticing her and she'll all but melt to the ground in front of you. It's not rocket science.

Without meaning to, his mind has slipped back to the thing he can't stop thinking about, and his practised smile becomes a grin. He's grinning like an idiot, and he knows he has to stop before the estate agent arrives.

Who'd have thought it could be so easy?

Granted, it hadn't gone totally as expected, totally as planned. But so what? Wasn't that even better? The element of surprise – something unexpected happening, something thrilling to perk things up?

Wasn't that why bored city workers did extreme sports? And fat-wanker bankers had sex with sluts in the cleaning cupboard? 'Course it was.

Although this *isn't an extreme sport. He knows that. He can't pass himself off as some weirdo schizo and pretend like he doesn't know what he's doing. He knows exactly what he's doing.*

His smile fades as he admits this to himself and, as he checks his watch once more, he thinks, maybe I should call it a day. She was scared. Even doped up, she was really, really scared.

He had harboured a small hope that she might kind of get into it.

Because, that could happen, right?

But, no. That wasn't how it had gone. So maybe best to leave it at that, find other things to do.

But then a thought occurs to him.

Suppose the next one gets into it? Suppose she's been waiting for something like this? For someone like him. That could happen. It was possible.

A silver BMW Z3 pulls up alongside him, and a harried-looking woman in her mid-forties climbs out, approaches his driver's side door.

She's carrying a stack of papers and is holding them in front of her open blazer, trying to conceal the fact that her ugly belly is straining her skirt to bursting.

He opens his door, looks directly into her eyes and smiles. She averts her gaze, trying to gather herself. 'I'm so sorry to have kept you waiting, Mr—'

'Not at all.' He shrugs to indicate that it's been no bother and holds out his hand. 'Call me Charles,' he says, trying to pull himself back to the business of charming this feckless woman.

But it's hard.

Hard because his mind is still on the girls and he's thinking: Of course it's possible that the next one will play out differently.

I mean, anything's possible, right?

8

FOUR YEARS AGO, we'd been invited to Kate's for a dinner party. Something that had never happened before or since. There were to be six of us – Kate and Guy, Alexa and Adam, me and Joe. Kate had not long since moved her children back into the state system and though we'd always kind of known each other over the years, this was her doing what people like Kate do – expanding her social circle to include the parents of her children's new friends.

I was eager to go in that way you are when you're invited to something new and different. No one I knew had dinner parties. Certainly not the other parents in school, who, probably like me and Joe, couldn't face the thought of tidying up and cleaning the entire house on a Friday night *as well as* cooking, and after a full week at work. Or maybe they were all secretly having dinner parties and just didn't invite us. Anyway, I'd never been to one, so I was both excited and anxious.

Kate, I was pretty comfortable with by then and Guy, I knew from saying hello to at school and around the village. Alexa, I was intimidated by. I confided this to Joe as we made our way up the front path, and rather than settle me and give me words of reassurance (as was his usual way), he looked at me with a pained expression, whispering, 'Why are we here, baby?'

Before I could reply, Guy answered the door, bottle of wine in hand, and immediately I felt deflated. My shoulders slumped, my chin poking forward in a pathetic posture.

He greeted us exuberantly, almost shouting, 'Hello, the Kallistos! Come in, come in!' His face was a perfect show of warmth and welcoming, deftly masking what he'd instantly noticed as our first major gaffe: our outfits.

Joe had worn his only suit, a cheap black Burton's thing he put on when he was required to drive someone to a funeral. With it, he was wearing a new white shirt and a spotted tie. He did look lovely, as he always does in a white shirt because of his dark colouring, but Guy had on faded jeans and a round-necked jumper.

I was wearing a new dress I'd bought that day from Next. It was strapless and cut above the knee, made from shiny red fabric with great big black roses all over it. And for reasons best known to myself, I'd been and had a spray tan.

I dreaded to see what the women were wearing.

I shot a panicked look at Joe as Guy beckoned us in, and he said, 'Well, we're here now,' tenderly touching my bare shoulder briefly, guiding me, encouraging me to move forwards.

I was like my old grandad – he was dead now, but for the last ten years of his life he had suffered from Parkinson's. Whenever he was faced with walking through a doorway, he'd freeze. The top half of his body would be leaning ready to go, but the bottom half was stuck fast, as if his shoes were glued to the carpet. The only way we could get him moving was to march him steadily to the tune of 'Onward, Christian Soldiers'.

Surprisingly, I began humming, and it worked for me as well.

Kate and Guy had not long moved into the house, so there was the smell of wood shavings and linseed in the air. They were having oak flooring installed throughout, and I wasn't sure whether I should remove my heels – reckoning if I knackered an eighty-quid-a-square-metre floor with a pair of cheap stilettos, it would be just about the worst thing ever. But Guy didn't say anything so I kept them on. Just tried to walk on the balls of my feet.

Music was coming from the kitchen, a dreamy acoustic female artist I didn't know. As we walked in I found Kate and Alexa by the Aga, tasting and stirring, both wearing similar outfits of pale linen, both wearing minimal make-up, both with their hair pinned up loosely, as if they were in a Nivea or a Neutrogena commercial. I felt like a total idiot as they turned around, their broad smiles not matching the alarmed look in their eyes as they regarded first me, and then Joe. Then, chiming more or less together, 'Wow, Lisa, you look . . . fantastic! I love your dress, where is it from? . . . Joe! So great to *see* you.'

Embarrassed, I mumbled an answer, thrusting the bottles of wine we'd brought at Kate, saying something along the lines of *Thanks for inviting us.* Then I quickly pulled out a stool from the kitchen island in an attempt to hide myself.

Joe said a quick hello, gave the ladies a peck on the cheek and did the obligatory, 'How nicely the house is coming along, Kate,' while Kate did her best exasperated expression, sighing dramatically, replying, 'Well, we're *getting there*,' as if they were not renovating a home but were in fact building a school in Namibia and were struggling to locate a clean water supply.

'I'll open another bottle,' Kate said, walking across the room. Turning, she added, 'Joe, you go and join the boys – leave us girls to gossip. Adam's brought a stupidly large selection of bottled ales for you to get through.'

Alexa had turned her back and was taking another taste from the pot on the stove. 'Kate,' she said, her voice snippy with criticism, 'these onions are not completely softened, you can't serve the tagine like this, it'll be awful.'

Kate, over by the fridge, didn't comment.

'You should do what I do,' Alexa went on. 'I soften a ton of onions, sometimes shallots, at one time. Then I freeze them in batches, and I use them as I need . . . it saves ever such a lot of time . . .'

'I'll remember that,' said Kate, smiling tightly.

'I do it with peppers and aubergines as well,' Alexa added. 'They freeze a lot better than you'd imagine.'

Quietly, I said to Kate, 'I'll eat anything, I'm starving. I've not had anything since breakfast.'

Work had been crazy. Fridays are always the most popular day for adoptions. Then I'd had to go straight through to Ambleside to pick up Joe's mum, who was babysitting. Joe was still on a job at that time, so he couldn't get her. Then I had to feed everyone, because even though Joe's mother is more than capable, she won't use our cooker because she says she's unfamiliar with it. And it's easier to go along with it than to cause a problem.

'Gosh,' said Alexa, leaving the tagine and sitting down opposite me, 'you are a busy bee, Lisa. Are you still at the animal shelter?'

I nodded. Took a big gulp of the white wine Kate had set in front of me. 'Lovely,' I said to Kate. 'Just what I needed.'

Alexa took a sip of hers, saying, 'I've been working myself, actually, at the gallery around the corner from the cinema.' Again, I nodded. 'All helps towards the school fees!' she quipped.

This was absolute nonsense, because everyone knew Alexa's mother-in-law paid the children's school fees, because her mother-in-law told everyone. Dorothy Willard, Adam's mother, was one of those noisy, aggravating women who volunteered at the charity shop a couple of mornings a week and loved telling anyone who'd listen about her talented grandchildren. About how they were *positively thriving* at the superb school she and her husband paid for. 'Well, it's what one does for one's offspring,' she'd say as I'd dump down a hardly worn winter coat on the counter, or else a stack of Mills & Boons that my mother liked to read. I'd smile at her, saying, 'You must be very proud,' and she'd go all mock-modesty, replying, 'Well one shouldn't boast, but—'

I think Alexa liked to work to pass the time, or just to get out of the house, but was ashamed to admit such frivolity to the likes of me – the type of person who works because she has to eat, and so forth. I didn't hold it against her. No point. The Lakes has always been littered with two extremes of women: the ones who never work . . . and the ones who never stop.

'How many days do you do at the gallery, Alexa?' I asked, because I couldn't think of anything more interesting to say to her.

'Oh, just two or three mornings. I fit it around my MA.'

'Your MA?'

'My master's,' she replied. 'I'm doing a master's in cultural studies.'

'Sounds . . . difficult,' I said.

'It is. It's taking up far more of my time than anticipated. Adam keeps complaining that he's lost me to the world of academia *once again*.'

I noticed Kate was not commenting on Alexa's degree and, sensing I knew the reason for this, didn't say anything further.

Alexa, as well as doing silly, pointless work to fill her time, loved to study. I have no idea what a master's in cultural studies actually is, but I can guess the reason she's doing it. So little people like me will think: Wow, not only are you incredibly beautiful but you're really, really clever as well! How is that even possible?'

She's not the only attractive woman I've met with this affliction. I want to say to them, 'Stop. *Please*, just stop. You already have what we all want. You *got the beauty*, you already got the free pass. It is enough.'

'Will you be a doctor when you finish this one, Lex?' Kate asked her.

'No,' she replied. 'Gosh, imagine that! Two doctors in the house,' and, as if on cue, the men came in, carrying their beers, looking for food.

Alexa's husband, Adam – Dr Willard – was dressed casually, wearing similar clothes to Guy. When he entered the room I immediately became self-conscious again.

Kate said, 'Lisa, have you met Adam? No? Oh, Lisa, this is Adam. Adam, Lisa.'

I nodded at him politely, and he smiled in my direction. He was what I'd describe as kind-looking. Not handsome, but his face had a softness that was appealing. 'Hi,' he said. 'Nice to meet you. You're the animal-sanctuary lady, yes?'

'That's right.'

'Bet that's a tough job, dealing with the general public in that way.'

I was about to tell him a couple of anecdotes but, before I could answer, Alexa cut in. 'Oh, isn't it just the worst? You wouldn't believe the silly things people ask for at the gallery. And why does everyone think they can bag a bargain? I blame those haggling programmes. Gone are the days when they're willing to pay a fair price for something.'

Adam ignored her, kept his gaze on me. 'What's the biggest problem you come across at a place like that?'

'Money,' I said. 'Well, the lack of it. The vet fees can be in excess of twenty thousand, and then there's the food costs and the—'

'Where does the money come from?' asked Alexa.

'Private donations, mostly. Some kind, rich old ladies leave us their estates. The rest we find from fundraising, and a little from a regional animal charity that pays us to take in cats and dogs from other branches.'

Joe was smiling as he watched me speak. He had his proud face on. He hadn't done what I thought he might – that is, removed his jacket and tie, undone his top button. He remained the same as when we'd arrived, and I felt a flush of love for him. He was grinning at me shyly, which meant he was trying to hide that he'd downed at least three beers already. He does that when he's not quite comfortable. Actually, he does it if the beer is put in front of him. He's like a kid who can't say no.

An hour or so later, and the tagine with the uncooked onions had been eaten, the wine loosening us up sufficiently so that the conversation was free-flowing, the stilted awkwardness of earlier gone.

I was in the middle of recounting the basic plot of a BBC drama I'd been following, saying to everyone, 'And it's the banter between the two detectives which makes it so lifelike,' when Alexa cleared her throat and slapped me down, informing me that, '*We* don't really do TV, Lisa. Most of us here are readers, aren't we?' And I felt the energy in the room change.

Nobody challenged Alexa. And, naturally, I felt stupid and gauche, but as I looked around the room, everyone avoided my eyes and I wasn't sure if I'd been making a fool of myself for a while (and they'd all been too polite to say), or if it was Alexa's comment that they were embarrassed by.

I glanced at Joe, but he was no use. He had that loose, devilish expression that told me he was so drunk he was either about to start singing, or else fall asleep. Checking my watch, I saw it was still only nine thirty. I knew then there was no way he'd make it through to the end of the evening.

Kate lightened things momentarily by serving up Delia's strawberry-shortcake ice cream, which everyone declared an absolute success. More wine was poured, and Guy ushered the children, who'd been watching TV in the den (not readers, then), upstairs to bed.

Things went downhill after that.

Alexa, sensing perhaps that she'd killed the conversation earlier, took on a real gossipy air, leaned in at the table and began telling us about a couple they all knew who were having marital difficulties.

'Of course, Tammy's not admitting it, but everyone knows she's secretly seeing another man. I saw her buying new underwear in the village . . . a sure sign she's up to something. Especially when she's the type of woman who doesn't even wear mascara. I said to Pippa that I *bet* she—'

'You don't know that,' Kate cut in unexpectedly, her face stony.

'*Everyone* knows, Katy—'

'You don't know for certain she's having an affair,' finished Kate, and Alexa rolled her eyes at her, meaning: Don't be so naïve, which made Kate shout: 'Think about the children! Don't start spreading ugly rumours when you have no evidence. Think about Tammy's children.'

The table fell into uncomfortable silence again. It was Kate's tone. So unlike her. I'd never heard her speak that way before.

Alexa stared at her, affronted. 'Think *what* about the children, Kate? If they are not happy, then the last thing Tammy and David should do is stay together for the sake of the children.'

Kate put her glass down. 'How can you say that?'

'Because it's true.'

'It's not true! That's what everyone says, that it's okay to just up and leave whenever the mood takes you. They say, "The children will be all right!" "Better for them to be brought up with divorced parents than in an unhappy home." Well, *you* should know, Alexa, that it's *not* all right. You of all people should know that.'

Alexa sighed, as if she was thoroughly bored. 'Not this again.'

Walking into the room, Guy cleared his throat. 'Ladies, ladies—'

'Shut up, Guy,' Kate snapped.

I'd dropped my head, furtively glancing around the table. Joe was smiling openly – he loves it when people are drunk and they start arguing, especially family. Alexa's husband, Adam, sat there pretending nothing was happening at all and was scraping up the last of his ice cream.

'If two people want to have an affair, let them,' Alexa continued. 'Christ, Kate, life is bloody short, love is thin on the ground. People need to take love when and where they find it. If Tammy's got a little romance in her life, let her have it, and don't be so fucking sanctimonious.' Then she said, 'You lose your prettiness when you get all tense like this, Kate. Really, it's not good for you.'

Kate was shaking now. Quietly, she said, 'I can't believe you're pretending to forget what it was like.'

'It's life, Kate. Get over it.'

I went to stand, saying, 'Does anyone want anything from the kitchen?', but Alexa shot me a look.

'Sit down, Lisa,' she said. Then, addressing Kate again, 'We're not the only people to have divorced parents, you know. And you can't go around hating everyone who puts their children through it.'

'I don't hate them,' Kate replied. 'I hate the way they act so blameless. I hate the way they bring strangers into the house, acting as if it's fine when you know it's not. Don't you remember what it was like for us? To come out of the bathroom when you were thirteen and find a man in the hallway? It was excruciating, Alexa, you know it was. And if you want to pretend otherwise, that's fine. But I can't.' She gave a small sob and got up, leaving the room.

For a while nobody spoke. Then, finally, after a minute, Adam looked at Alexa, saying, 'Was that really necessary?'

And she threw her wine at him.

'Oh, fuck off, you pathetic little man,' she shouted, and stormed off as well.

The men all sighed and sat back in their chairs. I didn't know what to do. 'Should I go to them?' I asked. 'Should I see if they're okay?'

'Not if you want to keep your teeth,' Guy answered. He refilled the glasses. 'From experience, I'd say it's best to let them sort it out. If you go in there now, you'll only end up coming off worse. Believe me, Lisa, you don't want to come between them.'

Joe chipped in, slurring, 'It's siblings, Lise. You don't understand, being an only one.' And he was right: I didn't. But his comment was still a little wounding, probably because I was drunk and slightly irrational. Also because *it is* wounding when someone says you're incapable of understanding just because you have no experience of something.

I replied by saying, 'Oh, like you do understand, Joe.'

Joe got on just fine with his sister, mostly because he never saw her. He shrugged, his face blotchy from the booze, then, narrowing his eyes at me, he said, 'Maybe if your dad hadn't fucked off when he did—'

'*Joe!*' I said, and stared at him. We didn't discuss this. We never discussed this in front of people. Especially not people like this. But Joe had passed over into that territory I referred to as Nasty Pissed. And though generally Joe was a sweet drunk, once the eight-pint mark had been crossed, he became argumentative and hostile.

I felt uncomfortable. Suddenly, the dynamics had changed. I was the only woman, alone at the table, with my smashed taxi-driver husband and a well-spoken, rich property developer and a consultant dermatologist. It all seemed wrong and awkward. If

Adam hadn't given me a consolatory smile, a smile to say, *Don't be upset*, I think I would have left.

And I should have. What I should have done was go and find Kate and Alexa and check that they were okay. Looking back, that would have been the right thing to do. But I didn't. I stayed, and I continued to drink. And by the time Alexa came back forty-five minutes or so later, we'd all kind of forgotten about her and Kate. Joe had passed out (as I knew he would), on a lovely striped easy chair. And I'd got a bit over-friendly with the two men.

I'd kicked off my shoes and was dancing to MTV in my stockinged feet, holding my glass, and we were laughing and shouting. Alexa stood in the doorway and said, 'You're spilling out of that dress, Lisa. You should sit down,' and, stupidly, I sniggered at her. Which was not the best thing to do, because she got mad. Understandable, but it had just felt so funny that she was telling me off.

Glaring at me, she shouted, 'You look like a fucking trollop, Lisa! Sit down!' Which made me stop in my tracks.

Then she turned to her husband. 'We're going. Get your coat from upstairs and ring for a taxi. Kate is fine now, thank you all very much for asking.'

Guy approached her, his arms outstretched. 'Oh, don't be like that, Alexa,' he boomed. 'We're only having a laugh.' He tried to hug her, but she pushed him away, marching over to the corner to get her handbag.

I backed out of the doorway, saying, 'Excuse me, I need the loo,' and I made for the stairs, thinking I could hide up there until she left. I felt like a teenager at a house party when the parents returned home and switched the lights on.

Seconds later, I crashed into the bathroom, fumbling with the lock, before sinking to the floor against the bathtub.

The room was beautiful. All enamel and chrome, marble and

mirrors. I looked around dreamily, wishing I could afford even the hand soap, never mind the thick, fluffy towels stacked neatly on the built-in shelves. God, I would die for this bathroom, I was thinking, when the door handle began turning slowly.

Adam leaned his head around the frame, and said, 'Can I come in?'

My eyes were wide. 'No,' I hissed, automatically adjusting my dress. 'Of course you can't.'

'Please,' he persisted. 'I just want a quick word. It'll only take a minute.'

'Oh, okay, but be quick. Your wife is waiting.'

'Guy's calmed her with a drink.'

He edged in and closed the door. I wasn't sure if I should try to stand but, to be honest, I was disastrously drunk. My limbs were loose and not to be counted on.

'What is it?' I asked him.

'I hate her,' he said flatly, and I couldn't help it – I burst out laughing. Had to put my hand up to my mouth to stop.

'It's not funny,' he said. 'I really fucking hate her.'

'It kind of is,' I said, still laughing, then: 'Sorry, sorry, I'll stop now.'

He knelt down, too close for me to focus. I was moving my head backwards and forwards, trying to get his image to sharpen. 'Sorry,' I said again, and without warning he pressed his lips to mine.

Horrified, I said, 'Stop. You can't do that.'

'Let me . . . please.'

'I'm married.'

'So am I.'

'Yes, but—'

He kissed me more deeply, and I was too shocked to stop him. I wasn't kissing him back, but I wasn't pushing him off either. I was just kind of numb. Numb and confused. It was as if I were watching this scene play out from somewhere across the room. Not actually partaking in it.

Then he stopped and he looked at me.

'I'm really, really drunk,' I said helplessly, and he hushed me, putting his finger to my lips.

'You're beautiful.'

And I wanted to say, 'No I'm not, I'm cheap.' But I didn't. I liked hearing his words, even if I knew he didn't mean them.

Instead I said, 'What about your wife?', and he shook his head as if their relationship were a lost cause.

'You've seen her, you've seen how she is,' he said. 'She attacked you because she couldn't stand not to have all the attention.'

'She attacked me because she thinks I'm stupid. And she's right. I am stupid compared to the likes of her.'

He kissed me again, whispering, 'You're way off.'

And this is the part I'm most ashamed of. This is the part, when I think about it, I hate the most. I hate who I was in this moment.

Because I let him.

I let him kiss me. I let him push my dress up and pull my knickers down over my stockings, around my ankles. And I could lie and say it was because his wife made me feel worthless and crap, and I hated her for it. That would be true, but not the only reason. Really it was because I'd looked at Joe, pissed and daft in the corner, and I'd looked at Adam and Guy, eloquent and charming, and I couldn't believe Adam could *want* me. Want me and be willing to risk being found out. He was clever and funny and handsome, and, Jesus, he had money. He was all the things I was never, ever down for. The things I could never, ever have.

Before I knew it he was inside me and moving and I was gasping. The whole thing was raunchy and thrilling and desperate.

And then, as I opened my eyes in sweet anguish, there was a face peering around the door, watching me. Us.

Then it was gone.

9

IT'S ALMOST ELEVEN A.M. I've called the animal shelter and told them I won't be in until . . . I don't actually give them anything firm. My office door will be kept shut, and there'll be no animal adoptions today.

I have to sign off on all the adoptions. I do the home visits first to check we're not sending our cats and dogs to a hellhole. And I have a personal rule that if you've brought more than one dog back to us, you can't have another. I don't care if your personal circumstances have changed, I don't care if you've got more time now, that you really regret giving up the last pet. Two strikes, and you have to go elsewhere.

Joe puts a cup of tea on the bedside cabinet and gives the top of my head a quick kiss. I sit up and lift the rim of the cup to my lips, but my hands are shaking too much to take a sip.

He's just had a phone call to say there's a police officer coming to see us shortly, to talk about what we know. I'd protested. Said to Joe that we didn't *know anything*, and wouldn't we be more use out looking for Lucinda?

But Joe had stroked my face, saying, 'They need to talk to us. Don't worry, it won't be that bad.' As ever, he knew the true meaning behind my words. He knew what I was really saying: *Don't interview me and blame me. Don't blame me again.*

'Come on,' says Joe. 'You best get downstairs. They're not going to want to talk to you while you're in bed.'

We go down to the kitchen, and the doorbell rings.

Joe answers it quickly, and I hear a woman's voice.

'Mr Kallisto? Hello, I'm Detective Constable Aspinall.'

Joe murmurs something and, seconds later, she's in my kitchen. The three dogs are immediately around her legs, sniffing and fussing. I go to apologize but, before I get the chance to shoo them away, she says, 'It's fine. I don't mind dogs.'

Joe tells her the kettle's boiled and asks if she would like a brew. She accepts. Strong tea, one and a half sugars.

'How are you bearing up?' she asks, because she can see by my face I'm a mess. I'm crying even when I don't know I am. 'I'm told that Mr and Mrs Riverty assumed that their daughter was here for the night. Is that correct?'

I nod sadly, sitting down, gesturing for her to do the same. The scrubbed pine table is still littered with this morning's debris. Grains of sugar, rings from the bottom of cups and glasses. I put my elbow into something sticky then move it again.

'It's my fault,' I tell her and she doesn't say anything in return. Not: *It could happen to anyone.* Or: *Try not to be too hard on yourself.* None of the things I would surely say to someone in my situation.

She's a chunky, squat-looking woman in her parka and flat shoes. It's only when she takes off her coat that I see it's her bust making her appear much bigger than she actually is. Her dark hair is held back in a ponytail at the nape of her neck. A few strands have escaped around her face. I'd put her at about my age, thirty-sevenish. There's no wedding ring.

Joe hands her the tea. 'Do I stay?' he asks. 'Or do you want to speak to us separately?'

Neither of us has had any dealings with the police before, and he's flapping. 'Stay,' she says kindly. She takes out a notepad, flips through the pages.

'Kate's not doing too well,' I tell her.

'To be expected.'

'They had to get the doctor. That's why we left. That's why we decided it was best if—' I stop myself. *I'm* flapping now. Telling her stuff she doesn't need to know. Trying to explain why we're not round there doing something to help.

I change tack and ask her if it was she who interviewed the family earlier. 'Did you see Kate?' I say.

DC Aspinall starts writing in her notepad while she speaks. 'I saw Mr and Mrs Riverty this morning.' She says this without looking up. 'Then I went on to Windermere Academy to talk to the teachers and find out what time Lucinda was in school until. We're piecing together her movements just before she disappeared.'

'My daughter's at school there,' I blurt out. 'Did you talk to her? She's called Sally, she said that the police were going to—'

'My colleague's interviewing the students.'

I feel as if I'm doing this all wrong. I want to come across as sensible and capable. Not like a silly woman focused on all the wrong things.

She looks up. 'Okay, let's get started.'

I'm expecting her to run through the events of yesterday, expecting her to want exact times, arrangements, phone calls made, texts sent. I'm expecting her to want *the full minutiae*, so when she says, 'What kind of mother would you say Kate is?', for a second, I'm floored.

'Sorry?' I stammer. 'I don't understand.'

'Kate?' she repeats. 'What kind of mother would you say she is?'

And, without hesitation, I say, 'The best. She is the best kind of mother.'

I think back to the health problems she's had with Fergus, her seven-year-old. 'Her son's been sickly for as long as I've known them,' I tell her. 'He had some kind of an eye problem no one could seem to resolve. And where I would be frantic, not coping and worrying about everything, Kate would make their trips to London to see the specialists an adventure. She'd make them something for Fergus to look forward to.'

I can remember Kate letting Fergus dress up as a superhero or a knight or a warrior. She'd create maps and games and quests for them to complete together on the train. I never once heard her complain about the disruption it caused them; never once did she act like it was a bind.

I look at DC Aspinall. 'Kate is the kind of mother you want to be, the kind you wish you had.'

'What about Mr Riverty?' she asks. 'Would you say that he's also a devoted parent?'

'Of course.'

She holds my gaze before flipping to another page in her notebook.

I chance a quick glance at Joe, and he raises his eyebrows. He's thinking the same thing as me, that she might be suspecting Guy of something. Which is ridiculous.

I don't know Guy *that* well – apart from that one time we went over there for dinner, we're not the kind of couple who socialize 'as a couple'. You know the types – where the men get together and talk about whatever it is men talk about, and the women stand in the kitchen complaining about how little their husbands do around the house. Joe and I tend to have separate friends. I see Kate socially and at school, but Joe and Guy would never go out for a pint together. Now that I think about it, I wonder why that is. I feel a stab of irritation, although I'm not sure exactly why.

'How well do you know Mr Riverty?' DC Aspinall asks.

'How well do you know anybody?' I reply, and I see immediately that philosophizing is not the way to go with her.

She says nothing and waits for me to answer the question appropriately.

'Not that well,' I say, 'but well enough to get the measure of him, if that's what you're asking.'

'We're just trying to get a picture of them as a family at this stage.'

'You don't think he's involved, do you?' I say, and immediately Joe admonishes me.

'*Lisa!*' he says sternly.

'What? It's what they do, isn't it? The police? First they check out the family.'

DC Aspinall looks to Joe and then to me. She speaks slowly and carefully.

'An enormous number of children go missing each year,' she says. 'Most are runaways, so we need to establish as fast as we can if the child has any reason to disappear of their own accord. That's why we examine the relationships within the family – it's important to know the dynamics before we start.'

'So you're asking me if I think Guy could be responsible for Lucinda running away?'

She tips her head to one side slightly, as if to say, *Could that be possible?*

'Not a chance,' I answer.

'How can you be so sure, if, like you say, you don't know him very well?'

'Because I know Kate and . . .' I pause, not sure whether to say what I want to say. 'I don't know how to word this, so I'm just going to spit it out . . . Let's decide that Guy is some kind of weirdo who makes his kids uncomfortable – Kate would be on to it like a shot. She watches those kids constantly, she tends to everything, she knows the name of every child in Fergus's class, she knows all the families of Lucinda's friends – where they live, what they do. She makes it her business to know. She misses nothing. Those children are her life. They come before everything.'

'Okay,' DC Aspinall says, and she takes a gulp of tea. She nods at Joe. 'Good brew.'

He smiles. 'She's got me well trained.'

'Let's go back to yesterday then,' she says. 'It was normal for the girls to have a sleepover on a school night?'

'Yes,' I reply. 'They're great friends, they—' Then I stop. 'Actually, it's not normal.' Confused, I turn to Joe. 'Has that ever happened before, Joe? Lucinda staying here on a school night?'

'No idea,' he says, shrugging. 'She's here a lot, so I can't say I've ever paid it that much attention.'

I stare at DC Aspinall blankly. 'I don't know.'

'Who arranged it?' she asks. 'Can you remember?'

'Yes. Sally. She said she and Lucinda needed to work on an assignment together. I think it was a group thing. Kate would know. Anyway, Sally asked if Lucinda could come here for the night so they could work on it together, and then stay over. I can't say I thought much about it, because, like Joe says, she's here a lot.'

'What about getting to school the next morning?' she asks. 'Would Mrs Riverty just assume you would take the girls?'

'What? Oh, no. Both girls get the minibus. It picks up all the children in Troutbeck and takes them to school each day.'

'What firm is that?'

'South Lakes Taxis,' I say, and she jots it down.

'Can I ask something?'

'Go ahead.'

'*When* did Lucinda disappear? Did she make it into school yesterday? Or has she been missing for a full twenty-four hours?'

'We're almost certain she went missing at the end of the school day. The register was taken at the start of the final lesson and she was marked down as present. But we're re-checking that with the students themselves. Would you say it would be usual for Mrs Riverty to contact her daughter during a sleepover?'

'I would have thought so, knowing Kate.'

Had Kate tried to call Lucinda and not received a reply? It happened often enough with Sally. The first few times we went ballistic, but then, like I'm sure most parents of teenagers do, with time, we let it go.

I choose my battles with Sally carefully and I gave up on this one a while back, probably around the time I gave up on nagging about the state of her bedroom.

'Kate sent a text to Lucinda, but it went unanswered,' DC Aspinall says. 'And I wondered if, as a parent, that would make you worried enough to call? To try to make contact with the parents?'

I thought about this. Could she really be putting some blame on Kate for not following up on a text?

'There have been times when Sally has stayed over with Lucinda and she's not replied to my texts. Girls get giddy, they get carried away in whatever it is they're doing. You know what it's like.'

Seemingly, DC Aspinall doesn't know, because she makes no gesture of agreement.

'But, to be honest,' I say, 'because I know she's with Kate, I've never really worried about her if she's at Lucinda's. Perhaps if Sally stays at someone else's house, perhaps if she's with a friend I know less well, maybe that would make me call the parents and check on her.'

This seems to satisfy, because DC Aspinall stops with this line of questioning and she goes on to ask me about what sort of girl Lucinda is. Could she be hiding anything from her parents? When I sense we're done I ask the thing I've wanted to know since she walked in.

'What do *you* think's happened to her?'

'Impossible to say,' she replies.

'But if you had to say. If you had to call it one way or another, would you say you thought Lucinda—'

'At this stage we're exploring every avenue.'

I nod. A large part of me has been hoping to hear DC Aspinall say she thought Lucinda was a runaway. Then my guilt wouldn't be quite so all-encompassing. But of course Lucinda hasn't left of her own accord. Why on earth would she?

'One last thing,' DC Aspinall says, matter-of-fact, as she goes to stand. 'We'll be needing an account of your whereabouts, both of you . . . from around three o'clock yesterday afternoon.'

'So, Charles,' – the estate agent regards him, blinks – 'are you wanting to view properties like this one? Properties right on the lake? Or are you open to anything?'

'I'd prefer something with lake access if possible. Actually, I'd really like a boathouse – but I suppose if the right property came along then I'd be happy to go for anything—'

'I understand,' she says, nodding. 'Though I'm sure you're going to love this one – it is exceptional.'

He hangs back as she unlocks the front door and deals with the alarm. No one home then, he notes. Once she's inside the hallway, she turns, beaming at him, waiting for him to ooh and aah. Waiting for him to gush about the oak panelling and the original features. As if she herself had some hand in building the thing.

'Impressive,' he says, to appease her, but he doesn't really think so. Whoever owns this place doesn't have any real taste. The stair carpet is cheap, and the stained glass fitted inside the porch is tacky.

'Let me show you the kitchen,' she says. 'It's amazing.'

Her stilettos move fast across the parquet floor. He watches her walk and sees that the hem of her skirt is hanging low. A thread of black cotton has come loose and is snaking down her calf.

'It's a wonderful room, flooded with light,' she says. 'A perfect family room, wouldn't you say?'

He doesn't even bother commenting on that. Feels like he's in one of those aggravating relocation programmes where the women declare the kitchen to be the 'heart of the home'. The kind of women who want a 'usable space where we can all be together', and their teenage kids look on as if they couldn't imagine anything worse.

The agent moves towards the wall of windows beyond the dining area and asks, 'Where are you living at the moment?'

'Grasmere,' he answers.

'Oh? It's just I'm not familiar with your name, so I assumed you weren't from the area.'

She's clumsy in her quest to figure out if he can really afford this place. She's smiling at him, waiting for him to divulge more information. He doesn't.

He examines her: all that loose flesh squeezed into something that's supposed to pass for professional attire. Look into this woman's face and you'll see her life. He pictures her running out of the house in the morning, stuffing a Mr Kipling's French Fancy into her mouth, pretending she's not wearing yesterday's knickers, climbing into her car, which is littered with crisps and bits of crap.

They move back to the kitchen and she runs her hand across the rose granite worktop.

'What line of business are you in?' she asks casually. Before he answers he notices the wedding band on her left hand is cutting into the flesh.

'Commercial property, hotels,' he says.

'Oh,' she answers brightly. 'Which ones?'

'I'd rather not say at this stage, because I'm thinking of selling, and I don't want it to be common knowledge. Often guests don't like the idea of staying somewhere that's for sale.'

'I assure you I would never discuss a client's affairs outside of—'

He smiles. 'I'm not really a client though yet, am I?' he says mildly.

'Prospective client, then.'

Suddenly she's looking at him from beneath her lashes in a flirty, girlish way. 'Is there another hotel you're looking to invest in?'

'I'm trying to get away from the hotel business, actually. Too tying. I can't find decent managers, and then there's the problem of the great British public . . . No, I'm thinking of trying my hand at an online business. Importing goods that are already selling well within the US.'

She nods seriously and, not for the first time today, he marvels at how willing people are to believe whatever you tell them. They really want to believe, even if their insides are screaming doubt. He's enjoying himself now and relaxes his guard a fraction.

'Do you have a property to sell?' she asks.

He snatches his head around. 'W–what?' he stammers.

'A house? Are you renting right now, or do you have something to sell before moving?'

Why didn't he prepare an answer to this? Why not look up some addresses before coming here?

He shakes his head, looks away. His palms begin to itch.

'Can I take a look at that?' He motions to the literature she's brought with her about the house.

'Oh,' she says, 'you don't have one of these? Sorry, I thought you'd already seen this.'

She moves towards him and lays the brochure open on the work-top. As she gets in close he catches a whiff of her, and his stomach heaves.

The room is warm and, as she leans forward, her jacket is pulled open a little, filling the air with a pungent smell of oniony sweat, fake tan and stale old fag breath.

What the fuck does she think she's doing getting this near to him?

He shifts slightly. His palms are itching furiously now. It's a deep, crawling sensation beneath his skin. He tries to step away from her, but she's oblivious. She's running her fat index finger, the one with the fleck of polish near the cuticle, along the text. Suddenly she's talking at break-neck speed about freehold leases and mains water and private drainage. His head is scrambled and he can barely breathe because this disgusting woman is taking up all the oxygen.

He swallows. 'Please move away from me.'

'I'm sorry?'

'Move away.'

Affronted, she does as he asks.

'Is something wrong? I can assure you this house is priced very competitively, if you look at other lakeshore properties you'll find very little difference between—'

He's holding up his hand, signalling for her to stop. He closes his eyes and takes one long, slow breath. 'Thank you,' he says, 'but I'm finished here,' and begins making for the door. Before he reaches it, though, she speaks, and what she says makes him pause.

'You can't afford this house.'

He turns, tries to make sense of what she's saying.

She continues: 'You've wasted my time. Jesus! It's not like I've not got enough to do.' She clenches her jaw and looks him up and down, disdainfully.

Which sadly leaves him no alternative.

He walks towards her and, pulling back his arm, he forms a fist. It gives him no pleasure at all to do this; he's not a natural when it comes to violence, but when he hits her square in the face, the force knocks her to the floor three feet away from where she was standing. She comes to rest by the American fridge.

She's too stunned to make a sound and perhaps she couldn't even if she wanted to, because her nose has exploded across her face. Her grotesque mouth is now so full of blood it's possible she'll drown in her own juices.

She lifts her hands to her face in horror, gagging on the secretions in her throat.

He shakes his head. 'You are not the right person for this job,' he says resignedly, and walks out, his bloodied hand thrust deep inside his jacket pocket.

10

I LOOK AT MY WATCH. It's only twelve twenty. I feel like I've lived five lifetimes already this morning. Joe has gone to join the search. Local residents have arranged three different parties. One in Troutbeck, covering the fields between the school and Kate's house. This is a few square miles, but they're using quad bikes, the ones the shepherds use for dealing with sheep high up on the fells. The next search party is covering the school grounds, playing fields and the wooded area that runs down from the school to the shores of Lake Windermere. The last is covering the area between the school and Windermere village itself. Plenty of students walk back to Windermere village after school, calling at Greggs, the Co-op, the library (if they've not got Broadband at home). It's just over a mile, and the thinking is that Lucinda could have headed this way if she had in fact decided to run away.

But I know it's all fruitless.

Lucinda didn't bunk off and go into Windermere. Lucinda has been taken to a place and raped. Just like Molly Rigg.

I think of Lucinda, and my insides coil tight. She would never run away and put her parents through this. Not in a million years. Sally often complains that Lucinda can be such a goody-goody. It upsets her, the fact that Lucinda never gets told off, that she never comes to lessons unprepared, that she always wins the prize for neatest uniform.

Lucinda would never leave of her own accord. Never.

Suddenly, I'm filled with a blind panic and a deep need to have my own children right where I can see them. I run downstairs, my heart pounding, frantically searching for my car keys. I need to get my children and have them at home with me. Safe where no one can touch them. Screw school; they should be here.

I toss papers, gloves and hats and unpaid bills from the cabinet by the front door. Eventually I find them in my coat pocket and it's only when I get outside and see the car's not there that I realize it's still outside Sam's school. From when Joe picked me up earlier this morning.

Temporarily, I'm powerless. I go back inside and call my mother. It's the only thing I can think to do.

It's ringing, and she picks up.

There's a pause as she takes a long deep drag of her cigarette before speaking. 'Hello?' she says, then coughs.

'It's me.' As expected, my voice cracks.

She knows what's happened. It's a small place, and news travels fast. My mother cleans the NatWest Bank in the morning before it opens and, from there, she goes straight to one of her cash-in-hand jobs. She could clean three houses fewer a week if she didn't smoke forty fags a day. Her answer to that is that they're her only pleasure, and without them she can't open her bowels. So I don't get on at her too much about it.

I tell my mother about needing to bring the kids home, about being scared someone will steal them and, 'Lisa,' she says firmly, 'leave them children at school. It will do them no good whatsoever being home with you. Not with you in this state. No one's going to steal them today, anyhow. Not when everyone's on high alert.'

She's always been good in a crisis. I suppose because she's had to, being that we were my dad's second family, his *other* family.

He lived in Wigton, in the north of the county, and we saw him once every three or four weeks. We lived pretty much in poverty, my mother doing scraps of jobs to make ends meet, my dad providing what little money he had spare. But he had another four kids to support back in Wigton, and there wasn't much to go around.

The winter was a harsh one, and a group of us kids on the estate had made a sledging run on the pavement outside our house. No one had sledges then, just tea trays and black bags. I can remember one kid bringing a swimming-pool lilo.

We were lining up for our turn on the sledging run when a car crept around the corner. It was a taxi, one of those huge Rovers – a three and a half litre, built like a tank. It pulled up beside us, and a woman got out.

She was well-dressed. Posh. She wore a woollen, camel-coloured coat with a cameo brooch on the lapel, and her hair was pulled neatly into a bun on the top of her head. She carried a patent-leather handbag, a trapezium-shaped thing, the type favoured by Maggie Thatcher and the Queen, and as she cast her eyes over the ragtag and bobtail group in front of her, she shocked us all by saying, 'Which one of you lot is Harold's little bastard?'

A few of the older boys sniggered at her use of language. She meant me, of course. I wasn't exactly sure what 'bastard' meant, but I'd been referred to as it before, and knew it wasn't a good thing.

When no one spoke, she moved among us, picking her way through the snow towards our front door. My mother opened it, and the woman disappeared inside.

Then it started to snow. Big clumps of snow the size of small oranges and, because I was dressed in just a thin anorak, something you'd dress a child in on a rainy day in June, I went in.

The woman was perched on the edge of the sofa in the lounge – the only room besides the bathroom that had any heat – and as I entered she jumped up, clapping her hands together. 'Lisa! I'm so glad to meet you,' she sang happily. I looked to my mother for direction but she seemed as baffled by this woman as I was.

'I'm your daddy's wife,' she said, still smiling. Then, to my mother, 'We should have some tea, Marion. How about some tea while I give the child her gifts?'

My mother obliged and went out to the kitchen. A moment later I remember hearing the back door slam as she nipped next door to get milk, or sugar, or tea, or cups . . . whatever it was that we were short of that day. My dad's wife reached into her handbag and produced two packs of Opal Fruits and a large Mint Aero.

Then, as I sat chewing happily in front of the fire, she reached back into that bag of hers and she whipped out a Stanley knife. She waved it around a couple of times with a flourish, saying, 'Lisa, I want you to make sure you tell your daddy *all about this*,' and I nodded seriously – assuming she meant the sweets, not knowing what the Stanley was for.

Then she did the unthinkable. Carefully, she pushed up each sleeve of her camel coat to the elbow, revealing her milky-skinned arms, and began cutting deep, deep gashes into her wrists.

I was too frightened to move, and by the time my mother came back in to ask how she liked her tea, my father's wife was slumped on the sofa, her blood pooling upon her knee like a blanket.

'Go next door,' was all my mother said, calmly, succinctly. Then she added, as if to no one in particular, 'I told him this would happen. I knew it would come to this.'

We never saw my father again. Any crisis that came our way,

my mother dealt with alone. And she did it in the same way she's handling me now, in a straightforward manner, no fuss, no drama.

'What should I do?' I ask her, my voice hysterical, my head throbbing.

'About what? I've told you to keep the kids at school.'

'About Kate. I have to do something. I can't just stay here going crazy.'

'Joe's out there searching,' she says. 'What else *can* you do?'

'I told her I'd find her.'

She takes another long drag. 'Well, that was a bloody stupid thing to say. What on earth made you promise that?'

'Because Kate said, "Find her." What was I supposed to do? Say no?'

'You'd better make a start, then.'

'I've got no car.'

'You've got legs, haven't you?' she says. 'Use those.'

I set out with the rough notion of heading over to Kate's side of the valley to do my own search. It's a bit vague and I'm not holding much hope of finding anything. But like I told my mother, I can't just sit and do nothing.

It should take around twenty-five minutes to walk across the valley to Kate's. I've got my hiking boots on, because there's no grip left on my wellies, and I'm wrapped up as thickly as possible while still maintaining the ability to move. If I weren't feeling totally overwhelmed by what's facing me at the moment, it would feel strange heading out without the three dogs. As if I were cheating them by going for a walk alone.

I slide a couple of times when I get to the main road. The asphalt is glassy and shining. The sun, so low in the sky, is hitting the ice crystals on the pavement surface, making it glisten. My shadow stretches out before me. I'm around twenty feet tall and my head is the size of a tennis ball.

It was around this time yesterday that Lucinda disappeared, and I find myself wondering if she was dressed for this weather. Most days I have a battle on my hands getting Sally and James to wear coats for school. '*Nobody* wears coats,' they chime, in the same way James now refuses to wear anything from Gap. 'Gay and Proud, Mum, that's what it stands for.'

'That's not what it stands for,' I argue, but by then he's backing out of the room, my opinion not relevant.

He's twelve now, but I can fast see the teenager he is about to become. He's taken to sneaking around the house to avoid conversation. I walk into the kitchen, and I hear his footsteps creep off upstairs. I remember the fear I felt just before his birth, the paralysing certainty that there was no way I could possibly love this second child like I loved Sally. How on earth could I generate that level of love twice? But then there he was. And then there the love was. I didn't even have to try. Now I endeavour to lay that love on him, but he writhes away. He doesn't need it right now. Doesn't need me.

My mind volleys to Lucinda again and I wonder if she left without a coat yesterday. You could not survive a night at these temperatures. Typical Lake District weather is mild, and unless you do something particularly stupid, like go up Great Gable or Scafell wearing flip-flops, you could probably survive a night in the open. You wouldn't die of exposure.

Not in this weather, though. Not last night.

Suddenly I have an image of Lucinda lying dead against a drystone wall, dumped and discarded. Stripped to the waist like that other girl.

But, unlike Molly Rigg, Lucinda is dead. This girl he decided to kill before chucking her out of the car and driving off.

I'm in the shadow of the valley now, making my way up the other side towards Kate and Guy's house, trying to shake the images from my brain. It's colder, and even though the day is crisp and bright, it's dark on this side. Eerie.

My mind's playing tricks. I keep seeing flashes of colour amid the white. Keep jolting my head around at the sound of the jackdaws in the trees, expecting to see Lucinda up there, smiling and waving.

At the top of the road I turn left and all at once I can hear noise. Commotion, voices. Quickly, I make my way along the road and after the next bend I see what's causing it.

There are vans. Cars. Newspeople. There are cameras and satellite dishes on the tops of vehicles. The road around Kate's house is almost blocked.

Jesus Christ, I think, they've found her! And I break into a run.

But they've not.

They've found nothing. Kate and Guy are doing a press conference at the front of the house by the big red door.

Guy is speaking; he's doing the talking. He's the one giving out the information, and Kate stands by him, silent. She has that look on her face. Haunted. As if she's gone missing, too. There's no life left behind the eyes, no movement, not even a twitch in the muscles of her face. It's empty.

I hang back so as not to draw attention to myself. Alexa sees me and glares, furious that I'm here.

Guy is talking and talking, but I can't hear his words. His mouth is moving fast, like he's giving a running commentary, and he's gesticulating and pointing down the valley. As if this will somehow give the watching public an idea of where his daughter might be. Then he looks at his wife's face, and he stops, unable to go on.

It's the worst thing I've ever had to watch.

Worse than watching the vet euthanize an abused dog, because it's kinder to kill the thing than to keep it alive. Worse than watching my father's wife slitting her wrists right there in front of me.

There's nothing as bad as a missing child. Nothing at all.

He drifts along the aisles trying to look as though he's browsing, like everyone else in here. Killing time in the DIY store. He can't decide if he would be less conspicuous buying the supplies he needs now, or if he should chance using the hardware shop in Windermere.

Both have drawbacks. Here, it's the cameras. There, it's the nosey, chatty staff.

He wouldn't have this problem in a city. No one gives a shit what you need rolls of polythene for if you live in Newcastle or Liverpool.

He takes a detour outside and makes like he's comparing the sizes of the bags of ornamental gravel while he decides. He doesn't want to hang around for too long in one place, because people notice.

And he's got an admirer.

A sad-looking redhead in a denim jacket and spike-heeled boots keeps following him. So far she's put caustic soda, mildew remover and a four-pack of decorator's dust sheets in her trolley. He suspects she needs none of these items and he's tempted to stay by the gravel a bit longer. Just to see how she fares hauling a 30 kilogram bag of aggregate.

Back inside, he makes the decision to split his shopping trip between two stores. The cleaning products he'll get from here, the protective sheeting he'll get from the builders' supply yard. He's just remembered that the staff there couldn't be less interested in what you're purchasing.

He runs through the list in his head. Bleach. Cloths. Black bags. Might as well get a mop and bucket to make the job faster.

His wife likes those Vileda mops. Says the floor dries quicker than with the old cloth types, so he's probably best to pick up one of those.

11

KATE SEES ME hanging over by the road and stares back at me blankly. I'm about to turn and go back the way I've come, because it's immediately obvious I've made a mistake. It was stupid to show up here.

I think I had some half-baked notion that if they could see me searching, if they could see just how much I want to put things right, it might go some way towards helping them to forgive.

Stupid. Stupid and self-centred. I'm embarrassed I came.

I turn to go, take a few steps, and hear, 'Excuse me?'

A woman is making her way towards me. At first I start in her direction but then I see she's a reporter. She's immaculate, clearly not local press – she has to be national news to be dressed in this way: navy cashmere coat, flawless hair and make-up. 'Do you know the family?' she asks.

'I'm a friend.'

'What can you tell us about the missing girl? What kind of girl was she?'

I stare at her. '*Is she*,' I correct. 'You mean to say, what kind of girl *is* she.'

'Of course. Apologies,' she says briskly. 'Do you know the Riverty family well?'

I nod, but I'm feeling hugely uncomfortable. I shouldn't be speaking to this woman, and I glance to the house to see that Kate and Guy have retreated back inside. 'I'm sorry,' I tell her, trying to walk away, 'but I really must go.'

'Please, just one moment, it won't take long.' Her eyes are full of kindness. Is it fake? I can't tell. 'I won't take up any more of your time than I have to, but the media plays a crucial role in finding missing children. We can get information to the public in an instant. It can *really* mean the difference between the child being found alive . . . and—'

She doesn't finish the sentence. She doesn't have to. She knows she has me.

'What do you want to know?' I say.

She whips out a recording device from her handbag. 'State your name and spell it as well, please.'

I'm spelling out K-A-L-L-I-S-T-O when I see Kate in the drawing-room window.

'I'm sorry,' I say, 'I'm not sure I should be doing this,' and the reporter's face hardens in an instant.

'Okay, but can you just confirm something for us?' She doesn't wait for an answer. 'Is it true that Lucinda Riverty has an older boyfriend? A much older boyfriend. Can you confirm that?'

'What?' I say, shocked. 'No.'

'No, as in *not true*? Or, no, as in you can't confirm it, because you don't know?'

I stammer something along the lines of it not being true but, to be honest, I'm thrown. Where has she got this from? Who is telling the press this stuff?

I look at her levelly, because all at once I'm annoyed. 'Have you seen a picture of Lucinda?'

'Yes, a school one. We could do with another, actually.'

'So if you've seen a picture of her then you know she's not the kind of slutty girl you are making her out to be—'

'I did not suggest for a second she was slutty.'

'Yes you did. Lucinda's running around *with a much older*

boyfriend. You go printing crap like that and instantly people stop caring. People think, oh, well, she's obviously *that kind* of girl. She'll probably turn up dead.'

She goes to interrupt, defending her job, but I continue on.

'That's what journalists do. You write, "Mr So-and-so, who was the victim of an armed attack *at his eight hundred thousand pound home.*" It's the same deal. You're telling people how sorry they should feel for the victims instead of just reporting it. You make me sick.'

'That's what news is . . . Mrs—' she pauses, and I remind her, answering 'Kallisto.'

A faint smile crosses her lips. 'Oh yes. That wouldn't happen to be the same Mrs Kallisto who was supposed to be looking after Lucinda Riverty, would it? . . . At the time she disappeared?'

Shocked into silence, I glare at her.

'That's not what happened,' I say finally. 'That's not how it was—', but she's moved the digital recorder back towards my lips.

'How about you tell me, in your own words, exactly *what did* happen?'

I glance towards Kate's house. She's still there, in the drawing-room window, beckoning for me to come up.

I turn to the reporter. I know I'm guilty. I know that Lucinda's disappearance is my fault. But saying it out loud to this woman? Saying it out loud to the nation, and having them judge me, having this vile woman put words into my mouth? I can't do it. It's the coward's approach, but I can't bring myself to form the words.

'Mrs Kallisto?' she prompts, and, short of something intelligent and cutting to say, I tell her to piss off and make my way to the house.

Kate is standing right there in the hallway when I go in. For a second I hesitate. She sees my apprehension and embraces me.

She feels so tiny beneath her clothes that I think: When did this happen? When did she get so thin without my noticing?

'What did that reporter say to you?' she asks.

'Nothing,' I reply uneasily. 'Just if I knew you. I told her I did but that I couldn't answer her questions.'

'I've been watching her.'

'She's very businesslike. I suppose you've got to be if you're to survive in that game.' I don't tell Kate what the reporter said to me.

'They're here fast,' I say. 'The media.'

'It's because of that other girl,' Kate replies. 'Because Lucinda's the second one to disappear.'

My voice is weak and shaky. I want to ask Kate how she is, but I can't bring myself to do it, because it's such an inadequate question. Because you know they're not all right. You know they're holding on to the edge, their fingernails scratching to keep a hold.

She looks at me as if sensing what I'm thinking and says, 'I'm so scared, Lisa. I'm so fucking scared.'

My heart is breaking for her. 'I know,' I say softly. 'I know.'

'Where is she?'

'They'll find her.'

Kate rubs her face with her hands. She's exhausted. We move through to the kitchen. I can hear the quiet pitter-patter of footsteps signalling there are people upstairs, but compared to earlier, the house is deafeningly quiet. Everyone must be out searching.

We sit down at the kitchen island. There's a huge lean-to conservatory that runs along the back of Kate's house; it's flooding the kitchen with white light from the snow-covered garden.

From where I'm sitting I can see the children's playhouse. It's painted in nursery colours to look like the gingerbread cottage from Hansel and Gretel. Sally and Lucinda spent whole days out there when they were nine or ten. Making up clubs, and secret codes, and whatever it is girls do at that age. It seems so painfully long ago now.

'I know this sounds stupid,' Kate says quietly, 'but I never thought this would happen to me. I never thought I'd be the woman on the news, the woman you never want to be. I always thought I was protected somehow. I always thought I was shielded from things like this.' She tries to smile. 'Stupid, really.' Her eyes are red-raw, her skin almost see-through.

'Kate, I'm so sorry. I don't know how to tell you how sorry I am.'

She takes my hands in hers. 'Stop saying that, Lisa. Please. You've said it already. This is not your fault. It's nobody's fault. *I* should have checked as well, if we're looking to apportion blame.'

I shake my head. 'I don't know how you can do this,' I say, truly staggered by how she's dealing with the situation, by what she's saying. 'I don't know how you can be so discerning. Is that really how you feel?'

'What's the use?' she says softly. 'I've not got the energy for anger right now. I just want her home.'

'She will be.'

And she looks at me, the dark shadow across her face lifting for a second. 'Do you know what?' she says, 'I really think she will. I think she *will* come home. I'm at the stage now where I don't care what's happened to her as long as I get her back. We can get through anything as long as she's alive.'

I do my best to put what I hope is a positive expression on my face. Try to show: *Yes, absolutely, Lucinda is coming home.* But I don't know if I pull it off, because I don't really believe it. How can I believe it when I've watched family after family go through this on the news? Split open with grief when their child turns up dead.

I stand and hug Kate again. 'Where's Fergus?' I ask her.

'Upstairs with Alexa.'

'How is he?'

'He knows an awful thing has happened, he knows Lucinda's not here, but he doesn't understand the consequences of it. He's no idea of the danger she's in and we've purposely not told him.'

'Of course.'

'How's Sally?' she asks.

Typical of Kate to be concerned about my kids at a time like this.

'Pretty awful, but I've not spoken to her since this morning. I tried calling. The police were at school interviewing them and I've heard nothing since. She blames herself, as you'd expect.'

'Why was she off yesterday?'

'Stomach pains – nothing serious. I couldn't stay home with her 'cause there was too much going on at work and so she—'

'You should have called,' Kate says. 'I would have kept an eye on her—' and then she stops.

Because we're both thinking the same thing.

If only I *had* called her.

There's an extended moment of silence as we both consider the what-ifs, the if-onlys, then I shudder as I hear footsteps coming from the floor above.

Kate senses my anxiety. 'She's just using the loo. She's not on her way down here.'

She means Alexa, of course, and I let my breath out slowly.

'I'm sorry she was so fierce earlier,' Kate says. 'It's just her way. To blame, I mean.'

I avert my gaze. What I always do when Alexa is the subject of conversation.

'She was right to blame,' I say quietly, but Kate's mind is suddenly elsewhere. She's looking past me to the corner of the room, and her eyes have glazed over.

12

DC JOANNE ASPINALL walks up the steps to the doctor's surgery. It's 5.40 p.m.

Missing girl number two, day one, and the pressure is building. She had been going to cancel this appointment. She had been going to stay at the station, keep working. But her boss told her they weren't going to get any further with the investigation today. He sent Joanne home, telling her to call at the Rivertys' while she was heading back that way. 'Let them know we're doing everything we can. Take some more details, speak to the press if necessary.'

Guy Riverty had been out with the search parties and Kate was being looked after by her sister. Joanne hadn't stayed long.

Detectives usually work office hours – nine to five; staying late if the case warrants it. Sometimes Joanne missed the shifts of a WPC – she used to get more errands done when she worked nights. She sees her reflection in the glass doors at the top of the steps and touches her hair briefly. It has all but come loose from her ponytail. She can't remember the last time she had a proper cut.

The waiting room's full and it's Joanne's instinct to drop her head. She keeps a low profile in Windermere. She knows better than to advertise the fact she's CID.

She'd read something recently about 'Making the police more visible'. Some daft government adviser suggesting that, because of the cutbacks, they should make the most of police officers. Cultivate a greater perception of police presence – bobbies on the beat and all that.

The idea was that police officers should travel to and from work in uniform. Joanne had laughed out loud when she read it. You go in and out of your *house* in your uniform and it won't be more than a day before your windows are egged and your tyres are flat. And that's in a nice area.

Joanne punches her details into the computerized thing on the wall that lets the surgery staff know you've arrived. The old people never use it, so you can sometimes jump the queue a bit while they wait for the receptionist to deal with them. She takes a seat next to a smiling old lady, who says to her, 'Flu jab?', and Joanne says yes. Just because it's easier.

There's a pharmacy within the surgery, which Joanne thinks is a terrific idea. No more driving round in the pouring rain, clutching your prescription, nowhere open after 5 p.m. This pharmacy keeps the same hours as the doctors, so you're done and dusted all in one go.

Joanne spies a copy of *World of Interiors* – which her Auntie Jackie calls 'World of Inferiors', and bypasses it, opting instead for the December issue of *Good Housekeeping*. Unusual to find an up-to-date copy in here, she thinks, and muses over ways to liven up Christmas dinner: Why not try goose? Or guinea fowl? Her eyes settle on a salmon terrine (suitable for diabetics), but her thoughts are never far from the missing girl.

When Joanne first moved to CID she found it hard to live alongside the job. She wasn't like those TV detectives, the ones who never switch off, the ones who drink heavily, who go against the boss and lose their family to the force in the process.

Joanne's problem was more subtle than that. She found she suffered from a heavy guilt the minute her thoughts drifted elsewhere, the minute she went back to the mundane tasks of normal living.

If she wasn't thinking about her current case, she felt that she *should* be.

She was more used to it now. She managed it better. She'd come to liken it to the creative process she'd heard artists speak about. When their attention was diverted by other things, their subconscious was busily working away on their behalf, figuring things out, solving problems.

Joanne found that if she let her mind wander, if she let it relax, then ideas and answers would pop up like traffic cones. One minute they were absent and the next they were everywhere she looked.

She hears the buzzer signalling they're ready for the next patient, and her name appears. The old lady next to her seems a bit perturbed that Joanne is going in ahead of her, but Joanne doesn't bother to explain she's not really having the flu jab after all.

She's nervous because she's going to have to undress. She's not prudish, not even shy, she just doesn't like to see the look on the face of whoever she is undressing *for*.

She knocks once before going in, and Dr Ravenscroft, Joanne's GP since childhood, greets her. 'Joanne! Good to see you. Take a seat. How are you today?'

'Well, thanks.'

'And how's your aunt? I've not seen her in a while.'

'Same old, same old – they don't call her Mad Jackie for nothing.'

He chuckles.

'She's still living with you, then?' he asks.

'Think I'm going to be stuck with her for ever.'

He smiles sympathetically. 'And what about you? Are you still busy fighting crime?'

'Trying to.'

'Wonderful. Wonderful.' He starts typing, bringing up her notes. 'Now, what can I do for you today?'

'I'd like a breast reduction.'

He doesn't look up. 'Not really a fan of them myself,' he mumbles absently, and Joanne's not sure what she's supposed to say to that. 'You're having upper-back pain, sweat rashes?'

'Pretty much,' she answers. 'The back pain's not continuous but it's vicious when it hits. My main problem, though, is here,' and she motions to the area between her neck and shoulder.

'Trapezius,' he says. 'Gets quite tight in there, does it?'

Joanne pushes her thumb in. 'It's almost solid. I've got permanent indentations on each side from my bra straps.'

She reaches beneath her blouse and hooks the right strap out from where it's become embedded within the muscle. The relief is temporary as she gives the skin a quick rub. She slides her index finger inside the groove the strap has made; it's half an inch deep. It feels fiery hot to the touch.

'Does it affect your work?' he asks.

'Sometimes.'

She doesn't want to tell him in what way. Doesn't really want to share that she can't run without feeling humiliated, can't conduct an interview without first feeling embarrassed. She's done her best to put a brave face on things in the past and not let this get in the way, but it seems now that she's approaching her late thirties, the fear of being viewed with ridicule is not so easy to shrug off.

Doctor Ravenscroft nods gravely. 'You know you won't be able to breastfeed.'

'I don't even have a boyfriend . . . breastfeeding's not exactly top of my agenda.'

'It might be one day,' he says, his tone suddenly breezy. 'Nice chap comes along, sweeps you off your feet . . .'

Joanne just looks at him.

'Never say "never"!' he says. 'Lovely girl like you, there's bound to be some fellow waiting in the wings, ready to take you home and make you his wife . . .'

'But where would I put the unicorn?' Joanne says flatly.

Joanne gets her referral to the plastic surgeon.

Leaving Dr Ravenscroft's room, she walks past the phlebotomist, past the treatment room where all the oldies are having their flu jabs, past the cleaner's store cupboard and back through to the main waiting area. She's about to leave through the double glass doors when she hears something that makes her stop.

'Do you pay for your prescriptions?' the assistant in the pharmacy is asking the man.

'Yes,' comes the reply. Then, 'Oh, actually, no. I don't pay for this one . . . it's for a child . . . see?'

Apologetically, the assistant says, 'Of course it is. It'll be ready in just a moment.'

It's Guy – Guy Riverty – who's waiting for a prescription. What is he doing here? Wasn't he supposed to be out with the search parties?

The first thing that pops into Joanne's head is that he must be picking something up for Kate. Something to calm her nerves, to make her sleep. But then he's just said it's for a child. No prescription charge. It's exempt.

Joanne decides to wait inside her car.

She climbs in, and the temperature gauge reads minus seven. She turns the ignition to get the heat going and automatically there's a blast of music. One of Auntie Jackie's Michael Bublé CDs that she's been listening to. 'Smug bastard,' Joanne mutters, and kills the stereo.

She switches her headlights on so she can't be seen so easily inside the car, and remembers something Lisa Kallisto said earlier in the day. She said Kate's son had health problems. 'Been sickly for as long as they'd been friends,' was more or less what she'd said, and Joanne decides that's the reason for Guy being here.

So she calls it a day. Guy must be here for a prescription for their son, she thinks, and dips the clutch, puts the car into gear. Just as she edges forward, though, she sees Guy Riverty emerge. He's looking harried.

To be expected, she thinks.

He's glancing around furtively.

His daughter's missing, she reasons.

He drives off in his Audi Q7 V12 – a hundred grand's worth of car – without his headlights on.

Yeah, well, he's distracted.

But then, at the top of the road, instead of taking a left towards home, he goes right.

Bit odd, Joanne thinks. So she follows him.

13

JOANNE KEEPS WELL back. Stays a safe distance behind Guy Riverty. If he were to slow down for any reason, and she were to get too close, he'd see her in his rear-view mirror. He has a personalized numberplate – GR 658 – and his huge Audi, bright white in colour, is lit up like a Christmas float. If you were up to something dodgy, it would be the last car you'd want to be driving. It's about as conspicuous as you can get.

They drive through Bowness village. It's the busiest place in the National Park in the summer months, but now, in these dead weeks of mid-December, there's no one around. The shops are shut. Joanne remembers they tried staying open till seven this time last year in the run-up to Christmas. 'Shop Till Late!' they advertised, but no one had bothered this time around. There's no money now. Everybody's skint.

She sees Guy pull into a space just along from Bargain Booze, so Joanne parks about twenty yards away from him. He gets out, disappears inside, and a minute later he's back out again, lighting what looks like a Café Crème cigar. Then he climbs into his car and drives off without checking his mirror, almost colliding with an old Peugeot 206, before tearing off down the hill.

The road's been gritted heavily, but still, he's driving too fast. Even by Joanne's standards he's driving too fast. It's a narrow road, cars parked up on the left-hand side, and in these conditions he's not leaving any room for error.

But Joanne can forgive that. Your daughter's been abducted, you're allowed a bit of leeway.

He approaches the mini-roundabout and he should turn right here. If he's heading back home, he needs to do a right.

He doesn't. He heads on towards the lake, and then it's as if he knows he's being followed because he pulls a quick left on to Brantfell Road.

'Fuck,' Joanne whispers.

Brantfell Road is steep. Must be about a 30-degree slope, and it won't have been gritted properly. It's not a real thoroughfare, just leads to housing, so it's not a priority. Guy Riverty has disappeared up there out of sight in a matter of seconds, and Joanne can't even get her Mondeo to tackle the first part.

She puts her foot down on the accelerator and her tyres spin uselessly. There's an old guy standing watching. He has an ancient black Patterdale Terrier shivering at his feet. The old guy shakes his head at her. Then he starts circling his finger, telling her to turn around, telling her she won't make it up Brantfell.

'Yes, okay, okay,' she mouths at him, irritated.

What is it with old men?

Sometimes they stop to watch her parallel-park on the street where she lives, shaking their heads if they deem the space she's trying to get into to be too small. You'd never get a woman doing that. You'd never get a woman stopping to say you were about to hit something, or taking the responsibility upon themselves to wave you in, directing you like you were the pilot of a bloody aeroplane. Women just walk on past when she's trying to get into a tight space, perhaps throwing her a look of *Rather you than me*, but they'd never stop to watch.

Joanne forces herself to smile at the old guy when, really, what she wants to do is slam her fist on the dashboard. She's lost him. She's lost Guy Riverty.

The old guy approaches the driver's-side door and motions for Joanne to lower her window.

'Too icy for you up there, my love.'

His nose is purple, his eyes milked over and pale.

'Looks that way,' replies Joanne.

'You could try Helm Road instead, but if it were me, I'd leave the car down here. I wouldn't be chancing it.'

His terrier is looking up at Joanne. It's gone grey around the muzzle, a dead ringer for Spit the Dog. Joanne smiles at it, feeling kind of sorry that he's dragging it out in these temperatures.

'It's proper icy underfoot,' the man tells her. 'I've only made it down with these on,' and he lifts his foot, showing her the plastic ice grips he's attached to the sole of his boots. 'Like snow tyres for shoes, these,' he says proudly.

Joanne knows she won't make it up there on foot in her work shoes. They're not good on ice.

'Do you live on the hill?' Joanne asks him.

'Yep, Belle Isle View. I shouldn't be out really, broke my fibia when we had this weather last year, but Terence gets nowty if he's not had his evenin' walk.'

Terence looks like he's about to drop down dead, she thinks.

'You ever see that white Audi around here?' she asks him.

'That car what just went up?'

'Yes.'

'Don't think so. Doesn't live there, that's for certain. I know everybody up there and no one's got one o' them. There's a couple o' Range Rovers, though.' He smiles at this. '. . . Folk who can't really afford 'em, just showin' off. Reckon they'll all be gone soon enough, when the money's dried up. They're all on the tick, you know.'

'Isn't everything?' replies Joanne. 'So you can't remember seeing that car before now?'

He shakes his head. Then he cocks it to one side, looks at her kind of puzzled. 'Why d'you want to know anyway? You his wife?'

Joanne laughs. 'Just interested,' she says, and tells him thanks.

She lets the car roll back a little before attempting to turn, the wheels spinning a few times more than she'd like, but finally she makes it.

As she's about to get going again the old guy starts waving at her from the pavement.

Great, more driving advice, she thinks.

'I've remembered something,' he shouts. 'I've not seen that car up 'ere before now, but I have seen *him*. He used to drive summat else flashy, can't say what, but I remember the little cigars. Always got one in his mouth when he passes.'

Joanne shouts back, 'Much obliged,' and she can see he's pleased he's helped her.

Joanne gives him a small wave, and she's gone.

'That you, Joanne, love?'

Joanne steps in through the front door and the heat hits her. She walks straight to the thermostat and turns it down. Her Auntie Jackie has this place like an oven. Says she can never get warm. But every night, as soon as the two of them have eaten, they pass out on the settees with the heat. Like a couple of Magaluf tourists after a late lunch and a jug of sangria.

Mad Jackie's been living with Joanne for almost a year now, since declaring herself bankrupt. Shortly before she moved in, Martin, Joanne's boyfriend of three years, moved out. He decided he didn't want to take the relationship any further.

Joanne's friends rallied round, calling him a bastard, taking her out to get pissed – the usual cure for a broken heart. All of them were certain he had someone else, some slag somewhere.

Turned out he didn't, though. Turned out he didn't have

anyone else and he was still on his own. This was something Joanne struggled with privately. She didn't think it could be worse than being dumped for another person ... but it absolutely was. She felt humiliated. Especially when she saw him around Windermere and he pulled this kind of pained expression, as if he were physically hurting from letting her down like that.

Joanne had taken to flicking the 'V's his way when they caught sight of each other. Silly, but it made her feel better.

'Yes, it's me,' she shouts to Jackie, kicking her shoes off.

The lounge door opens. 'Your tea's in the oven,' says Jackie, arms folded across her chest. 'Why are you so late? Thought you'd be back an hour since.'

'Got held up.'

Auntie Jackie looks comical in her uniform. She's a carer. She wears a lilac dress, white tights and white clogs. And she's no lightweight. Jackie's had a ton of stress this last year and, like a lot of women, she swallows her stress along with any carbs she can find lying around the kitchen.

'You heard about that missing girl?' Jackie asks.

'Yeah, I've been up there today. Me and Ron Quigley are on it.'

Jackie's leaning against the lounge door. Her face is flushed pink. She's probably had a couple of Bacardi Breezers already.

'D'you think you'll find her?'

Joanne shrugs. 'Hope so. What's for tea?'

'Breaded fish. It's a bit dry. There's some tartare sauce in the fridge. Oh, and I got some nice strawberry trifles for afters.'

Joanne smiles at her. 'How many've you had?'

'Two. Saved you one, though.'

Jackie follows Joanne through to the kitchen. It's a mid-terrace house in the centre of Windermere. Two up, two down, with a kitchen extension at the back. 'I've just watched the girl's parents on the news. How were they doing when you saw 'em?' Jackie asks.

'Gutted. Scared. What you'd expect. Their name's Riverty – do you know them?'

Jackie shakes her head.

'They thought she was staying over at her friend's house after school, but that girl never went to school that day so . . . you know, crossed wires. I went up to interview the mother, the mother of the girl where she was supposed to be staying, and—'

'What's she called? She local?'

'Lisa Kallisto.'

Jackie's face drops and she blows out a sigh.

'You know her?'

'Yeah. Nice woman. She runs the animal shelter. I was only in there a couple o' days ago, dropping off the cat of a dead client. She's taken a few off my hands this past year . . . when I've not been able to get the relatives to take 'em, that is.'

'Client' never seems to be the right word to describe the people Jackie deals with. They're old folk in their own homes, folk who need help getting up, getting dressed, who need their commodes emptied.

Whenever Jackie mentions 'a client', Joanne imagines her handing out legal advice or completing tax returns. Not wiping arses and checking leg sores. Jackie can be difficult to deal with sometimes, but Joanne knows she's good at her job. She does the extras the young carers don't do. Like painting ladies' fingernails and calling to the library for audio books . . . and rehoming pets when she finds 'a client' dead in their bed.

'Lisa Kallisto's a grafter,' Jackie says. 'She's a good little worker, an' she's proper caring, too. She'll be beside herself if she thinks she's caused this.'

'They're friends – her and the other mother – good friends, I gather.'

Jackie sucks in the breath through her teeth; the air makes a whistling sound. 'That's awful,' she says. 'Imagine that! Your friend's kid goes missin' on account of you. That's really shit, that is.'

But Joanne couldn't imagine how it would be, because she didn't have kids. She wanted them, but she didn't hold out much hope. She knew of a woman in the village who'd paid to become 'inseminated', as she termed it, down at a private clinic in Cheshire.

'*Inseminated?*' Jackie had said, truly staggered, when Joanne told her about it. 'Why'd she not just go out and shag someone?'

Jackie's son worked abroad. Dubai. He'd cleared off after all the trouble of last year and hardly rang his mother any more. Joanne knew it broke Jackie's heart, but she never spoke of it. She was too ashamed about what had gone on.

Joanne opens the oven and sets her plate on a tray. She'll eat it on her knee in front of the telly and watch *Emmerdale.* Jackie's in the fridge getting the wine out. Officially, Jackie limits herself to half a bottle a night (because of the calories), but Joanne usually finds that she's drunk the other half by the end of the evening without really realizing. Jackie looks at her. 'Do you think it's that same pervert who raped that young girl and left her in Bowness? Do you think it's the same guy?'

'We were working on that presumption, but he only kept that girl for a few hours . . . and then he let her go.'

'So this one should have been back by now? That what you're saying?'

14

IT'S AS IF WE'VE been dropped into a new world. A world so unfamiliar and bleak that we don't know how to survive in it.

Me, Joe and the three kids are sitting around the kitchen table. The younger two, the boys, are shovelling their food down, racing against each other, as whoever finishes first will get to go back on the PlayStation. They feel the atmosphere and can't wait to escape.

Sally and I are pushing the food around our plates. We can't eat. Joe is hungry, but he's not speaking. He's been out searching all afternoon in the cold and will be going out again in an hour. They're meeting up at the village hall to continue looking for Lucinda throughout the night. Mountain Rescue have joined the search now, and they're bringing the dogs, the collies they use to find bodies beneath the snow and stuck in ravines. I can faintly remember putting some money in a box for them recently. Like all of us in the charity game, they're struggling for funds.

Sally talked briefly about being questioned by the police. She said the officer she spoke to was nice, and was relieved when he just wanted her to tell him what she knew. I think she'd been expecting a telling-off, to be blamed.

I sense there is more, though. Sense she's hanging on to something, and I'm waiting for Joe to leave the house before I push her. This is how I play it with Sally. I can tell immediately, the minute I set eyes on her, if there's anything wrong. But I wait. I've learned. I might ask if school's okay. 'Any gossip from today?' I might say, and she'll say no. But then, later, when I'm clearing away after tea, making tomorrow's sandwiches, she'll appear. And, after a gentle prod, it'll all come pouring out of her.

The thing I mustn't do if I'm to get to the bottom of things is to judge her friends. If I were to say *one* thing to slight them, one thing that suggests I'm being critical, then her back is up and she shuts down. She's incredibly loyal. So I tread carefully. And I listen.

We've had junk for tea; all of us on chicken nuggets, chips and beans. It was the best I could manage under the circumstances. Sally scrapes the leftover chips from her plate into the dogs' dishes. I see her take two out and pop them into the next bowl so they're divided equally. Joe has gone to the woodshed at the back to make sure I'm stocked up for the evening and Sally turns to me.

'Mum?'

'Hmm.'

'Do you think Lucinda could have gone off with someone, like, I mean, on purpose?'

Carefully, I say to myself. *Tread carefully.*

I do my best to keep my voice even. 'What makes you say that?'

'I was just thinking, that's all . . . I mean, it's not like she's a little kid. So it would be kind of hard to steal her.'

I cock my head to one side, make it seem like I'm weighing up what she's said, rather than what I'm actually thinking, which is: *Do you know something? Tell me. What do you know?*

'You're right,' I say. 'It would be hard to take Lucinda against her will in broad daylight, but I don't think that's how it would've happened. I think if a man wanted Lucinda to get into his car, he would have been more subtle than that.'

'Like how?'

'Well, usually what happens is they trick them.'

'But Lucinda's not stupid. She's not going to climb into his car if he tells her he knows her mum or something.'

I know what she's getting at here, because this was what I used to warn my kids about when they were little. It crosses my mind that I've not had this talk with Sam for a while. And boys are daft. They don't listen when you tell them. You have to keep reminding them.

You say, '*Even* if a person says they know your mummy, you don't go off with them, okay? *Even* if they say, "I know your mum, she's called Lisa, and she asked me to collect you from school today," you *never, ever* go with them. You find a teacher, all right?'

And they look at you soberly, and you think, *Yes, that went in. I think they got it.*

But then their face changes, there's a glint in their eyes, and they announce, 'It's okay, Mummy, because *if I did* get into the car, then I would bash him! And punch him! And make him crash. And then I'd run! And he'd never catch me because I'm really, really fast and . . .'

And your heart sinks. Because your child has descended into fantasy.

I stop what I'm doing and face Sally.

'They don't try to trick a teenager the way you'd trick a child, Sal. They talk to them, and flatter them, they—' I try to think how to put this so she'll understand what I'm getting at. 'A man would pretend to fancy a girl so the girl will think, *He likes me*, and because he's older, and teenage girls are often insecure, they fall for it. They fall for what they tell them.'

I don't tell her that abductors really do fancy teenage girls, that part is not a trick.

Sally starts nodding. 'I get it,' she says softly.

I put my hand on her shoulder. 'I love you, Sal,' I say, and her eyelids flicker.

She looks away, and I realize she's trying to blink back tears that are forming. 'It's okay,' I tell her. 'You're bound to be upset.'

She looks so young and vulnerable, and my insides ache for her. Her world is changing out of all recognition and—

'Mum, that's what's happened!' she cries suddenly. 'Lucinda . . . this man, he's been talking to her on the road after school. And, well, she said she was going to meet him.'

'To *do what*?' I say, astonished.

'I don't know!'

I sit down, the breath knocked out of me. 'Why didn't you tell us? Why have you kept this a secret? You know better than that. Christ, Sally, have you not listened to anything I've told you?'

'Yes, but—'

'But what?'

'Lucinda didn't want anyone to know. She didn't want her mum to—'

'Jesus, Sal, this is *beyond that*. It's beyond keeping a secret. You can see that, surely?'

She's crying. 'Don't shout,' she sobs.

Joe comes back in. 'What's going on?'

I turn to him. 'Don't speak, just for a moment. Just stay there.' He stops, mid-stance, rooted to the spot. He's holding the big plastic bucket filled with split wood; he doesn't even lower it to the floor.

'What's happened?' he asks quietly.

'Lucinda's been meeting a man and Sally knew all about it.'

'Did you tell the police?' he asks her.

She shakes her head. 'No.'

'What?' I yell. 'What is *wrong* with you?'

'They didn't ask me! They didn't ask about it, and I didn't

want to come out and say it, because her mum doesn't know, and what if she blames me when—'

'What if she blames you? Sally, she's probably dead. Dead. Do you understand that? Nobody is going to give a shit about blaming you. But they might *now*.'

'Enough,' says Joe, and I glare at him.

'Don't protect her, Joe. She should've said something sooner.'

'What difference would it make?' he asks me.

'Well, there wouldn't have been three separate search parties for a start. *You*,' I say, pointing a finger at him, 'wouldn't be wasting time searching through the scrub and the woodland in minus-God-knows-what temperatures when she's obviously not going to be found anywhere near here.' I close my eyes. 'Fuck,' I say. 'Fuck.'

Sally is crying pitifully and I know I should stop, but I just can't believe she's been so stupid as to keep this to herself.

I look at her sharply. 'Pass me the phone. I'm ringing Kate.'

Joe puts the wood down. 'Hang on,' he says.

'Why? She needs to know.'

'Ring the police first. Ring that detective, speak to her first. Then ring Kate.'

I dial DC Aspinall and get her voicemail. 'It's Lisa Kallisto. Please call me as soon as you get this.'

Then I take a breath and I look at Sally. She can't meet my eye. 'Why did you not tell us this, Sal?'

Her shoulders heave up and down twice. 'Because it's not always the way you think it is,' she sobs. 'You think everyone's like us, you think they're all like me . . . and they're not.'

'I don't know what you mean . . . tell me what you mean.'

She glances across at Joe, and bites her lip.

'Would you prefer to tell me this without Dad in here?'

She nods.

I throw Joe a quick look and he shrugs, because he doesn't have a choice.

He leaves, and I say, 'Okay, go on. You can tell me, I won't be mad, I'm sorry I got mad. It was frustration, that's all. And I'm scared, too, Sally. That's why I lost my temper.'

'You think that because I don't have a boyfriend, and none of my friends have boyfriends, you think that everyone at school is so innocent. And they're not. They're really not, Mum.'

'Honey, I know. There's a world of difference between some thirteen-year-old girls and others. Same back when I was at school. Some were having sex, but most weren't.'

She cringes when I say the word 'sex'. I've tried over the past year to think of a different way to say it, but it all sounds ridiculous, so that's what we're stuck with.

Sally blows her nose. 'There's pressure on us,' she sniffles. 'The boys are laughing at us if we've not *done* anything, they're saying we're—' She stops here. Instead she says, 'It's hard, Mum. It's really hard sometimes. They can make it unbearable.'

The plight of the teenager. No one can possibly know how hard it is. Especially your mother.

'They don't stop hassling us. They've been calling Lucinda frigid and posh, and she hates it.'

I can see why the lads have seized upon Lucinda. She can come across as a little haughty and holier-than-thou sometimes. And she speaks differently to the other kids. It's partly because Kate used to have her in the private prep school and it's partly down to Guy. Guy's not from around here, he's from the south, so Lucinda and Fergus lengthen their vowels and mimic his speech patterns, something Kate has always encouraged.

I explain to Sally that these boys, these relentlessly nasty, awful boys – the chavvy boys, as she calls them – are the ones who'll want to sleep with her in around a year's time, and this is just their way of getting her attention. But she dismisses this totally, looks at me as if to say, *Are you insane?* So we drop it.

I get the phone and ring Kate.

I punch the numbers in. Sally's standing forlornly next to me. 'Tell her I'm sorry,' she whispers, and I nod. 'Course I will, I say.

But the phone rings and rings.

I shout out to Joe, 'How can no one be answering the phone at Kate's?', and he comes back through from the lounge, the petroleum smell of firelighters and woodsmoke wafting into the kitchen along with him.

'Leave it ringing,' he says. 'They'll be dealing with the search party or the police.'

So I do. I let it ring thirty times. And then I ring her mobile. She doesn't answer that either.

He's been watching for long enough now to pick out what excites him without having to study them for too long. It's almost immediate.

The difference between them is astounding, as if they're not even members of the same species. Like breeds of dog, he supposes. All different. Tall, short, fat, thin, and coming in almost every shade.

Funny how you don't know what turns you on before you've tried it. He'd had an idea, but it wasn't until he'd sampled it that he really honed his preference. And who knows? Maybe he'll change it after a while. Try one of those leggy, pale girls instead. See how it feels to lower himself in between the soft, white gooseflesh of her thighs. See if it's as cold as it looks.

But that's later. For now, he's made his choice and, he's got to be honest, it's been so incredibly easy. It was as if she'd been waiting for him. As if she wanted to talk to him, to get to know him. She was a little reticent at first, but he preferred that. He'd never really gone for loud girls; he found their gaucheness unappealing, their language repugnant. They gave him an ugly, fetid feeling that made him want to escape, made him want to get home, get straight in the shower.

He came across a lot of women like that at work. Casual workers from further south who thought their filthy Kerry Katona mouths would talk him straight into their knickers. They sickened him. They'd stand around talking, leaning on radiators, while he checked their work. 'Let the heat warm up my arse!' they'd laugh, and he'd have to look away.

One had been coming on to him this past week. Chelseigh from Crewe. And, yes, it really was spelt like that. She'd come and find him, start chewing on her nails when he was trying to read something, and he'd catch sight of the scuddy nail beds, the swollen skin of her fingertips which she'd picked to bleeding, and he'd want to slam his fist into her. But he didn't because, one, he'd have had to touch her (something he couldn't bear to do), and two, it was beneath him to lose control like that unless absolutely necessary. She'd asked him to come and check a damp patch in her room in the staff house, and when she got him there, she sat on her single bed asking him questions, running her tongue along her lower lip as she spoke. It was as if she thought he was just going to jump on top of her then and there. And the more he ignored her, the more suggestive, the more crude and shameless she became.

Chelseigh said she liked him because he was shy. When she said the word 'shy' she parted her mouth, holding her lower lip open in a pout. And he thought of all the idiotic famous women wearing that same ridiculous pout whenever they were photographed. What was the purpose of it? To show they were never more than a few short seconds away from giving a free blow job? Pathetic.

Chelseigh mistook his shyness for avoidance. Because, when he was where he wanted to be, and with who he wanted to be, he wasn't shy, he was charming.

All he had to do was wind down his car window and get their attention and . . .

15

I TUCK THE CHILDREN into bed. The boys share a room and as I go in I have to pick my way through the debris. The floor is littered with Wii remotes, Lego, *Simpsons* DVDs (not in their boxes), crisp packets. A wet towel lies across the end of James's bunk. 'Night, honey,' I say to him. I'm not allowed a kiss.

'Night, Mum.'

I bend down and adjust Sam's covers on the lower bunk. He's lying there, eyes screwed shut, smiling his gummy smile. He hasn't lost any teeth yet. His baby set are worn down to tiny nubs. 'Mummy,' he says, without opening his eyes, 'do you know any times tables?'

'A few,' I tell him, and give him a squeeze and a kiss on his cheek. He still has the juicy cheeks of a toddler; he tries to pull away as I kiss him too fiercely, too hard.

When I go to Sally's room I find her lying on her side, still fully dressed. Her face is tear-stained and she has a look of complete hopelessness.

'C'mon, Sal, you need to get into bed.'

She nods but doesn't move.

'I'm scared, Mum,' she says, and I tell her I know. And I hold her.

When she's settled, I go downstairs and try Kate's number again, but there's still no answer. I think back through our conversation earlier that afternoon, trying to recall her mentioning being away tonight. And once again I'm flooded with admiration at the person she is.

How is it possible not to apportion blame under these circumstances? Where does she draw the strength from, not only to have me in her house but to reassure me that Lucinda's disappearance is not my fault?

It's not the first time Kate has opened up and shown me the depths of her understanding. Not the first time she's made the rest of us appear primordial by comparison.

We had never discussed that night, Kate and I. We'd never discussed the fact that she saw me with her sister's husband, Adam, on the floor of her bathroom after the dinner party.

She'd never raised the subject and asked me to explain.

And, at first, I'd *really wanted* to explain.

At first, I thought it would kill me *not* to get the words out. I needed to say *something* to her, to give her a sense of what happened, of how we ended up in that situation. But each time I'd get her alone, I would go to talk and she would evade. There's no other word for it: she'd evade every single attempt I made to explain my actions.

So, with time, I stopped. As the months passed I realized that neither she nor Adam had any intention of bringing up that night again, and I learned to bury it along with them. I took the cues from Kate, the cues which seemed to say: *Leave well alone.*

But, unlike them, I couldn't do it. The guilt and the shame would surge up in me.

Joe knew something was off but put it down to my being tired. I came within inches of telling him so many times. But just when I thought I couldn't stand it any longer and I had to confess, at the last second I wouldn't.

I like to think it's because the thought of wrecking our marriage was too painful, and I suppose that's true to an extent. But really it's because I'm a coward – a coward who'd been let off the hook by her friend, because, for whatever reason, she'd decided not to tell on me.

Eventually, though, I found I *had* to talk to Kate about it. It was around a year ago and Kate and I were at the swimming gala, and I don't know what prompted it but suddenly I couldn't hold it in any longer.

The noise in the stand was cacophonous. Kate and I were surrounded by parents, all of us shouting encouragement at our six-year-olds. The kids at the poolside were bug-eyed in their goggles, skinny, white limbs turning a faint blue in the chilly, damp air.

I turned to Kate. 'Why did you never tell Alexa about what happened?'

'About what?'

'*You* know,' I said shiftily. 'That night Joe and I came for dinner, you came in and saw me and Adam in your bathroom.' Kate's face became serious but she continued to keep her eyes focused on the pool. 'Every time I tried to talk to you about it, you wouldn't let me.' I dropped my voice then and leaned into her ear. 'What did you *think* of me, Kate?'

Above the shouting, she said simply, 'I thought you were lonely.'

'That's it?'

She tilted her head.

'That's it? That's all you thought?'

Reluctantly, she said, 'I thought my sister had bullied you. I thought she'd bullied you for almost the entire evening, making you feel insecure, and I thought she'd done the same to her husband . . . and so, inevitably, you found some comfort in each other.'

I stared at her, surprised at the matter-of-fact way she was speaking about what had occurred that night.

'Why didn't you out us?'

'Because I couldn't stand to see either of you destroy what you've got – just for one moment's bad judgement. It would be wrong to decimate two families for one indiscretion, and it certainly wasn't my place to do it . . . If you or Adam decided that you wanted to out *yourselves*, then that would be up to you. But I didn't want either of you thinking that you had to on account of me.'

She turned back towards the swimmers. 'Thanks,' I found myself saying, lamely. And we never spoke of the episode again.

I glance at the clock now and see that it's after nine. Picking up the phone, I try Kate once more. Eventually, she answers and tells me she had to go to Booths to get something for supper.

'Booths?' I say to her. 'You went to the supermarket? Tonight?'

'Yes, Lisa. We still have to eat.'

'Of course,' I mutter in response. 'I should have brought you something over,' I say, and it comes out sounding like the pathetic gesture that it is. Kate brushes it off as if I'm not letting her down on every possible level. Anyway, when I think about it, what would I have given her? Chicken nuggets? Kate wouldn't feed her family on crap like that, whatever the circumstances.

I exhale. 'Kate, you need to prepare yourself,' I say carefully, and when she doesn't speak, I plough on, get it over with. 'Sally told us earlier that she thinks Lucinda might have gone off with someone. Somebody older. A man.'

Still she doesn't speak.

'Kate, are you there?'

'I'm here,' she says, and I can hear the fear clear in her voice.

'I've called DC Aspinall, left her a message telling her what Sally said. I imagine she's been trying to get hold of you as well.'

'Yes' is all she says.

I imagine Kate standing in her lovely hallway by the telephone table. The family photos, the ones of Lucinda and Fergus rising in age as the stairs ascend. I see her staring at the pictures, hearing my words, feeling as if her guts have been ripped out of her.

'I'm so sorry, Kate. God, as a family, we've let you down so badly. I can't describe to you how I feel about this and how I wish I could *do something*.'

I hear Kate take a breath in. 'Why did Sally not tell us this sooner?'

'She was scared. She was scared that if you found out it would make things worse. Lucinda had made her promise not to tell anyone. She's so sorry, Kate. I've really blasted her for this, as you can imagine, but it's a bit late now.'

'Don't be too hard on her . . . I . . . I . . . think I might have already known.'

My voice is soft: 'Yeah? How?'

'I'm not sure. You know how sometimes you just do? You sense something isn't right, you can tell they're up to no good. I asked her a couple of times if she was okay, but I didn't force it out of her—'

'You can't with girls . . . the more you push, the more they close up.'

She agrees. 'I suppose I was waiting for her to tell me what was going on and' – her voice quivers now as she re-lives it – 'God . . . Lucinda and I are *best friends*, Lisa. I shouldn't have waited, should I? If it had been Fergus I would have sat him down and forced it out of him. *God!*' she says again, crying.

'Kate? Are you alone there? Do you want me to come round?'

'No,' she answers. 'Guy's here. He's not gone on the search

again. It's too hard on him. He's frightened he'll find her. I know that's what he's thinking. And anyway, Alexa's coming back shortly. She's just gone to make supper for Adam and put the children to bed. She'll be back to spend the night here. She's been a godsend with Fergus. I couldn't have dealt with him today, not like this.'

Kate goes quiet and I hear her take a raggedy breath in.

'Lisa?' she says.

'I'm here.'

'I'm going to hang up now. I really need to cry, okay?'

'Okay,' I tell her, and the line goes dead.

I rub my face with my hands and look around the room. Two dogs are asleep on the opposite sofa. There's a cat nestled in Joe's lumberjack shirt on the armchair. I turn on the TV, trying to distract myself from my thoughts and flick on to Sky Plus.

I see Joe has recorded *Kes* again. Twice. There's *Bladerunner: The Final Cut* – something he watches almost monthly. Two episodes of *Nazis: A Warning from History*. And a selection of old football matches on ESPN.

For a second this makes me smile.

I'm remembering Kate coming over to ours one time and, on seeing Joe watching something like Manchester United versus Liverpool from 1977, Kate, totally perplexed, said, 'Is this *old* sport?' and looked at Joe as if there was something wrong with him. 'Why would you watch *old sport*?' she asked. 'Don't you already know who wins?'

Joe simply smiled.

I flick channels and my heart stops when I see Kate and Guy on the news. I hit the standby button automatically because I can't watch it. I just can't.

I get up, unable even to stare at the blank screen knowing that the two of them are really there inside the TV, and go to the kitchen. Hanging my head over the sink, I start to pray. Pray to God that I won't be spending the rest of my life saying sorry to Kate because her daughter never came home.

Then I do the only thing I *can* do. I drink.

DAY TWO

Wednesday

16

YESTERDAY I WOKE up feeling sorry for myself because I was tired.

That's it. Nothing at all wrong in my world except I was tired. '*Jesus*,' I whisper into the pillow.

I hear footsteps coming up the stairs. The clink of crockery. Joe appears, carrying my breakfast.

'It's toast,' he says, 'on a bed of plate.'

I manage half a smile.

Joe hates all the cookery programmes we're bombarded with, the hoity-toity food that we're never going to cook.

He particularly hates it when Nigella pretends to raid her fridge in the middle of the night. You know, as if we're supposed to think that her food is so yummy, and she's so happy celebrating her curves, that she just can't resist? Joe watches that little charade and says, 'You think she'd be shitting herself there's a cameraman still in her kitchen, wouldn't you?'

'How are you feeling?' he says to me now.

'Crap,' I reply. 'I drank too much wine. Couldn't help it. What time did you get back?'

'After twelve. June made us all hotpot and gave us a free pint.'

June is the landlady of the pub in the village.

'Nice of her,' I say.

'Yeah, well, it felt a bit like we were going through the motions after a while, so we called it a night.'

'Because of what Sal said?'

He nods. 'Yeah. No one really believes Lucinda's gonna be found around here. They're just turning out for Guy and Kate, to show some support.'

I go to sit up and the pain in my head slams me back down again. 'Stay there,' Joe says. 'It's only half six, we've got ages before we need to get moving. You going into work today?'

'Got to.'

'I'll get the kids up. You have another half an hour.'

'Joe?'

'Hmm.'

'What are people saying? What are they saying about me? Do they say it's my fault?'

He shrugs. 'If they are, they're hardly gonna tell me.'

'I suppose . . . Joe?'

He stops. 'What?'

'I thought she'd be back by now. I really thought she'd be back at home.'

He smiles at me softly, his eyes sad. 'Me too, baby.'

Last night I drank till I was absolutely sure I could drink no more. I wanted to be certain to pass out. I didn't leave any room for thinking. I wanted my brain to stop.

Of course, now I'm paying for it.

I feel my stomach heave and I'm too shaky to move. Frightened that if I stand upright I'll topple over.

I rest in bed a moment longer. Maybe I'll be okay. Maybe I'll get away with it. I almost smile at the lies I'm telling myself. My body needs to purge, I can feel it coming, and *still* I pretend it's not happening. I go suddenly hot and I know now I need to move. Might as well get it over with, I think, as I run towards the bathroom, stumbling against the wall as I go.

Two hours later, and I'm on my way to work. Joe is dropping Sam at school and is then heading to Lancaster Infirmary to take one of his regulars for some UV treatment on his vitiligo. I told him I'd nip to Asda at Kendal and pick up some bits and pieces for tea. Like Kate said last night, we've still got to eat.

I thought Sally would beg to stay at home today, but she didn't. She seemed better this morning, though she couldn't eat any breakfast. I think she needs to be around her friends. She needs to talk to them, not me. I tried digging a little deeper with her, tried to get her to tell me anything at all about Lucinda's behaviour of late, but she clammed up. I can't tell if she's hiding something more, or if she's feeling so bad that she simply can't talk about her.

Driving, I'm heading straight into the sun. The day is obscenely bright. Alpine-bright. Everywhere is still covered with snow. It's so cold that there's no slush yet, and even the snow banked along the side of the roads is almost as white as when it first fell, only a shadow of muck on it from the passing traffic.

Ordinarily, I would be filled with joy by such a morning, living in such beauty. I'd be listening to the traffic reports for all those poor sods in London stuck in four-hour queues, and I'd be driving along, smiling happily. Today, though, I don't notice the beauty. Today, the sun feels like sharp, fierce pain.

The windscreen is full of salt, and there's no antifreeze in my screenwash. Three times I have to pull over and rinse the glass manually with a bottle of Highland Spring – water I brought along for me to drink, to rehydrate. I'm praying I don't get stopped by the police. Not only am I unsafe driving with no clear vision, but I smell as if I'm fermenting. If they get one whiff of me I'll be breathalysed, be forever typecast as one of those pissed-up mothers still drunk from the night before.

Even with gloves on, my hands are freezing on the wheel. The air outside is still but dense. Cold is seeping into everything. Creeping through the stone walls of our houses, through the body of my car.

I get to Asda at eight forty-five and the car park is stupidly busy with Christmas shoppers. I see a woman in her early thirties get out of a Vitara she's parked in a parent–child space. She's childless and I'm overwhelmed with the urge to ram her. She's put on an air of aloofness. She knows she's in the wrong but she's pretending she doesn't care.

Eventually I manage to park in the overflow car park that's only ever busy at Christmas or Easter Saturday.

I haven't made a list but my plan is this: ready meals, lots of them.

That's why I've come out of my way and driven to Asda. It's cheaper for that sort of thing. I am in no state to buy ingredients and start constructing something from scratch. So I am going to make this easy. Lots of ready meals and stuff for tomorrow's sandwiches. That's it. Joe can do a proper shop on Saturday.

I see happy mothers, loaded up with goodies for Christmas – nuts, dried figs, dates, two-litre bottles of Coke.

There's a woman standing next to the fridge where I want to be; she has three kids under the age of four in her trolley. Usually, I'd stand and smile at the kids, make faces. Sympathize with the mother, saying, 'You've got your hands full,' or something along those lines. But today my face barely registers their presence. All I can think of is Lucinda. Where is she? And who is the older man she's been talking to?

I pick up three chicken kormas and rice, a madras for Joe that he can put his own bird's-eye chillies on, and a dopiaza for me.

You go out to eat with Joe, and the waiter says, 'On a scale of one to ten, how hot would you like your dish?'

Joe answers, 'Twenty.'

And he still takes extra chillies with him.

It used to bother me the way he put them all over every meal I prepared. 'But how can you even taste it?' I'd say, cross that he was somehow wasting my efforts. But now I don't bother. The only time it irritates me is when we're in company and the men get into a kind of macho I-Can-Eat-Hotter-Chillies-Than-You competition (but without actually saying it). It's playground stuff. Akin to I'm-A-Bigger-Manchester-United-Fan-Than-You. Joe has competitions in this as well.

I'm wondering how my mind has stumbled upon this nonsense as I'm running my debit card through the self-serve checkout. And then, as if from nowhere, just as I go to walk out of the store, a security guard approaches and grabs my bag.

'Come this way, madam,' he says, guiding me by the elbow.

I stop dead in my tracks.

'What are you *doing*?' I say to him, incredulous, but he ignores my question and pulls me along – much in the same way I would handle a reluctant, fearful dog.

I let myself be directed to a door by the toilets, an unmarked, brown, veneered door I've never noticed before. People are stopping to watch. Some are pretending not to, looking surreptitiously from behind the newspaper stand, from next to the stacked boxes of Stella Artois by the entrance. Some are just flat-out staring.

'Please,' I say to the guard. 'You've made a mistake.'

He's a big guy and I can smell the damp-mildew odour of several days' sweat upon him. He doesn't speak. Just opens the door and instructs me to take a seat at the desk, where there's a thin man in a suit. Actually, he's only a boy. His collar is too big around his neck and his shoes are the same ones my twelve-year-old has for school. He's wearing an expression of oily satisfaction.

'Can I take your name?'

'If you tell me why you've made me look like a bloody fool by bringing me in here,' I reply.

'We suspect you of shoplifting.'

I'm about to fly into a rage, about to send a barrage of insults his way, but, at the last second, I stop. Because, realistically, I'm in no state for shouting today. My head is killing me, my mouth is parched and, if I hadn't been drinking in my own home last night, I'd feel certain I'd bummed a few cigarettes off someone. Strong ones as well, Regal or Embassy Number 1s.

My tongue sticks to the roof of my mouth as I say to him, 'Will this take long?' But I don't say it outraged. I say it quietly. Sadly, as if I am actually guilty of shoplifting, such is my state of mind.

'Not if you are willing to cooperate with us fully, Miss—?'

'Lisa Kallisto. Mrs.'

He presses his lips together, gestures to my two carrier bags. 'If I could get you to unload these on to the desk here, and we'll take a look at what you've got.'

I look at him wearily. Inside, I'm thinking I might enjoy the apology he's about to give me. I might if this were a different day.

I stand. I take out a multipack of Walkers crisps, a loaf of Best of Both Hovis – my attempt to get some sneaky fibre into the kids – and a bumper pack of smoked ham which the cats go mad for.

I look up, raise my eyebrows. 'I've paid for all of this,' I tell him. 'Would you like to check my receipt?'

'That's not necessary. Please empty the other bag, Mrs Kallisto.'

One carton of orange Tropicana (no bits), the five ready-made curries – this is getting tiresome, I'm thinking, and then . . .

'Oh, shit.'

I stare at the table. I drop my head and cover my face with my hands. 'Oh, shit,' I say again.

When I look through my splayed fingers at him, he's looking right back at me as if to say, *Well?*

And I start to laugh.

'I don't find it very funny,' he says.

'You would if you were me.'

I've only bloody gone and packed the charity collection box from the side of the till. Put it in my carrier bag along with the rest of my shopping.

'We've had a spate of charity boxes go missing,' the boy says officiously. 'Two poppy tins were stolen last month and, as you can imagine, the patrons of this store are outraged. I assure you we'll be taking this very seriously. The police will be along shortly to question you, as this is the third box we've—'

I stop him.

'It's my box,' I say.

'I'm sorry?'

'It's my box,' I repeat.

I turn the yellow cylinder around so he can see the writing on the front. I point to the lettering. 'Rescue Me Animal Sanctuary. That's where I work. I run it. I'm on my way there now.'

He eyes me suspiciously.

'I'm sure you understand that we have to follow procedure here, and this is a very serious—'

'No, it's not. It's not serious at all. What's in there? Four, maybe five quid? Do I look like the type of person who would steal this? Do I look so desperate that I need to—' I don't bother finishing my sentence. I just look at him.

'People don't always steal because they need to, Mrs Kallisto. They do it because they have the *urge* to steal. There's sometimes no reason for it at all. They don't necessarily have to be in desperate circumstances. Look at Antony Worrall Thompson.'

'Fair point,' I concede. 'But I'm not Antony Worrall Thompson, or Winona Ryder, or whoever else you decide to reel out as an example of kleptomania. I'm a mother who's had a shitty couple of days, who's drunk too much Rioja last night and is not thinking straight. I packed that thing automatically in my bag without even knowing I did it. My best friend's daughter has been missing for two nights, and, well, you can imagine what's going through my head—'

He sighs out a breath. Looks to the security guard, who remains impassive. After a moment, he says, 'Have you got any identification to prove you work at this animal shelter?'

I peel back the lapel of my coat. I'm wearing a bottle-green polo shirt with an orange paw print over my left breast. Above the paw print, it says 'Rescue Me!' in jaunty, childish font.

He's in two minds what to do. I'm feeling he probably needs to check with someone senior, but he doesn't want to look like a tosser after doing the jobsworth routine.

'Listen . . . please—' I say. 'I'm really, really sorry about this. But I am not your thief.'

He clenches his jaw.

'You can go,' he mutters.

I gather my bags in my left hand, turn up the collar of my coat to protect my neck from the frigid air outside and, just as I'm about to leave, I lift the collection box to eye level, give it a little shake-a-shake.

'I'll pop back in to pick this up next week, shall I?' I ask him. 'Give you a few more empties?'

And he doesn't answer, just looks kind of defeated.

As I go out through the automatic doors I can't help but do a triumphant little skip.

Then I get to my car and burst into tears.

17

Detective Sergeant Ron Quigley sits in the passenger seat of Joanne's Mondeo eating a Greggs Steak Bake.

Bits of puff pastry are falling between the seats, into that hard-to-reach spot down the side of the handbrake. It's 9.20 a.m. and the smell is making Joanne nauseous. 'How can you eat beef for breakfast?'

Ron shrugs.

Last night, Joanne and Jackie had been watching a programme about Britain's alcohol consumption. The trend's now changed so that we're not so much a nation of binge drinkers, more like *constant* drinkers.

Joanne and Jackie had looked at each other, two empty bottles of Merlot on the table, and Jackie had said, 'Two glasses of wine a day is good for you. Two units a day, two times seven, that's fourteen units a week. We're only drinking our quota, Joanne. Women are allowed fourteen units,' and Joanne had agreed wholeheartedly.

Though she didn't mention the extra bottles each of them put away at the weekends. Nor the Bacardi Breezers Jackie knocked back before beginning her proper drinking.

And, anyway, Joanne and Jackie each having a bottle of wine was a world away from what Joanne saw at closing time on the streets of Kendal: women falling out of pubs, puking into rubbish bins, most, if not all, claiming to have had their drinks spiked when, in reality, they were just really, really pissed.

Joanne put it down to women having more money nowadays. Women of her mother's generation hadn't gone out boozing in the same way, because there was no money to go out boozing with.

The doctor on the telly asked the reporter how many units she thought was in a bottle of wine, and the reporter answered, 'Six?' He shook his head. 'There are ten units of alcohol in a bottle of wine.' And Joanne had shot a look at Jackie.

That meant they were actually drinking . . . she lifted her eyes to the ceiling as she totted up the numbers . . . shit, seventy units a week. Minimum.

Jackie said sheepishly, 'We'll start cutting back.'

Joanne says to Ron Quigley now, 'How much d'you drink, Ron?'

'Not much,' he answers. 'Same as anyone else, really. Never been that much of a boozer.'

'Rough estimate?'

'Five or six pints of an evenin'. Bottle of wine with the missus at the weekend. Although I had a few extra scoops last night, that's why I need a bit o' stodge to mop it up.' He shoves the rest of his Steak Bake into his mouth. A few flakes of pastry hang on to his tash, fluttering as he breathes.

No wonder the doctors are on at us, she thinks. We're all lying to ourselves. The nation's pickled and no one's admitting it.

She pulls a right off the A6 and heads towards Silverdale. They're scheduled to talk to Molly Rigg. See if she can't come up with any more details about the man who took her.

Bless her, Molly had tried her best during questioning the first time around, but she was what Joanne would call unworldly. Naïve. She'd been taken to a bedsit, she said; she didn't know where. She'd been drugged, raped, and dumped, and she couldn't even tell the police the make of car her attacker had driven. Nor the colour. Asked why she'd got into his car in the first place, she'd said she didn't know. She knew it was wrong, but she'd done it anyway.

Which set Joanne thinking that this guy, this kidnapper, must have something appealing about him. Joanne thought they were looking for not a loner, not your average paedo, but someone with a bit of charisma. Someone with a bit of charm. She was on her own with this theory, though. Her boss, Detective Inspector Pete McAleese, who was running the investigation, was more intent on them following up any leads on casual workers new to the area.

'What d'you make of this *Darling Buds of May* theory, Ron?'

'Waste o' time.'

'How so?'

'Well, this kid, Molly Rigg. You interviewed her, right?'

'Briefly.'

'And all she's said so far is the guy talks like Pop Larkin. Well, I didn't even know that was *supposed* to be a Kent accent David Jason was doing. I thought the programme was set in Devon or Dorset . . . so how's she supposed to know the difference? It's a non-starter.'

Joanne agrees with him. 'It is a bit thin.'

'I didn't think anyone still watched that crap, anyway. Do you think you might do better with this girl on your own?' he asks, shuffling around in his seat, trying to get something out of his pocket.

'Maybe. She's a shy little thing. Might be better without you in the room. D'you want to question the mother, see if she's got anything new to say?'

'Fine by me. What tack you going to take?'

'I want to know how he managed to get her back to his place, and out again, without anyone seeing. Or hearing them. That's the part that's bugging me most. I think if I can shed some light on that, we might start getting somewhere.'

Ron nods, offers Joanne a mint Tic Tac.

'And how is someone who lives in a bedsit able to afford to run a car?' she says. 'That doesn't add up either.'

'Probably not his bedsit.'

The satnav tells Joanne she's arrived at her destination, so she pulls the car over and cuts the engine. They're outside a bungalow, neatly kept, but it could do with a fresh coat of buttermilk paint.

There's not nearly as much snow here, it being by the coast, but someone's gritted the front driveway and chucked an extra load down by the gate. Thoughtful, thinks Joanne, as her shoes crunch on the salmon-coloured gravel.

Five minutes later, and Joanne sits with Molly in the kitchen next to an old boiler. It's turned up to maximum but the room is still cold. The floor is covered with maroon carpet tiles. One's been replaced recently, the one in front of the cooker; it's deeper in colour than the rest.

Joanne starts by apologizing. 'I'm sorry to bother you with this, Molly, but you've been told another girl about your age has gone missing?'

Molly nods without looking at Joanne. She's such a skinny little thing. She's like a Disney character. All big eyes, big lashes, tiny body.

'The reason I'm here is to see if I can jog your memory a bit. We really want to catch the man who abducted you, Molly, and at the moment you're the only person—'

'You want to catch him before he hurts someone else,' she states bluntly.

'Yes, that's true.'

Joanne's careful how she phrases the next part. 'But, really, the most important thing is to punish him for what he did to you.' Joanne doesn't want Molly thinking she's not the priority here. 'What did he look like? Can you remember?'

Molly shakes her head. 'He's blurry,' she says sadly. 'That drink he gave me made him blurry.'

'I know, honey. Is the whole thing blurry, or is it more that you can't remember some parts? More like when you've had a dream, and you know the memory is there, but you can't quite get to it?'

Molly looks directly at Joanne for the first time. 'That's exactly what it's like,' she says. 'I said he was blurry, but really I couldn't explain it very well. It's like I've got the *feeling* of what happened but I *don't know* what happened.'

'That's good,' says Joanne, encouraged. 'How about if I don't ask you specific questions but more how you feel about something? How would that be?' She sees Molly's not sure about this idea, so she adds, 'Not about what he did to you. We don't need to go through that again. What I'd really like to know is where he took you. Can I ask you about that?'

Molly begins biting her lip. 'Okay,' she says.

'Think back for me and try to tell me if the place felt dirty or smelly.'

'No,' says Molly automatically. And she looks startled for a second, surprised at how definite she is about this. 'No, it was clean. The sheets smelled of—' She looks off, over towards the kitchen window, as if trying to find the right word.

'Fabric conditioner?' Joanne offers.

'No. Not that type of smell, not washing powder. They smelled like heat, does that make sense?'

'Like they'd been burned?'

She screws her eyes up as she tries to retrieve the memory. 'When my mum dries the bath towels on the radiator – they smell kind of heated but I don't know how else to explain it.'

'Like laundered?' Joanne says. 'Like they've been to a laundry?'

'Yes. Like that.'

'Good,' says Joanne. 'And what about the room itself, can you remember if there were any pictures on the walls?'

'It was cream.'

'Just cream?'

'Bare. Not like a proper room.'

'Like a hotel room?'

'I've never stayed in a hotel.'

'But did it feel like a person lived there? Do you think the man who took you there lived there?'

'No.'

'You're sure?'

'Yes.'

'Why?'

'I don't know. I just am.'

'Okay,' says Joanne. 'You're doing brilliantly. All this is really helpful, but this next question is a tough one. And I don't want you to feel bad about it, but I really need you to answer it honestly. Is that okay?'

Molly tries not to look scared.

'When you first saw him, when the man first came to your school, did you . . . did you get into the car because you liked how he looked?'

She doesn't answer. Just drops her head.

'No one blames you, Molly. I just need to know what sort of person he is, and it would really help me if you told me. Did you fancy him . . . even if it's only a little?'

Her head still bowed, Molly nods. A single tear drops down on to her jeans. 'He looked nice. I don't really remember how he looked, but he looked nice . . .'

After a few moments, she adds, 'Don't tell my mum,' as she cries quietly.

Joanne reaches forwards and puts her hand on Molly's shoulder. 'Promise I won't.'

18

I'VE BEEN AT WORK less than half an hour when a scruffy woman in her early twenties with no coat on walks into my office. She's got a Staffordshire Bull Terrier with a length of blue nylon washing line around its neck that she's using as a lead.

'I don't want this dog.'

She's standing about two feet away and can't look me in the face. She's fidgeting. It's clear she's some sort of addict, because her pupils are pinpoints and she's skittish and jumpy, like the methadone patients at the local chemist. The ones who call the pharmacist by his first name, who act as if they haven't noticed all the other patrons giving them a wide berth.

'Is it your dog?' I have to ask this, because you wouldn't believe how many people bring in animals that are not theirs to give away. I've innocently rehomed dogs belonging to cheating, philandering husbands more than once.

'It's me dad's,' says the young woman, 'but he's not well. He can't look after it n'more.'

Inside, my heart sinks. Another Staffy. We probably won't get rid of it; we're overrun with them. I've been doing some work with the RSPCA recently: they're trying to get a law passed whereby a breeder must be nineteen and hold a licence. But they're barking up the wrong tree, so to speak. We need to be neutering these dogs en masse, because the problem is already out of control.

'He's got cats as well.'

'How many?' I ask.

'More than two.'

'Where are they?'

'In his flat. It's a bit of a dump. He's not really tidied up since me mam died. I woulda brought 'em in with me . . . but they've gone sorta feral.'

'Where's your dad now?'

'Helm Chase.'

Helm Chase is the local hospital.

'Will he be going back home again?'

'Doesn't look like. He's got a few problems. The flat's probably bein' sold.'

'Okay,' I say, passing her a pen and paper. 'Write down the address.'

She holds the pen in her fist – just like my middle child, James, used to. She writes using a mixture of upper- and lower-case letters.

'Will there be someone there to let me in? So I can get to the cats?' She removes a key from a heavy bunch she has clipped to her jeans and hands it to me. 'What do I do with the key once I've finished?' I ask.

'Bin it,' she says, and hands me the washing line with the dog attached. 'He's called Tyson,' she goes on, and I nod. Staffies usually are. I'll have to change his name, or we definitely won't find him a home.

And then she's gone. Doesn't want to fill in the paperwork, and there's not a lot I can do about it. I don't get too hung up on bureaucracy. I look down at the dog. 'Think we'll call you Banjo,' I say, and he seems okay with that. I have a list of about twelve, nice, soft-natured-sounding names that I use for the Staffies.

We replace the Tysons, Hatchets, Badasses and Tarantinos with the likes of Teddy, Alfie and Percy. A dog's name is only important to the owner. The dog will answer to anything and couldn't care less what you call it.

I squat next to Banjo, knowing he won't be neutered but hoping so all the same.

He's not. A scrotum the size of a pomegranate is hanging under there, and I sigh because, just once, just every once in a while, I'd like to be surprised by what I find. I give his head a little tickle, and say, 'C'mon, let's go get you settled in.'

Through in the kennel block the girls are busy hosing down and cleaning up. We open for rehoming at 9.30 a.m. so we like to be spick and span by then. Turds tend to put people off. You can understand.

Lorna, one of my two kennel girls, stops with the hose when she spots me come in with Banjo. 'Number seven's free,' she shouts above the barking. She gestures to Banjo. 'What's he like?'

'No history, seems calm enough. He was fine passing the others when I came in, so he should be okay.'

'Any news?'

'You mean about Lucinda Riverty?' I say, and she nods.

'None. You manage okay here yesterday? Any problems?'

'No, all quiet really. Clive was in, and I gave him the list that was on your desk. He picked up some timber for those fence posts that need replacing—'

'Did you pay him from the petty cash?'

Lorna smiles, and her eyes twinkle. 'He had some going spare—'

Clive Peasgood is what we in the trade call a godsend. He's a retired schoolteacher who can make anything, mend anything, build anything. *His way of giving back*, he says, and I take full advantage of him on a daily basis.

Occasionally, he'll help with the dog walking and kennel cleaning if I'm short-staffed, but mostly he keeps the buildings watertight and secure. When I try to pay him for materials, he's usually got *some going spare.*

His wife's a lovely woman who does a bit of fundraising for us – car-boot sales and whatnot – and whenever I see her I apologize for stealing away her husband when they should be enjoying their retirement together. Invariably, she answers me with the same line: Stop Clive coming here, and you'll stop him living. She's probably right, but that doesn't *stop me* feeling bad about how much he does for us. He put a new felt roof on the cattery last year and wouldn't take a penny.

'I need to do a pick-up later,' I tell Lorna. 'Cats . . . how much space have we got?'

Lorna pulls a face. 'Hardly any. We got those drop-offs yesterday, remember?'

'Oh, yes, I forgot. Shit. Maybe I'll have to ring Bill at West Cumbria, see if he can take any.'

'How many are there?'

'The woman didn't know. More than two—'

'Never a good sign,' says Lorna.

At first I think I must be at the wrong place. I'm outside a big old manor that's been converted into apartments. Not the usual type of dwelling I pick up wild cats from. I check the scrap of paper with the address: Apartment 6, Helm Priory, Bowness. Yes, this is it.

The snow has been cleared and I open up the boot of my car and get three cat baskets out. There's a woman watching me from the window of one of the ground-floor apartments. She's young, mid-twenties, looks a bit sad.

I retrieve my Bitemaster handling gauntlets from the flap behind the driver's seat and at the last second slip an odour mask in my pocket, just in case. I buy them from the painter's suppliers in Kendal. I've found them to be the best. If they can block out the smell of oil-based gloss, they can usually block out cat shit. In all the years I've been doing this job it's the one thing I've never got used to.

I smile at the woman, but she looks down as I approach the building, makes it obvious she's washing up by lifting her elbows in an exaggerated manner. She's possibly Polish.

For a time, they were everywhere around these parts, the Poles. Thin, pleasant girls, all dressed identically. All in just-a-bit-too-short black skirts and toffee-coloured tights, a colour my mother would have worn back in her twenties. I remember going to Asda one time, standing in the section marked 'Polish' and, after staring for a while at the borscht and kielbasa, it hit me that I wasn't going to find the Pledge or Mr Sheen there.

I lean into the front door, which opens into a porch area lined with letterboxes. The internal door beyond that is locked. I locate the Yale – the most likely-looking key on the bunch the girl gave me – and I'm relieved when it works without a hitch.

The entrance hall is pretty grand; plush, hotel-type carpet. There's a huge window at the top of the first flight of stairs, original leaded glass sending light bouncing every which way. A jasmine fragrance is discharged from a plug-in air freshener, and I find myself thinking for the second time in five minutes that I can't possibly be in the right place. It's too nice.

Apartment six must be upstairs. I take care as I climb, so as not to bang the paintwork with the cat baskets. At the top of the second flight there are two doors. On the right is apartment five. Flanking both sides of the entrance are two neatly trimmed bay trees, and on the floor is a pretty red floor mat, the message 'HOME IS WHERE THE HEART IS' printed on it.

I look to the left. Apartment six has a desiccated plant outside, its soil covered over with cigarette dimps, along with a few joints that have been smoked down to the roach. This is more like it, I think, as I put the key in the lock.

I open the door, and the stench hits me, so I close it while affixing my mask. I feel for the light switch and flick it, but nothing happens. The electric's been cut off. Cursing, I realize I've no torch with me and the hallway to the flat is dark; the doors to each room leading off are closed shut.

I think about heading in blind, just get it done as quickly as possible, but then I stop. Two years ago, I was removing a starving dog from a house in Troutbeck Bridge. The poor thing was yelping so much I wasn't thinking and I went straight on in. Treading on a needle. Which, if you can believe it, went straight through the sole of my trainer and punctured my foot. A needle-stick injury they call it, and I spent the next six months convinced I was HIV positive. Not something I want to repeat if I can help it.

I leave the baskets and the gauntlets outside the flat, pull the mask down around my neck and knock on the door of number five. No answer, so I nip back downstairs to the ground-floor apartment where I saw the woman earlier.

I knock lightly. She opens the door immediately, just a couple of inches, and eyes me warily. 'Hi, I'm from an animal-rescue charity and—'

'I don't have money,' she says in heavily accented English.

'No, I don't want money. I need a torch.'

'Torch? But is daylight.'

I gesture up the stairs. 'The man in number six, he is in hospital, I come to take his cats.' I am speaking with almost the same accent as her, I realize.

'You wait. I look.'

She shuts the door.

When she returns a minute later she has a baby on her hip. A big, bonny, blond boy about twelve months old. You would never put them together as mother and son if your life depended on it. I reach out to touch his hair, an automatic reflex I acquired on becoming a mother myself and say, 'He's beautiful. What's his name?'

'Nika.'

'That's nice – is it Polish?'

'Is from Georgia.'

I go to speak and at the last second realize she means the country below Russia, not the state next to Alabama.

She hands me the torch, a small black-and-yellow one made by Stanley and, as always happens when I see that particular brand name, I'm whipped right back to the day my father's wife slit her wrists with the Stanley blade in our living room.

'Leave outside,' the woman says, and I look at her, confused.

'Leave torch outside door when finished,' and I say, 'Ah, yes, okay, I will.'

I stand in the kitchen doorway and take a long, unsteady breath.

More than two, the woman said. I've spotted four adult cats already, and there's a litter of kittens in a cupboard over by the sink. I can hear them mewing pitifully. To be frank, this is really an RSPCA job. In instances like this, I usually make a phone call and they turn up with a local vet, ready to certify it's a case of cruelty. They gather all the evidence they need to move forward with a prosecution. But that takes time. And the owner's in hospital. Probably not coming out, from what the daughter said, so it's a pointless exercise.

I decide to gather up the cats in the kitchen first before checking the rest of the flat. One step at a time, or it'll be overwhelming.

The cats are a bit wild. They're really stringy things, all legs and claws. I pick up one female, a mangy tortoiseshell with three white paws, and feel a pregnant bellyful of kittens inside her.

One female cat is capable of producing twenty thousand kittens if all her offspring go on to breed. That's why a huge bulk of our budget goes on neutering – to prevent scenes like this. If owners would neuter their pets at six months, instead of 'letting them have one season', we could almost put an end to unwanted pups and kittens. Of course we'd still have to deal with the fall-out of those who believe neutering is interfering with nature, but I tend to think if that crowd weren't causing trouble for the likes of me, they'd just be causing it elsewhere. Cock-fighting probably. Maybe wife-beating.

I double up, putting two cats in each basket, then I go to the sink. I'm guessing the guy who lived here was a drinker because, even though the place is a cesspit, there's not much food around. Just empties. I say a silent prayer of thanks, because I don't think I could have faced moulding scraps and rancid meat today.

There must be over sixty tins of Special Brew scattered about the work surfaces, as well as countless empty bottles of gin. I don't recognize the brand so I turn it over in my hand and look at the label on the back. It reads: 'Specially produced for Aldi stores'. An image of the drinker pushing his trolley filled with gin forms in my mind: thin as his cats, with yellowed corneas and that hypermobile lower jaw alcoholics seem to develop. I hear another tiny, strangled meow from the cupboard beneath the kitchen sink.

There are five kittens in a cardboard box. One dead; the other four are not far off.

Fleas. They're riddled with them.

The fleas have sucked off so much blood from these tiny beasts that I'll be lucky to save them. Their gums are white as alabaster and their little bodies are limp. Only two are able to make any sound. They're a mix of black and white. The hardest to rehome at the moment, I don't know why.

People are going a bundle for ginger toms and tabbies; they come in asking if we've got those silver tabbies off the Whiskas advert, not knowing those are pedigrees and sell for around four hundred quid.

I don't bother putting the kittens in a basket just yet. They're too weak to go running off, so I leave them in the cardboard box. I go and check the rest of the flat and find two more adult cats. Both black, both semi-feral, and one is pregnant. I have a quick look round in wardrobes and behind chairs, but I can't find a trace of anything else, so I head off down the stairs with two of the baskets and lock them in the car before returning for the others.

The Georgian woman is pretending to wash up again and I give her a half-wave, but she's trance-like. I think about giving her another knock to return the torch, but she was adamant: *Leave torch outside door when finished.* So I do that. Some people just don't like visitors.

I collect the rest of the cats and have one last check round before leaving. Then, propping the porch door open with the third basket, I check my pockets for my car keys and the bunch belonging to the man's apartment, making sure I've got everything.

And it's then that I notice the name on the letterbox belonging to apartment two.

Riverty.

'G. Riverty,' it says, in small, neat letters. As in Guy Riverty. As in Kate's husband, Lucinda's dad.

Guy and Kate have lots of cottages scattered around the Lakes, but I didn't know they owned anything here.

They've never mentioned it. Then again, I think, closing the door, why would they?

19

'BUT WHAT IF it's not the same guy?' DS Ron Quigley asks the DI.

'Too many parallels,' he replies. 'The girls are the same age, same type, similar area, went from around school. Too much for us to not work on that assumption.'

'But he'd let Molly Rigg go by now. He only kept her for the day.'

Detective Inspector Pete McAleese sighs. 'Ron, it's not atypical for the crimes to escalate as they go along. You've seen that for yourself enough times. First time, they test the water, see what happens, then they move up a gear.'

They are in the operations room. It's packed with bodies, but Joanne still has her coat on because there's a frost on the inside of the windows. She's warming her hands on a mug of strong tea, hoping they are still dealing with a clever rapist and not a clever killer.

Joanne clears her throat, addresses McAleese. 'I know we've got to move quickly with this new information Lisa Kallisto's given us – about Lucinda meeting with an older man – but I agree with Ron. What if it's not the same guy taking the girls? I think we need to take a closer look at the father.'

'We always do,' agrees DI McAleese, wearily. 'But in this case we can rule him out. One, because his alibi stacks up: he was with his family when Molly Rigg disappeared. And two, we've shown a picture of him to Molly and she says it's not him.'

Joanne puts down her tea. 'I re-interviewed Molly this morning and she doesn't know *what* she knows. She was so drugged up with Rohypnol. How can she give a sure negative when she can't recall any of it?'

'Like I said, his alibi stacks up. So even if you've got the hunch of your life, Joanne, you're going to have to let this one go for now. So, that leaves us with—'

'What DNA we got?' Ron asks.

'No semen, no skin, no hair. We're limited to a suit fibre found around Molly's genitals. It's not definitive, but the lab reckons it comes from something with a silk thread in it. A pinstripe maybe.'

'Great,' Ron says, leaning towards Joanne. 'A dapper paedo . . . that's all we bloody well need.'

Joanne senses the meeting is about to come to a close. 'Sir,' she says quickly, 'I really feel it would be a mistake to ignore the father here, even if he's got his alibi—'

McAleese holds up his palm. 'Joanne, listen, you know what we're dealing with – thirteen-year-old girl, white, middle-class, missing from an area of outstanding natural beauty. The second girl to disappear in a fortnight. So, yes, I'll be looking at the father, and, yes, I'll be putting someone on to that, but remember: everyone's watching us. The whole country's watching us. We've got to find the bastard who's taken this girl *today.* Not tomorrow. And that means following up what we actually have to go on right now.'

Joanne nods. 'I understand.'

'You and Ron get yourselves back to Windermere and go and interview Sally Kallisto,' instructs McAleese. 'See if you can't get her to give you more about this mystery man, see if anything correlates with what Molly Rigg's said this morning.'

Joanne stands, and she and Ron gather up their things as McAleese delegates more house-to-house.

She's just about to leave the room when she doubles back and stops beside McAleese, interrupting him mid-flow. 'Molly Rigg was taken to a place with laundered sheets,' she says quietly. 'Guy Riverty's got rental properties. Is anyone checking them out?'

Weird to be back here, Joanne's thinking, as she and Ron are directed to the deputy head's office.

'Brings back all the old memories, does it?' Ron asks her.

'Yeah. Which school did you go to, Ron?'

'Lancaster Grammar.'

'You're cleverer than I had you down for.'

'I was pretty sharp when I took the eleven plus, deteriorated straight after that, though. Came out with nowt at sixteen, so I joined the force . . . I only signed up on account of all the sport.'

Joanne casts Ron a sideways look. He's not what you would call a fine physical specimen. He can get out of puff tying up his shoelaces.

'I know what you're thinking' – Ron smiles – 'I don't play so much any more, but I did use to play a lot of cricket. This police scout came round to our cricket club and told me he had the perfect career for me. Said I could play all the sport I wanted if I joined the police cadets.'

They are walking down the main corridor of Windermere Academy. The place does bring back old memories for Joanne. Memories of being thirteen, of being shit scared she might trip up and make a fool of herself. Of catching the eye of a fifth-form boy and blushing hot for the rest of the day every time she thought of him.

The deputy head has made his office available for Joanne and Ron to speak to Sally Kallisto. Joanne looks around at the bland decor, at the veneered desktop, at the once-white vertical blinds, now a soiled, creamy-grey.

She'd sat in here on one occasion before, way back, twenty-odd years since, when there had been a particularly brutal fight between two fourth-form girls. One had had her earring ripped straight from her ear, splitting the flesh of the earlobe in two, and Joanne was brought in because she'd seen it. But she didn't say anything. She'd feigned ignorance because she'd been brought up believing that you never grassed on your mates. Ironic she was here now, about to ask Sally Kallisto to grass on hers – though, admittedly, the stakes were considerably higher in this instance.

Sally is ushered into the office along with a pasty-faced young teacher – Miss Murray – who looks more frightened than the child.

Sally looks nothing like her mother. She's the spit of her dad. Straight, black hair, smooth, dark skin, beautiful, deep, chocolate eyes.

'I'm Detective Joanne Aspinall . . . and this is my colleague' – she gestures towards Ron – 'Ron Quigley. You met each other yesterday.'

'Hi,' Sally answers quietly.

Joanne's arranged the chairs into an L-shape. She sits with her notepad open on her knee, and Sally sits down on the chair next to her.

'Before we ask you some questions, Sally, you're quite sure you're happy to be accompanied by Miss Murray? Because we can wait a little longer, try to get hold of your parents if you'd prefer for them to be here instead. Your mum's out collecting cats, the shelter told us, so she should be back soon. But I can't seem to get hold of your dad. He's not answering his phone.'

Sally's tights are bunched a little around her ankles. She pulls at the fabric of each leg as she answers, doesn't make eye contact with Joanne. 'Can we do it now?'

'Of course.'

'It's just . . . it's just that—'

She doesn't finish.

Joanne glances at Ron. They're both thinking the same thing: Girl doesn't want to talk in front of her parents? She's got something useful to say.

Joanne smiles. 'Let's get straight to it then.'

Joanne begins by running through the events of Lucinda's disappearance, to check nothing's been missed by Ron when he spoke to Sally yesterday.

When she's finished speaking Sally looks directly at Joanne. 'Do you think she's still alive?' she asks.

'I'm really hoping so. Do you?'

Sally shakes her head.

'What makes you think that?'

Sally drops her gaze. 'I don't know. I just don't see how she can be . . .'

'Because—'

'Because my mum says she's probably dead.'

'Your mum can't know that for sure. Nobody can, can they?'

'No, but I didn't tell you – I didn't tell the police – about the man Lucinda was seeing. I should have told you that, shouldn't I?'

'Yes,' says Joanne, 'you should. But that's why we're here, so you can tell us now.'

'My mum says it's my fault, she says that if Lucinda dies—' She pauses, tucks her hair behind her ear: '. . . do *you* think it's my fault?'

'No.'

Joanne leans forward in her seat.

'It is *not* your fault that Lucinda chose to get into the car of a stranger. But, Sally, listen to me, you're going to have to tell us everything you know about Lucinda for us to be able to help her.

Even if you think you're betraying her. Even if you think that she will be so upset and angry with you that she'll never speak to you again. You're going to have to tell us her secrets. Do you understand that?'

Sally nods and takes in a trembling breath. Suddenly she's trying her very best not to cry, and the skin on the back of Joanne's neck prickles. They are close. She can feel it.

Joanne prompts her. 'Cry if you need to, Sally. Don't hold it in.'

Ron produces a clean handkerchief from his breast pocket and passes it to Sally. 'There you go, love,' he says gently.

But Sally manages to hold on to her tears. 'I've never seen the man she talked to,' she begins. 'I've never been with her when she met him. She said she'd seen him three times, and he wanted her to go somewhere with him, he wanted to take her shopping.'

'Did she seem at all frightened of him?'

'She was excited.'

'So he hadn't tried to hurt her?'

'No.'

'Did you ever see his car?'

'Not properly. Just the back of it one time.'

'When was this?'

'Two weeks ago?' She phrases it as a question. 'I'd stayed to talk to a teacher, so I was late.'

'Can you describe it for us?'

'It was silver.'

'Definitely silver?' Ron cuts in. 'Could it have been white?'

Sally looks to the side. 'Maybe,' she admits. 'I'm not completely sure. I didn't know it was him until I got to Lucinda, and she told me he'd just asked her out.'

'Asked her out?' Joanne repeats. 'Does that mean to be his girlfriend, or to go somewhere?'

'She didn't know. We talked about it a lot, but we were never really sure if he meant it, like, as in to be his girlfriend, or what.'

Ron says, 'So you've never actually seen this man for yourself.'

She shakes her head. 'Never.'

Joanne jots down the car colour and raises her head. 'What else can you tell us?'

'Not much.'

'Nothing at all?'

Sally shrugs.

'Come on,' Joanne encourages. 'I know what girls are like – you discuss *everything*. Every tiny detail to do with boys.' Sally is momentarily wounded, so Joanne adds quickly, 'It's no different when you get older, you know,' and she shoots a glance at Miss Murray. 'Is it?'

'Oh no,' replies Miss Murray, flustered. 'I can spend hours and hours talking about my boyfriend.'

Sally doesn't take the bait, though.

She stares down hard at her lap. Her body's rigid, and it's almost as if she's been threatened not to divulge anything.

'What is it, Sally?' Joanne asks finally. 'Has Lucinda told you something about him, something you're frightened to tell us?'

She shakes her head. 'I've told you everything I know.'

'You're certain about that?' Joanne asks this while at the same time feeling deflated. She was certain there was more to be had here.

'I'm sure,' confirms Sally.

Ron goes to shift in his seat but, without thinking, Joanne reaches her hand across to his knee, a gesture to tell him to stay put.

'Sally,' she says carefully, 'remember what I said. You need to tell us everything, or we can't find her. You're not helping Lucinda by keeping her secrets safe. Not now.'

Sally looks up, and all at once begins blinking rapidly. She tries to take a breath in, but the air shudders into her lungs as if there's a blockage inside her trachea.

Her eyes lock with Joanne's. Then suddenly brim with tears as the words come spilling out of her in a rush.

'It's to do with her dad,' she says. '*That's* her secret. That's what I'm not allowed to tell anyone.'

20

I'M BACK AT WORK trying to syringe-feed some fluids into these kittens, but it's no use. I know I'm hurting them, and I'm reaching the stage when it's going to be kinder to go ahead and get the vet to give the blue juice. I'm pissed off and sad, but trying not to let myself get angry about the bastard who's left them like this. It takes too much out of me. One good thing to come of it, I suppose, is that we know Banjo the Staffy is okay with cats. That'll improve his chances of rehoming. Even if prospective owners don't have a cat, they're not keen on the idea of adopting a dog who'll happily eat one.

The buzzer goes, meaning there's someone outside in the office, so I leave the kittens and go on through. I could do with a break from them anyway, maybe have a cuppa.

It's Mad Jackie Wagstaff.

People call her Mad Jackie because she was prone to thumping people on a regular basis, particularly when she was going through a bad time a couple of years back.

Her husband frittered away all of their money – re-mortgaging the home without Jackie knowing it – and getting them into a whole heap of financial trouble. To get them out of it, he had the bright idea of raffling off the house. It was a nice property, valued at about three hundred thousand, and everyone (including me and Joe) bought tickets at twenty-five pounds a go. Apparently, they sold close to eight thousand tickets, after putting adverts in the *Gazette* and dropping fliers about the village, which gave them close to two hundred thousand pounds in total.

Then Mad Jackie's husband ran off with the money. Disaster.

And suddenly everyone was gunning for Jackie. She says people still cross the street when they see her coming; she's lost the friends she'd had for over thirty years.

Now Jackie works as a carer, bringing me the pets of those that have died.

I look at her surprised when I see she's standing in the office, empty-handed.

'What?' she says, then realizes. 'Oh, don't panic, I've not brought you anything today. I've come to see you. See how you are. Our Joanne said that missing girl was staying with you when she disappeared.'

'Yeah, she was, kind of,' I tell her. Then: '*Your* Joanne? You mean Detective Aspinall? Is she your daughter?'

'Niece.'

'You never said.'

'Yeah, well, she doesn't like me advertising the fact. Paranoid, if you ask me. She thinks if everyone knows she's CID she'll have her tyres slashed. Anyway, our Joanne said you were pretty cut up about it – the girl – so I thought I'd just look in on you, see if you're okay, since I was passing.'

'Trying not to think about it, if I'm honest. Well, trying not to imagine what's happened to her. It's helped coming in here. You don't want a cat, do you?'

'No.'

'Kitten?'

'We're not allowed any pets.'

'You could sneak one in. No one'd know.'

Mad Jackie laughs. 'The landlord would. Anyway, it's Joanne's house, not mine. She's only letting me stay there 'cause

I can't afford to live on my own. She won't let me have a cat.'

'Fair enough. I've got to try. We're stuffed to bursting at the moment and I just brought in a load of half-dead kittens . . . I've got nowhere to put them if they *do* survive. What a day,' I say to her. 'What a bad couple of days.'

'What do they think's happened to the missing girl?'

'You probably know more than me.'

'What? You mean Joanne? Oh, she tells me nothing. She's not allowed to and she's a stickler for the rules. How's the mother doing? Joanne said you and her were friends.'

'Did you see the press conference?'

Jackie nods.

'I couldn't watch it,' I say sadly. 'It's bad enough knowing the agony I've put them through, I couldn't stand to watch them go and—'

I stop because the door opens and a woman walks in with a West Highland Terrier.

She's wearing one of those padded gilets in shiny fabric, expensive jeans tucked into pink Hunter wellies and a silly furry hat with ear flaps – like she's been out trapping beaver.

Mad Jackie gives me a look, moves away from my desk to let the woman approach.

'Good afternoon,' she says. She's about mid-forties. 'I've brought Hamish in because we're relocating – we're moving to the Middle East – and I wondered if you would like to buy him from me.' She says this in such a bright, sunny manner you'd think she was offering me a free holiday.

Jackie coughs.

'That's not really what we do,' I explain, and the woman tilts her head to one side.

'But he's ever such a good dog, very clean and well-behaved. I have his pedigree papers right here,' she says, and gives a little wave of an envelope.

Patiently, I tell her how we work and what we do and, though I'd like to say this is a one-off occurrence – someone wanting payment for a pedigree – it's not. It happens at least once a fortnight. They really think the same rules apply as if they were selling a plasma TV. Why would you not want to buy it when they're offering it at such a reduced rate? When it's such a bargain?

I give a kind of helpless shrug. 'Sorry,' I say to her, 'but we're a charity.'

Her pleasant, jolly demeanour is suddenly no longer there and her expression is one of deep concentration. She's faced with a problem she wasn't anticipating.

'You could still leave him with us,' I try. 'I have space for one more dog, and I'm sure he'll find a lovely home.'

'I told my husband we'd be reimbursed,' she says, frowning. 'We've spent a great deal of money on him and we were hopeful of recouping some because—'

All at once Jackie pipes up. 'You're dumping this poor animal here, and you want *paying* for it?'

I could feel it coming, could feel Jackie getting heated, but I had hoped she would keep it under wraps.

The woman's indignant at Jackie's tone. 'I am not *dumping* anything,' she replies. 'My husband has been headhunted and we have no choice but to relocate.'

'There's always a choice,' answers Jackie. 'Just depends on your priorities.'

'My priorities are with my family – that is why we're going! Now,' she says, turning back to me, 'we paid fourteen hundred pounds for this dog, it will make someone a lovely pet, it doesn't need much walking and it's very clean.'

Jackie's eyebrows are raised. '"It"???' she's mouthing.

'I'm quite sure someone would be happy to pay for it,' the woman continues unabated, 'and if this shelter is not prepared to offer me some money, then I'll simply put an advertisement in the Westmorland Gazette. Somebody will.'

Jackie wanders over to the door and looks out. Then she turns round, all innocent. 'That your Lexus out there, then?'

The woman says yes. Yes, that is her car.

'Forty grands' worth o' car and you're farting around in here trying to get some fool to buy your bloody dog? . . . A dog that you no longer want?'

'It's not that I don't want him, as I've explained—'

Jackie, walking back to the desk, cuts her off. 'Yeah, yeah, you've said . . . Well, let *me* explain to you, because Lisa here is far too nice to do it. Let me tell you what should happen when you can't care for your dog any longer . . .

'You come in here all friendly and apologetic,' Jackie tells her, 'and you say, "Please, nice lady, who gets paid next to nothing to mop up after ungrateful shits who don't give a damn about their pets, please, nice lady, could you take this dog from me and find him a good home, because finding a good home for him is the *most important thing*. A home where he'll be loved and cared for." And then you say, because you are so grateful to the nice lady for taking away your problem, you say, "I'd really like to give a donation to the shelter, because it must cost an awful lot of money to run this place. Why, you must have *food costs*, *vet bills*, *heating costs*. How about I write you a lovely big cheque right now? What? No, of course I don't mind! My husband's loaded! He's been headhunted by a bunch of Arabs, so we're gonna be minted. No! I don't mind at all." '

Jackie folds her arms across her substantial chest and glares at the woman. '*That's* what you say.'

The woman storms out, dog in tow, and I look at Jackie and shake my head. 'You can't go dealing with people in that way.'

'Who says?' she snaps. 'She had it coming. I can't stand women like that. Think they can walk away from their responsibilities just 'cause the mood takes them. I don't know how you do this job, Lisa, I really don't . . . Anyway, did you see that hat?'

21

YOU'RE NOT SUPPOSED to have favourites.

I know that. But sometimes you can't help it.

Currently, we have an old Bedlington Terrier at the shelter named Bluey that nobody wants. We have him in a kennel on his own, because he's the nervous type and what he's truly craving is companionship in the human form – he's not really one for other dogs. He tolerates them, he's not aggressive – Bedlingtons rarely are – but he'd just as soon be left alone.

Bluey's been at the shelter for five months, and the reason no one wants him is because he's old. No one wants to take on an old dog, what with the increased chances of illness and vet bills. But every time I walk past his kennel my heart aches for him. He's forever standing by his gate, never sitting or lying, and he's waiting. Always waiting. He's like one of those horses left out in the rain, the ones you see tied up outside the saloon in Westerns. Head dropped, hind leg crooked, eyes half closed, waiting.

I talked to Joe about Bluey last week and we decided that if he doesn't get rehomed in the next fortnight we'll find space for him back at ours.

But then, as of two o'clock this afternoon, I decide *there is a God after all* because, just when I'm spiralling downwards, what with no news about Lucinda, and three dead kittens on my hands, in walks a guy who tells me he wants to adopt a dog in need.

Immediately, I tell him about Bluey, and he seems not put off by his age; in fact, he says he'd prefer an older dog because he's not got time for a pup at the moment.

'I can't tell you what a lovely boy he is, so calm and gentle, the perfect dog,' I tell him. 'Have you owned a dog before?'

'Not since I was a kid. I've just got kinda lonely these last few months, I'm new to the area, so I thought it would be a good way to meet new people.'

I nod in acknowledgement, like, *Yes, I know how that is.* But inside I'm thinking I can't imagine this guy having trouble meeting people. Without meaning to, my eyes move to his left hand. There's a barely noticeable band of paler skin where a wedding ring once lay, so either he's newly separated or he's taken it off to play away from home.

He's wearing a shin-length Barbour wax coat and a striped woollen scarf. The scarf is knotted in that way the well-heeled tend to knot them nowadays – where you fold it over lengthwise, drape it around your neck and insert the loose ends through the loop. Some folk look as if they're being strangled when they wear them in this way, but on this guy it looks chic.

I'd put him at around thirty-four. He's attractive. And he knows it.

'Can I take your name?'

'Charles Lafferty.'

I go to write but for a second both of us are startled into silence by a Tornado jet flying low overhead. The whole room shakes and I squeeze my eyes tightly shut. It's the third one this hour, and it gets a bit wearing. On bright days it can seem as if the RAF deploys every single one of its fighter jets for a mad whizz around the Lakes.

Charles Lafferty is also wincing from the assault of noise. When it passes, he asks, 'Do you have many dogs for adoption?'

'Too many,' I say. 'And no doubt we'll have a load more in after Christmas.'

'Really? Do people still buy pets as presents? I thought they'd know better by now – after all the "A dog is not just for Christmas" warnings I see in car windows.'

I look up briefly. 'Apparently not . . . Mind you, we don't tend to get the unwanted pups in till about June. That's around the time the Christmas pups have turned into destructive, crazy adolescents. We get a deluge of dogs after New Year because Christmas is such a stressful time for people. They find it hard to cope, and often the first thing they do – to make things easier – is get rid of the dog.'

'Poor things,' he says earnestly. 'I wish I could take more than one.'

'One is brilliant. Believe me. If everyone could just take one dog then it would be so much—'

I'm babbling.

'Let me take you through to meet Bluey,' I say firmly. 'I've been talking you into this dog and you haven't even seen him yet.' I roll my eyes at my own ineptitude, expecting him to laugh along with me, but he doesn't. He regards me in a strange way, keeping his gaze fixed on mine. And then, as if he's all of a sudden remembered how to do it, he smiles at me warmly.

'Follow me,' I tell him, and we make our way past the first few kennels, stopping in front of Bluey's.

The dog's standing in his usual spot. You couldn't find a sorrier-looking animal if you tried. 'Here he is. This is Bluey.'

Charles Lafferty squats down. He's wearing good, expensive, pinstripe trousers and soft calfskin loafers. He seems very out of place on the utilitarian tiles, the sharp smell of Jeyes Fluid around us.

'He looks so sad,' he comments.

'He needs an owner.'

'He's okay, though?' he asks. 'He's not got depression or anything, has he?'

'Just lonely. He really needs some company. Shall I open the kennel and you can have a proper look? He tends to come alive more when he has a bit of a fuss made of him.'

Charles stands. 'Yes, please do. Let's see what he's like.'

The cast-iron gate makes a low, groaning sound as I pull it open and Bluey is snapped into alertness. The dog views me and then Charles, and I swear, if a dog could smile, then Bluey is doing it right now.

'Look at that!' says Charles excitedly. 'He looks almost happy, doesn't he?'

I give Bluey a deep, kneading kind of rub on the front of his chest where I know he likes it, and instantly his eyelids drop down a fraction again as he relaxes under my touch.

'May I?' asks Charles.

'Be my guest. Just don't stroke him round his tail-end area, he gets a bit cross.'

'He's housetrained, is he?'

'Oh yes,' I say confidently, while at the same time thinking, *Actually I have no idea.*

It's impossible to say whether they are fully housetrained or not, because all the dogs have to crap inside their kennels. We haven't got the manpower to get them outside four times a day. When in doubt (and in circumstances such as these), I find it's best to lie. Because Bluey needs all the help he can get.

I stand back to give them both some room to get to know each other. Charles is scratching Bluey behind his ear, which sets Bluey's back leg off in that circling motion they can't help but do. And I feel a little choked by the spectacle. I almost have to blink back the tears.

I'm certain he's going to take him. It's very rare you get

someone fussing over a dog in this way for them to turn around and say they'll think about it. *Please*, I pray . . . *Please take him.*

Charles stands, and his eyes are shining. 'I'll have him,' he says decisively. 'Can I take him now?'

''Fraid not,' I reply. 'There are a few things we have to go through first. I need a copy of a utility bill – you know, to prove you actually have a home and you're not sleeping in your car or something – and when I get that I can do a home visit, just to check that it's suitable for Bluey.'

'Oh, absolutely,' he says. 'I fully understand. You can't just go sending them anywhere, can you?'

'Not really. Do you happen to have any proof of address on you right now? Then we can get that hurdle out of the way, and I'll be able to do the home visit as early as tomorrow, if that suits.'

'Heck,' he says. 'No. No, I've not. How disappointing. But what about if I come in tomorrow morning, give it to you then. And you could do the visit in the afternoon? How would that be?'

I exhale, smiling. 'That would be wonderful . . . you don't know how relieved I am that you're giving him a chance. He's been a real worry for us. We all adore him.'

He bends to tickle the curls on top of Bluey's head. Then he straightens up, saying, 'He's going to be the perfect companion for me. Aren't you, Bluey?'

'Do you live alone? I only ask because I don't think he would be great being poked by young children – some of the senior dogs prefer a quiet household.'

Bluey would be fine with young children, I'm sure. And even if he wasn't, I'd be happy to send him to a busy household, just to get him out of long-term kennel life. The reason I ask him if he lives alone is because I'm being nosey.

'Yep,' he answers. 'Just me. I do work fairly long hours, but I can bob back home several times a day – my office is just round the corner from my house, so it shouldn't be a problem.'

'What is it you do?'

'Solicitor. Actually, I haven't yet asked her, but my secretary's a real animal lover, and I'm hoping I'll be able to sneak him in with me a few days a week and she can keep an eye on him. What do you think?'

'Bluey is *the* perfect office dog. I'm sure he'll curl up underneath her desk.'

'How does he walk on the lead? Does he pull at all?'

'Not one bit.'

'Could I take him out for a walk now? I know it's a bit cold, but I'd really love to go for just a short while.'

'That's no problem. In fact, we encourage people to try a walk with the dogs before reserving them. It's important to get the right dog. After all, you're going to be together for a long time. I'll get you a lead. And I think we might have a coat to fit Bluey somewhere too.'

'Excellent,' he says.

'There is one thing we've not discussed – bit awkward, actually, I'm never good at this part – but as a charity we're not allowed to accept any payment for the dogs we rehome, but we do ask for a donation. Whatever you can manage is great—'

Usually, at this point people start fishing around for their wallets, telling you how they'd be more than happy to give blah blah blah, but this guy stays stock-still, his face a bit blank. Mildly uncomfortable, I continue with my rehearsed speech: 'Our vet bill can run upwards of £25,000 a year,' I say, 'so the donations go towards that, and of course Bluey comes to you fully vaccinated and neutered so—'

I raise my eyebrows and smile gawkily at him. Still nothing.

'The lead?' he says, prompting me, as if the last minute hadn't happened.

'Oh, yes,' I stammer. 'I'll just get it for you.'

And what is it when you know something is not right? When you know something is a little bit off, and yet you ignore it and continue on regardless? Is that stupidity? Or is it ignorance?

Both, perhaps.

I'm not sure what it is, but forty-five minutes later Charles Lafferty has not returned with Bluey and I'm getting nervous. It's minus six out. The ground is frozen and the air is raw. Exactly how far has he taken Bluey on this 'short walk'?

I go outside hoping I can see them returning and it's then that I notice there are only three cars in the car park. Mine, Lorna's and Shelley's – Shelley is the other kennel girl; she drives a clapped-out Fiesta.

Charles Lafferty has gone. There is no trace of him.

And, bizarrely, he's taken Bluey with him.

22

It's almost 5 p.m. and Joanne has spent the last couple of hours building up a picture of Guy Riverty. The plan is to head to Troutbeck to question him, just as soon as McAleese gives them the say-so. McAleese first wants the properties Guy owns around Troutbeck searched, then they'll widen it if that turns nothing up.

Ron Quigley's been assigned ViSOR – the Violent and Sex Offender Register – and he's not a happy bunny. He keeps tutting and shaking his head, periodically mumbling, 'Fucking sickos.' Which Joanne supposes is only natural.

Sex offenders must confirm their registration each year. Meaning they have to inform the police of any changes in their personal circumstances – their address, their job, and so on and so forth. Failure to do so results in a penalty of up to five years' imprisonment. Which should be a good enough deterrent.

But is it?

Do sex offenders really inform the police of their every move? Joanne supposes not.

Ron's looking for movement of individuals into the Cumbria area within the last six months. But, by the sounds of it, he's becoming sidetracked by their offences. Unsurprisingly, Guy Riverty is not on the register, but McAleese has told Ron to keep going over it, should this new lead on Guy amount to nothing.

Pushing the chair out from her desk, Joanne says, 'I'm getting a coffee, Ron. You want one?'

'Aye, okay. You've not got any Rennies in your handbag, have you? My stomach needs settling.'

'It's all that pastry you keep eating for breakfast. Get your wife to make you some porridge.'

Ron gives her a look. He is not really a porridge type of guy. 'I was fine before I started looking at these sick bleeders.'

'Fair point. I'll see if I can find you something.'

Joanne leaves the office as Ron's muttering, 'Like a needle in a haystack of Gary Glitters, this is—'

She walks down the hallway, past DI Pete McAleese's office, where he's shouting and bawling at someone on the phone. She's humming Gary Glitter's 'Rock and Roll Part 2', louder than she probably ought to . . . not really the done thing if you're working on a child-rape case.

Shame about Gary being such a fuck-up, Joanne muses. She always did like his music.

She presses buttons on the machine for two milky coffees and thinks about Guy Riverty. She can't shake the feeling he's involved somehow and so has been checking online which of his properties are occupied by holidaymakers. Not many. Most are empty right now, the next bookings coming just before Christmas.

They're nice, his properties. All high spec. Gone are the days of the cheap and cheerful B&Bs, the fifteen-quid-a-nighters, including a full cooked breakfast. That doesn't exist any more. The Lakes has a different clientele now. The walkers, hikers and outdoorsy types still frequent, but the place caters more for the country-retreat brigade. They want marble-tiled bathrooms as big as Joanne's house. They want Michelin-starred restaurants. They want midnight cruises with pink champagne.

Guy Riverty's holiday lets are all listed as five-star. He goes a bundle on a modern finish, and underfloor heating comes as standard. For a while this afternoon Joanne had become lost in dreaming up her ideal life in one of his cottages over at Hawkshead. Walking around barefoot, her feet padding softly on the solid-oak flooring, her hand running over the built-in espresso machine, across the wall-sunk TV. No wires dangling down to annoy her here. A faceless, nameless, good-looking Adonis lying on the bed upstairs, waiting for her . . .

That's when she'd snapped herself out of fantasy mode and got back to work.

She tracks down some Rennies for Ron from Mary, the station cleaner, and returns with his coffee to find him looking grave.

'D'you want the bad news or the bad news?'

She perches on the edge of his desk. 'Fire away.'

'Another girl's gone.'

'Shit. How?'

'No details yet, I've just heard. Which means—'

'Which means he's not let Lucinda Riverty go. Which means she's probably already dead.'

'Do you want the other bad news?'

'Go on.'

'Desk sergeant's fighting off the tabloid press downstairs. McAleese wants you to stand in on the statement, thinks it'll look best with a woman officer present . . . *and*—' he says, sighing out a long, unhappy breath.

'There's more?'

'Yeah. Your Mr Riverty was nowhere near where this one was taken. Sorry, Joanne, but it's just not him.'

The feeling inside him is growing to the point where he knows he can't contain it for much longer. This is the best part. The part just before. Right before.

She lies there, her eyes open, glassy. Seeing but not seeing. He would like for her to see him fully, but that's not possible. Perhaps later.

Her skin is paler in this light. There's not a blemish, not a crease. No lumpy flesh adorns her inner thighs. No silvery-white streaks crawl across her belly.

Instead there are two, sharp, angular hipbones jutting skyward. More like wrongly positioned shoulder blades than bones of the pelvis.

She doesn't speak.

He lies next to her. The cotton sheet slides upon the polythene beneath, the scratchy sound incongruous in the serenity before him. She moves her head. She knows he's here, but she's not scared. She wants him. Her mouth parts, but not in that trashy way he knows. She's communicating to him. If she could form words she would be urging him on, telling him it's time to begin.

Forming a light pincer grip between thumb and first finger, he circles his wrist in the air above her abdomen. He's removed her bra already and, as he suspected, she didn't really need it. Following her friends. Just fitting in. He really wished they wouldn't do that. Plenty of time for growing up later. Seems they all want to do it so fast, and if only they knew how wrong they were.

The air between his fingers and her body is warming now. The transfer of energy, a mixing of each of them, here in this space. Sacred space. The two of them joined together in the purest way.

Her mouth whispers inaudible guidance and it's time to remove his clothes. With his now-gloved fingertips, he gently parts her legs and takes his camera from the desk. Her neatness he finds astonishing.

Then he lies down upon her and lets her take him to where he needs to be.

23

IT'S JUST AFTER SEVEN in the evening and Joe and I are sitting at the kitchen table. The kids are upstairs. Sally is on the phone to her school friend, Kitty. She seems to have reached the stage where she needs to talk and talk – but not to us. The police spoke with her again this afternoon, about the man Lucinda's been meeting, but she's sketchy with the details, makes out like I'm pressuring her and tells me she's told me everything she knows already.

The two lads are playing Minecraft. This game seems to have every teenage boy across the country hooked, but I am yet to see its appeal. I feel a stab of guilt. Now and then I nag Joe about us doing more things together. 'We should play a board game, or have a meal out . . . we never spend any quality time with the kids.'

And Joe will say, 'We get fed up after half an hour of Monopoly, we haven't got a spare eighty quid *to eat out with*, and how many times do I need to tell you, kids *don't like* quality time?'

He's right. They don't. But then I watch *Supernanny* and feel shitty when she says parents only spend around forty minutes a day with their kids, and that's the reason for their bad behaviour. 'Those kids can't behave,' Joe says, 'because their parents are idiots. We're doing the best we can, Lise. Let it drop, will you?'

Joe's exhausted today. He's driven to Lancaster (twice), not usually a big deal in itself, but a band of freezing rain came across late this afternoon – a meteorological event I have never witnessed before – and the roads are a nightmare. They are treacherous.

On leaving work, I'd assumed we'd had a brief respite from the snow, as everything was rain-covered, dewy-looking and clean. But then I stepped on to what I thought was a damp step, only to realize the rain had frozen on impact and the damp was in fact colourless ice.

I saw three cars in ditches and two accidents by the time I got home. And I could've cried at one point when I spotted an elderly guy crawling up to his front door on his hands and knees rather than risk trying to walk.

Joe came home and went straight out again. A group of his friends from the pub wanted to search along the river for Lucinda – without Kate and Guy knowing – and he's only just got back.

He's shattered, and he looks awful. There are deep creases beneath his eyes, his left eyelid is drooping slightly and his three-day-old stubble is growing through grey. This seems to have happened so suddenly. Almost overnight. As if the day he hit forty the black pigmentation was all used up. I put my arms around him from behind and kiss his neck softly. Then, as I straighten, I see a deep gash on the back of his head, visible through his hair.

'How did you do that?' I ask him.

'Twatted it getting out of the car. My legs slid from under me.'

I don't reprimand him for his use of language. Oddly, I don't mind the word 'twat' when used as a verb instead of a noun.

Needless to say, they found nothing on the search. Joe wore his golf spikes to give him some marginal grip on the ice, but the search party didn't stay out long. One guy lost his footing and slipped a good thirty yards, so they gave up and came back. And from what I hear, the police are no further along.

I'm telling Joe about the theft of Bluey and asking whether he thinks I should call the police and report it. But he rubs his eyes, saying, 'Reckon they've got a bit too much on their plates to be dealing with stolen dogs right now. Besides, Bluey's got a home. Which is what you wanted. The bloke probably just didn't want to give a donation – maybe he couldn't afford to.'

'But that's the thing,' I tell him, 'he comes in dressed all expensive and says he's a solicitor. He could clearly afford it.'

'What car did he drive?'

'Didn't see it.'

'People are weird, baby. Who knows what goes on? I'd let it go.'

He can't be bothered listening, and I can't blame him. He looks fit to drop. His skin's so grey it's like he's been dug up.

I clear away our plates. Joe's is littered with green stalks where he's bitten off the flesh part of the chillies, straight into his mouth. I check beneath his chair for any bits that might have fallen, because Ruthie, the Staffy cross, has a habit of eating them and then growling at the floor afterwards when her mouth is burning.

'School might be shut tomorrow,' Joe says, pouring himself a bottled ale. 'There's black ice everywhere. No one'll be able to get in . . . I'm thinking maybe we should switch your car for a Land Rover soon. It'd be safer—'

'Nice idea, but what with? I'm not swapping it for an ancient one because we can't afford to trade up.' Then I say half-heartedly, 'I suppose we could always get a loan.'

Joe doesn't answer. Our finances are bordering on disaster at the moment. We own nothing except our cars. There's no chance of us ever owning a property around here, and if we hadn't got this house through the housing trust, which provides affordable housing for people born in the area, we couldn't even afford to rent in the village. Not when rents average around two grand a month. My credit card is maxed out after buying the kids' Christmas presents and, well, it goes on and on.

Joe looks up. 'We'll put the car on the back burner,' he says decisively and I know as I sit back down at the table that both of us are thinking the same thing. A new car is immaterial when we have all three children, safe upstairs, here with us. Joe gives me a sad smile. 'Maybe we should offer to run Fergus to school tomorrow if it's open. Save Kate and Guy doing it.'

'Good idea. I was going to ring her in a bit and check on her. I'll ask her.'

James comes in and helps himself to a packet of crisps I bought from Asda this morning. We'll be lucky if there are any left by morning. Sometimes I think I'm housing locusts, not children.

James notices his dad's not his normal self and starts rubbing Joe's arm up and down in an uncharacteristically gentle, soothing way. I watch on bemused, because James is not a touchy-feely kind of kid. 'Dad,' he says, 'you might not know this, but I have some medical training . . . and I think you might be having . . . a *stroke*—' He laughs, still rubbing Joe's arm, tickled by his own joke. Then he takes off upstairs, oblivious, it seems, to the stresses of the past two days.

I run Joe a bath. The bathroom is like an icebox, because there's no double glazing in our ancient cottage and the insulation above that room is woefully lacking. You have to get in and out of the bath as fast as you can.

I've poured Joe another beer and leave it next to endless bottles of shampoo and bubble bath Sally's bought when she's been out shopping with her friends. I put Joe's pyjamas and dressing gown on the radiator in the bedroom, like I used to do for the two older kids, still do for Sam, and give him a shout to come and get in.

When Joe's soaking and happy, I go downstairs and phone Kate. Guy answers before it's even had a chance to ring twice.

'Guy, it's Lisa. Any news?'

'What?'

'Any news?'

I can hear noise in the background, a door slam, muffled shouting. It could be Kate, though I'm not sure.

'Guy,' I say gently, 'is everything all right?'

'What do *you* think?' he snaps, and I'm taken aback.

'I'm sorry—' I stammer. 'I rang to see if you needed any help with Fergus tomorrow. You know, what with the weather being so bad? We can take him to school if it's easier for you.'

Guy sighs out what sounds to me like a slow, scornful breath. 'It's really not a good time right now, Lisa.'

'Oh, okay, I'm sorry to have bothered you, I only wanted to—'

'Just go, would you? Just go, and get off the fucking line.'

'I . . . I—'

But he's gone. Put the phone down on me.

I stand there in the kitchen looking at the receiver in my hand, then someone starts hammering on the front door.

I rush to open it, thinking, *It's Kate! Or Lucinda!* But as I pull the door back a blast of bitter air hits my face and I see it's neither of them. There on the step, shaking, is Alexa.

'Alexa,' I cry, 'how on earth did you get here? It's not safe to be outside.'

'Where is Joe?' she demands, pushing past me, striding inside.

'In the bath – why? What is it, Alexa, what's happened?'

'Tell him to get out,' she says.

24

SALLY IS IN THE kitchen pouring herself some milk when Alexa barges in. 'Would you mind giving us some privacy, Sally?' she says.

Sally stares at me, because Alexa looks completely unhinged. She's wearing pyjama bottoms – blue flannelette with sheep on them – snow boots and a black, padded dealer's jacket. Her ordinarily silky blonde hair is damp, scraped back into a ponytail and starting to frizz around the temples. And she has black smudges beneath her eyes where she's not taken her mascara off properly.

I give a quick flick of my head to Sally, meaning 'Scoot,' and when she's left the room I say to Alexa, 'What's all this about?' But I've kind of figured out already that this is a whole different type of anger to what she displayed when Lucinda first disappeared.

Still, I want to hear it from her. I want to be sure before I fall apart. I give her my best poised, unruffled look.

Alexa's jaw is set. 'Get Joe.'

Five minutes later, and Joe's standing in his dressing gown, bits of shaving cream still welling in his nostrils and just inside his ears. Alexa turns to him. 'Joe, your wife and my husband have been having an affair,' she says.

Immediately, Joe snorts. Looks at me, ready for us both to collapse into laughter. When he sees I'm not smiling his face drains of colour. 'It's not true, is it?' he asks.

Before I can answer, Alexa shrieks, 'Of course it's true! Do you think I'd come around here like this?' – she gestures to her pyjamas – 'Do you think I'd come here if it wasn't true? Good God, Joe, what planet are you on?'

Joe swallows. After a long, silent moment, he says, 'How long?'

I hold up my index finger. 'Once,' I whisper. I can't look at him.

'Once? Fucking *once*!' Alexa screams. 'Well, if you think I'm believing that nonsense then you're a bigger fool than I had you down for. Of course it wasn't once. Who the hell does it once? . . . What, you did it once and then you couldn't live with yourself, is that it?'

'Something like that,' I mutter.

'When was this?' Joe asks.

'When we went round to Kate and Guy's that time for dinner.'

'But that was . . . that was ages ago,' he says, frowning.

'Three or four years,' I reply.

Alexa is looking quickly from me to Joe, me to Joe. 'Is that it?' she says. 'Is that all you're going to say to her?'

He shifts his feet around to face her. Exhaling, he says, 'What do you want me to say, Alexa? Why don't you tell me what you want me to say? Or, better yet, why don't *you* say what you want to say?'

'I want to know how many times. I want to know where they meet. I want to know *why*?'

Joe looks at me. 'Lise?'

'Once. It happened once. We don't meet anywhere, it happened that time and that was—'

'Oh, for fuck's sake,' Alexa says in disgust. 'You're as bad as him.'

'Who?' asks Joe.

'Adam.'

She's gripping on to the back of a chair; her knuckles have lost their colour. 'Is this what *you* decided?' she asks me. 'Is this some little plan you cooked up together with Adam before he came clean? "Let's just say it was a one-off, that it meant nothing, that it was one moment of madness. If we both say the same thing, then no one can prove otherwise, can they?" '

I stare at her. 'Isn't once enough?'

She doesn't answer.

'Why did you do it, baby?' Joe asks me softly.

I shrug hopelessly. 'I was pissed.'

'What sort of excuse is that?' Alexa hisses.

'A truthful one. I can elaborate if it makes you feel better. I can say the alcohol removed my moral compass, or say it blurred the boundaries, or that I lost self-control. But I was just really, really pissed.'

'Do you go fucking other people every time you have a drink?'

I look at Joe. 'I'm sorry,' I mouth to him, and he holds my gaze then closes his eyes slowly.

'Why did you have to choose *my* husband, anyway?' Alexa says, a tearful edge creeping into her voice now. 'Why Adam?'

'I didn't choose Adam.'

She glares at me as if to say, *Oh, c'mon.*

'He chose me.'

Wounded, Alexa turns back to Joe. 'Why are you not saying anything? Why are you not doing anything about this?' Then she starts to cry. 'What kind of fucking man are you, Joe?'

'I'd rather discuss this when you're gone,' he replies, ignoring the insult. Then, gently, 'How did you find out, Alexa?'

'That bastard told me. Couldn't keep it to himself any longer, he said. Said it's been tormenting him for years but he couldn't bring himself to admit it. What I want to know is, who else knows about your little affair?'

'It wasn't an affair.'

'Whatever. Who else did you tell? Obviously not your husband. But I'd like to know who's sniggering about me behind my back so I can be ready.'

I shift from one foot to the other. 'No one knows,' I lie, thinking of Kate. Jesus, if she finds out her own sister has been withholding this . . . 'No one,' I say firmly. 'I've never told anyone.'

Alexa dabs at her eyes.

Joe says, 'Why did he tell you now? Why *now*, after all this time? Doesn't make any sense.'

'That's what I said,' she snaps. 'But he said that with all the upset going on with Lucinda at the moment, and the police going through every inch of our lives, he couldn't handle having secrets any more.'

Joe nods. 'Alexa, would you like a drink?' he asks.

'No. No, I'll go. I don't know what I expected coming around here but, well, I have to say, Joe, you're dealing with this better than I am. I'll leave you to talk.' She turns to me. 'Do you have any diseases?' she asks, and I shake my head. 'Good. I suppose I'll have to take your word, won't I?'

'Sorry, Alexa,' I say weakly. 'If I could undo it, I would. All I can say is I never meant to hurt anyone. It's just something that . . . happened.'

She fixes me with a glare.

'These things never just happen. There's always some underlying pathology, as they say. You've been harbouring resentment towards me from the start. And I *know* Kate puts up with you. I know you're like her personal project or something. She has this ridiculous notion that she can save people, she thinks she can talk to the little people and make them feel important. And I warned her about it, I really did. I said to her, "Kate, we can't mix. There will be problems." But she didn't listen. And now look at us. Not only have you been fucking my husband but, because of you, Kate has lost her only daughter.'

25

We are lying in bed, the clock says 23.40, and we're both staring at the ceiling.

Joe's not spoken so far. I've tried to push him to talk, I *want to talk*, but he won't. And it's not that he's punishing me; it's worse than that. It's that he's physically unable to speak, as though if he lets himself acknowledge the enormity of what's happened to us, it will all be true.

I lie there, waiting. The heavy stone I've been carrying around in my gut since Lucinda disappeared has been replaced by molten metal. It's burning, corroding my insides. I hate myself. I hate what I've done.

I start thinking about Christmas and I worry now what a disaster it will be. Ridiculous to think about it, but will I even be here? Will Joe be here, or will he go, move out and live with his mother?

I can't believe this is happening to us.

All that love, all that love and work we've put in. Wasted. All the energy and commitment it takes to keep a family of five on the road, to keep our family running smoothly. And I threw it all away in the space of about – what? Three minutes? Three, short, disgusting minutes.

The bed between me and Joe is cold. I reach my hand across the old sheets, bobbled with wear. The space feels wider than ever before. I touch Joe's hand; he doesn't pull away.

'Just tell me this,' he says emptily, 'have I been kidding myself with what I thought we had together? Have I been living with you, all these years, thinking it's something it's not?'

'Never,' I cry softly.

'Then why? Why do it to me? You used to say it was the one thing you couldn't forgive. You said that there would be no way back for us if it ever happened, because it would make a mockery of us.'

'You won't want to hear this, but I still think that if you ever cheated on me, Joe, I'd leave. I couldn't handle it. I couldn't bear the thought of you inside another woman.'

'But it's okay for you?'

'It's not okay. It's the worst thing I've ever done. And to do it to you, the person I love the most.' I try to touch his face, but he flinches. 'I've felt sick with myself since it happened, I went to the doctor with irritable-bowel—'

'I remember that,' he says, and I don't know why this sets me off, but I begin to cry fully. Perhaps it's because I can remember the concern he showed at the time. He was worried there was something really wrong with me. And there was: I was falling apart. But I couldn't tell him.

We're silent.

After what seems like hours, he turns to me. 'Did you stop loving me, was that it?' he asks.

'Have you ever felt I stopped loving you? Because I never did.'

'No. I thought we were unbreakable. I thought we were more than those idiots.' He's meaning Kate and Guy, Alexa and Adam. 'When we went over there and they put on that stupid charade, each of them pretending to have what we have, I sat there and I actually felt smug watching you. Smug, because we were the real deal.'

'If you felt like that, then why did you drink so much?'

'Free beer,' he answers, and I can't help but smile a little.

'I thought you were as insecure as me. That stuff she said, Alexa, about us being the little people – that's how I felt. I know it sounded ridiculous when she said it downstairs, it made her seem like a total snob, but there is some truth in it. That's how I feel a lot of the time.'

'That they're better than you?'

'They *are* better than me.'

Joe sighs. 'Lisa, you're confusing the way they treat you with the truth. You think they're better than you because that's how they act. You think that because they've got more money—'

'It's not the money,' I cut in, 'it's everything. I can't manage things the way they can, I'm not as capable with the kids, and with—'

'They don't have fucking jobs, Lise. Can we just stick to the facts? Is that why you did what you did?' He touches my face, wipes the tears away. 'Is that why you shagged that dickhead?'

'I don't know, maybe. I think I was flattered by him. I was flattered he wanted me.'

'Of course he'd want you instead of her. Of course he'd want you, baby. How could he not *want you*?'

DAY THREE

Thursday

26

SLEEP.

One of the only things you can't buy.

Joe and I used to play the Who's-had-the-least-sleep? game.

Back when the kids were tiny and I'd go off to work unable to face another day, and Joe would start counting up the hours on his fingers. Invariably, he'd declare that I'd had at least two hours' sleep more than him.

We even had a tally chart going on the fridge at one point.

Then, I'd be driving to a pick-up, on my way to retrieve a load of wild cats from a stinking shed somewhere, and I'd see him: seat back, cap pulled down, snoozing happily in a layby. 'Waiting for a job to come in,' he'd say. It's the only time I can ever remember truly hating him.

Now I lie next to him as he snores softly, so grateful.

We'd clung to each other last night, me, wretched and emotional, overwrought, and him, tired and drained with it all. I'd all but put the phone call with Guy Riverty out of my head, but as we drifted into slumber it came back to me and I'd sat bolt upright, telling Joe how he'd told me to *get off the fucking phone.*

I know I don't deserve any real kindness from Guy right now, but the vehemence of his words really shook me. Joe, naturally, was the voice of reason, even in his depleted state. Said how Kate and Guy were under such unfathomable pressure, and we couldn't possibly understand how they were feeling. And, realistically, Guy was allowed to speak to me any way he liked. If he wanted to blame me and tell me to fuck off, then, okay, he could.

I feel better now I've slept and can see I need to stop being precious about it and take the shit. Their daughter is missing and however they behave is of course more than understandable.

I stand in front of the bathroom mirror and peer closely at my face. The skin of my eyelids and around my temples is covered in tiny red dots, like raspberry-coloured freckles. Immediately I panic I've got the meningitis rash and septicaemia, so lift my pyjama top expecting to see my white belly covered in the nasty-looking things, but it's unblemished. Nothing.

What is it then?

Trying not to wake Sally, I take her laptop from her room, climb back into bed with a still-asleep Joe.

Search: red-spots + eyelids.

I'm directed to a pregnancy forum and for a second I'm seized by a blind panic because I think this is some weird, little-reported symptom of pregnancy, a symptom I've never come across, and, Oh God, if I was pregnant now that would be just the *very worst thing*. I love my children more than anything . . . but I cannot go through it again. Please . . . no more babies.

Trying to stop from shaking, I read directly from the discussion forum: *These tiny red dots are a symptom of forceful puking. If you are fair-skinned, these burst blood vessels show up easily. Hopefully, you won't get them any more when the sickness subsides in the second trimester.*

I exhale.

I am not pregnant. Yesterday's hangover and subsequent hard vomiting has meant I burst the capillaries all over my eyelids.

Thank God. I thought it was something serious.

Joe stirs. 'Morning, baby.' His voice is sad, strained.

'Joe, I've got these spots on my eyelids. Check there's nothing on my back, will you?'

I lift up my T-shirt and he gasps like I'm totally covered. 'Shit,' he says, 'I can see . . . I can see Jesus's face!'

'Very funny,' I say, lowering it. Then I turn towards him and look at him levelly. 'Will we be okay?'

'You mean, am I leaving you?'

I nod.

'No. It hurts like fuck, though, Lise. Feels like you've ripped my guts out and you're twisting them around. But no, I can't leave you. You can't leave me either. What would we do? It'd kill me to see you with someone else.'

'I'm sorry I ruined it.'

'You've not ruined it. You almost ruined it. Maybe if you'd done it last week, or last month or, I don't know, last year. But we've had a long time being happy since you did it. You just did a fucking stupid thing, a really fucking brainless thing. But can this be end of them now? Kate, Guy, Alexa, all of them.'

'Not exactly a great time for me to break away from them, though, is it?'

'No,' he admits, 'but you're doing all you can to fix this thing. And it's possible you might have to come to terms with the fact that you *can't* fix it. It might not be fixable. She might never come back. Lucinda might never come home.'

'And what if they blame me for ever?'

'They will. And you won't be able to do anything about it.' He pauses. 'It might be better if you start backing off them a bit, just in case.'

'But how can that be the right thing to do?'

He shrugs. 'Just a thought. Let's see what today brings.'

I look down at Joe, and my whole being aches with how much

I need him. How I can't get through anything without him. 'Have another five minutes in bed,' I tell him. 'I'll bring the coffee up.'

He manages a smile of thanks. He still looks exhausted. Looks worse, if it's possible, than he did last night. When all this is done with, we'll go away. Find a cheap package to the Canaries and get a bit of winter sun.

I go downstairs and busy myself with the dogs' kibble and the children's Weetabix. I flick on Radio 2 and hear the pips signalling the start of the seven o'clock news. The lead item is the missing girls of Cumbria.

I stop what I'm doing and listen.

And that's when Guy's behaviour of last night makes more sense. Because another girl has gone. This one is from the private school in Windermere. Not far from here.

He must have known. Guy must have already known about it when I called.

Again, the girl is thirteen and, again, she's young-looking for her age.

An eyewitness claims she saw this girl speaking to a man before walking away with him; they're advising us to be extra vigilant. They think he may have lured her away with a dog.

A tall man with an old, grey dog.

I hold on to the kitchen worktop to steady myself. My hands start to shake. It's difficult to breathe.

Bluey.

I phone DC Joanne Aspinall and get directed straight to her voicemail, so I leave a frantic message. 'Please call me,' I tell her. 'As soon as you can. I think I know who the man is, I think I met him yesterday . . . please ring me . . . please.'

I'm breathing hard as I hear Joe come down the stairs. 'What's going on?' He's standing in just his boxers and is rubbing the back of his head where he whacked it when he slipped on the ice yesterday.

My words pour out in a gush. 'Another girl is missing. They think she went off with a man with a dog. A dog like Bluey. It's him, Joe. I told you there was something odd about him. *I told you.* It's him, it's definitely him. It's got to be.'

'It might not be,' is all he says, and turns to let the dogs out.

'*Joe—?*'

'What?' he replies. 'Don't get in a state, is all I'm saying. The chance of it being the same guy is slim.'

I stare at him. 'You're wrong.'

I leap up the stairs, thinking I know what I have to do. I'm going to get dressed and get round to Kate's and tell her. I don't care if Guy yells at me, I don't care. Kate needs to know this. I can tell her what the man looks like. Jesus, she might even know him! She might be familiar with him, and *that's why* Lucinda went off with him so readily, that's why she was able to take off without anyone suspecting anything.

I look at my watch.

I send Kate a text: *Need to see you, be round at 8 xx*

The bedroom door opens. Joe. 'What are you doing?' he asks.

'Getting dressed.'

'Why the hurry?'

'I'm going to Kate's.'

'Now? At this hour?'

'This is important. It doesn't matter what time it is.'

His face goes sullen; he can't believe what he's seeing. He spreads his palms wide in a gesture of 'Oh, what's the point?'

'Lisa, did you hear nothing of what I just said? You can't go tearing round there at this time. And what about your own children? You're getting to the stage where you're neglecting them. This is still all about—'

'I'm not neglecting my own kids.'

'No?'

'Why are you saying that? You're the one who's always telling me to stop feeling guilty about them, to chill out and leave them alone.'

'Lisa, stop. Look at yourself. It's still *all* about *them.* It's still *all* about *Kate.* You can't stand the fact that she's disappointed in you, so you—'

'Disappointed? Her daughter is gone, Joe! And it's my fault. I'm not worried that she's disappointed in me, I'm scared to fucking death. What the hell am I supposed to do? I need to tell her about this guy from yesterday, it could be the missing link to finding—'

'You'd better be careful then,' he cuts in, his tone self-righteous.

'What's that supposed to mean? Careful about what?'

'You take your eye off the ball again, Lise, and it might be *your* daughter next time.'

Forty minutes later and after scraping my car clean of ice I'm driving along Kate's side of the valley.

My tyres crunch on the gravel as I make my way up the hill. I skid twice but recover and, to be honest, I'm in so much of a hurry I don't care if my bumper slams into somebody's carefully built wall or takes out their hedge. I'm feeling skittish and desperate to get to Kate's to tell her what I know. I have a strong feeling that she is going to recognize the description of the guy who took Bluey and, not trying to get my hopes up or anything, I think there is more than a good chance of bringing Lucinda home.

I don't let myself consider the option of her not being alive. For now, I truly believe she is, and Kate is going to need me to be strong. I have to be positive for her sake.

I get to the top of the hill where the road splits and, as I turn slowly left, I think that I might just be able to right my wrong. If *I* could be the one to lead the police to Lucinda, then perhaps, in time, Kate and Guy will be able to forgive me, and—

I'm driving past the spot where the Rivertys park their cars. Guy's Audi is not there.

Just a little along the road from the house itself is their detached double garage. Like most families', it's so full of junk there is no room for the cars, so Guy and Kate park their 4x4s in front of it. Kate's Mitsubishi is there, but Guy's car isn't.

Where is he at this hour? Why is he not at home?

I dip the clutch and press the brake simultaneously, slowly, slowly, bringing my car to a stop on the roadside by Kate's front pathway. She didn't reply to my earlier text but I know she's awake because all the downstairs windows are illuminated.

Anyway, of course she's up.

What mother sleeps in when her kid is missing?

I stay where I am for a moment and watch. There's no movement from within the house, but I notice Kate has taken to switching her Christmas lights on again now – probably trying to keep things as normal as possible for Fergus.

The tree looks pretty in the front bay. They do that thing families do at the beginning of December and go and choose it together. Make a day out of it and stop at a country pub for lunch on the way home.

Our artificial one is still in the high cupboard above my wardrobe.

Throughout the year the cupboard has a habit of bursting open by itself, and I'll glance up to see a lone branch dangling down, taunting me, filling me with a sense of foreboding about Christmas – even if it's only June.

My whole childhood seemed to be spent waiting for Christmas to come around, and now I spend half the year dreading its arrival. Too much to do and not enough time to do it in. I'm always left feeling like a Christmas failure.

I look back again at Kate's car. Perhaps Guy has managed to park his in the garage after all, so he doesn't have to defrost it this morning. It took me for ever to do mine.

I get out and take tentative steps up the path. I remember reading once that the cartilage in human joints is three times more slippery than ice. But not this ice. This ice is like nothing I have ever experienced. I'm wearing some old ski pants I bought to go to Andorra with before I realized I was pregnant with Sally. We never did get there; so they've been used as winter dog-walking trousers ever since, and I'm grateful for them now. If I slip, at least my backside will have a little padding.

I press the doorbell and wait.

There's no sound. Usually, you hear someone thundering down the stairs or you hear Kate's quick, short steps along the hallway.

I press again, then start slapping my hands together to keep the blood flowing.

It's as if there is no one home at all.

Perhaps Kate is in the shower.

I decide to ring the house phone on my mobile; she might hear that if she's upstairs.

Two minutes later, and I give up because it goes unanswered. Then I have a brainwave. I bet they've gone to the police station. I bet they got the call about the new missing girl and they've gone to see if there is any more information. Yes. They must have taken Guy's car.

But why leave the house lights on?

I'm about to head home when at the last moment I give the front-door handle a turn, just to see. When the door opens I jerk backwards with surprise and almost lose my footing.

Stepping in, I hear music coming from the kitchen, so that's where I head. 'Kate?' I call out. 'Kate, are you here?'

It's Jona Lewie's 'Stop the Cavalry' playing, and it's coming from the sky-blue retro transistor radio, the one that matches Kate's other blue retro appliances.

Then my mouth drops open.

Kate is on the floor next to the kitchen table. She's in her Cath Kidston tea rose pyjamas and she's vomited all over herself.

On the table there are three empty pill bottles and a half-drunk bottle of sambuca.

Trembling, I squat down next to her. I don't think she's breathing.

27

JOANNE'S BRAIN IS fully alert but her body is still asleep.

She didn't make it back home until after eleven last night, when she had to abandon her car in Windermere village. Some idiot had abandoned *their* car outside the Co-op, blocking the road, and there was no way down. So Joanne had to make her way along, clinging on to parked cars like Velcro Woman, at one point thinking it would be easier just to give up and slide along on her arse. But even though there was no one else around, she couldn't quite bring herself to do that.

Of all the times for freezing rain, it couldn't have been worse. Two teenage girls missing and nine out of ten roads in Cumbria impassable.

The police have warned people to make essential journeys only – which of course is interpreted differently by everyone.

Joanne remembers seeing an American family being interviewed on TV once after a particularly bad ice storm in Minnesota. They were telling the reporter that they had *no choice* but to drive in the deadly conditions, because they had to eat – as in go to a restaurant – because, like a lot of Americans, they never cooked at home.

Life-and-death situations mean different things for different people.

Joanne untangles the covers and makes her first attempt at getting out of bed. She sleeps cocoon-like with the duvet pulled around her and tucked between her legs. That way she stays warm but her legs don't get sticky.

She shifts on to her back and runs her fingers underneath the lower rim of her sleeping bra. She's slept in a bra since she was fifteen years old and can't wait until she'll no longer need it.

There's banging coming from downstairs. Jackie's usually gone by now, showering at six, out of the door for six thirty, tending to the clients who need help getting up. Today she must be stranded also.

Jackie was already asleep when Joanne returned home last night. Joanne had popped her head around the bedroom door, but the sounds of Jackie snoring and grunting told her she was flat out, helped on her way by a bottle of Mateus Rosé. Joanne had found the empty in the bin.

Joanne pads down the stairs and finds Jackie eating toast and marmalade and watching breakfast news in the lounge. Her short blonde hair is wet and has that orangey hue that comes from home bleaching. 'Car's stuck,' she says, her mouth full. 'It'll need a man to get it movin'.' Joanne tells her that they're thin on the ground this time of year.

She's not told Jackie about her breast reduction because – well, she doesn't know why she hasn't, but she's just not. So when Jackie says, 'There's a letter come for you,' nodding her head towards the coffee table, 'says it's private and confidential,' Joanne doesn't have a suitable answer ready and tells her it's probably a bank statement.

'It's postmarked Lancaster,' Jackie says, eyeing her suspiciously. 'Bank statements don't come from Lancaster.'

Joanne taps the side of her nose with her finger, an action guaranteed to stir Jackie up into a frenzy, so she goes out to make some tea.

'I know you're up to something,' Jackie shouts from her chair.

As the kettle boils, she picks up her phone and curses as it's been set to go straight to voicemail. She listens to her messages, expecting something from the DI reprimanding her for not being within reach, but there's just one garbled message from that woman at Troutbeck. Lisa Kallisto.

Something about a dog and the rapist.

It's hard to hear properly, because Lisa's message is bordering on hysterical and Jackie's turned up the volume on the telly. Joanne has to plug her other ear to decipher what Lisa Kallisto is going on about. She'll call her in a moment, after she's had a mouthful of tea and at least woken up enough to hold a conversation.

'Another girl has gone, then?' Jackie's shouting from the lounge.

Joanne squeezes her tea bag against the side of the mug with a spoon. When it doesn't look strong enough, she drops Jackie's used bag in there as well. 'Yeah, yesterday,' she shouts back. 'That's why I was late home. Pressure's really on – we need to find something quick.'

'You missed seeing Nanna.'

Wednesday evening, they both visit Nanna at the nursing home. Well, she's *Joanne*'s nanna, she's Jackie's mother. Jackie's always called her Nanna, though. Probably since her own son was small and it was less confusing for him to know her just by one name.

'How was she?' Joanne asks as she comes into the lounge, spilling her tea slightly as her foot catches on a rumple in the carpet.

'The usual, coming on like she didn't recognize me.'

Nanna pulls this trick if they visit when there's a particular programme on she wants to watch.

They've learned to ignore it.

'Does she need anything?' Joanne asks. 'She all right for talc and stuff?'

'She could do with some new slippers if you want to get her a pair when you're next near Marks's; size three. And you owe me twelve quid for the hairdresser. She had a perm last week.'

Joanne and Jackie split the cost of sundries. Joanne's mother is supposed to contribute as well but, since she's been living in Lanzarote for the past four years, it's not worth the hassle trying to get her to pay her share. Thank God the state covers the nursing-home fees is all Joanne can say. At four hundred quid a week there's no way she and Jackie could manage it, and the alternative would be to have Nanna living with them . . . not really doable.

Jackie stops chewing and looks at Joanne straight. 'You having that breast reduction, then?'

Joanne looks to the ceiling and sighs. 'Does nothing get past you?'

'Sylvia saw you in the doctor's on Tuesday, and since you were keeping it to yourself, I thought that's what you must be going for.'

'He's referring me to a consultant. I've got an appointment after Christmas.'

'You're a bloody fool.'

'In your opinion.'

'Not my opinion. Fact.'

Joanne says nothing. She knows Jackie's thoughts on the subject well enough. She really doesn't want to go through it again right now.

Joanne's phone vibrates in her dressing-gown pocket. She pulls it out and checks the screen.

It's Ron Quigley.

'Joanne,' he says, wheezy-sounding and short of breath, like he's running up the station steps. 'Get yourself to Troutbeck soon as you can, love. That Riverty woman's only gone an' tried to top herself.'

28

THEY SAY TIME IS RELATIVE.

Slow time is waiting for the birth of your baby when you're twelve weeks pregnant; watching the hands move around the clock face on Christmas Eve when you're seven years old; it's waiting for the paramedics to come when your friend has tried to kill herself and the roads are slick with ice.

The longest minutes of my life.

The waiting was torture, because there was nothing I could do for Kate. Her body was stinking and lifeless, her breath barely there, her pulse shallow and erratic, and there was absolutely nothing I could do about it but stroke her head, helpless.

I hadn't realized when I'd first found her but as I tried to turn her into the recovery position I noticed her pyjama bottoms were filled with diarrhoea, and it spilled out all over the marble floor tiles. So I cleaned things up as best I could. Then I turned the radio off and I waited.

The first person to get here is a lone paramedic in a Land Rover emergency-response vehicle. I know the guy in passing; I'm used to seeing him around Windermere, picking up a sandwich, or at the HSBC. He has a kind face with a nose pushed to the side where he's taken a punch. Probably rugby. He's the right kind of build for it. He tells me there's an ambulance on its way but he'll get started with Kate because—' He pauses, says the next part apologetically: 'It'll be a struggle for them to get up here.'

'How long d'you think?' I ask, my voice shaking, and he shrugs, his expression again rueful. Hopefully not too long, he tells me.

He gestures towards the pill bottles on the kitchen table. 'That all she's taken?' And asks me to check upstairs, in the bathrooms, in the medicine cabinets, to see if I can find anything else she might have swallowed. They really need to know, he says.

The pill bottles on the table contained antidepressants. Amitriptyline and phenelzine. I'm familiar with the names, because my mother used to take them. I'd pick up the prescriptions for her if she needed me to. What's shocking to me is that Kate is on antidepressants and has been for long enough to stockpile them and then to go and do this. The date on two of the bottles is August; the other is October.

It seems that every time I think a person has got things sorted, every time I think a person has got everything under control and is holding their life together in far better ways than I could ever hope to manage, they turn out to be taking antidepressants. It seems I am very naïve about these things.

I am standing in Kate's beautiful kitchen, looking at her lifeless body, thinking, 'Why the hell was Kate taking them? Why, when she had *everything*.'

Of course I can see why she's overdosed, with the chance that Lucinda's now dead. I can understand that. But why were they necessary in the first place?

I am starting to comprehend that what I think I know about a person and what is in fact true are poles apart. And yes, I know lots of women take them. But why was Kate?

'What will they do with her?' I ask the paramedic before going to check for any more empty pill bottles around the house.

'If this is all she's taken, they'll give her charcoal, through a nasogastric tube. That's usually it . . . if we've got to her in time, that is. Depends on the complications. Is there anyone you need to call?'

'I need to let her husband know, but I haven't got his mobile number.' I wring my hands helplessly. 'He should be here . . . I don't know why he's not . . . they—' I start to tell him about Lucinda and all that's happened to this poor family, but then I stop. I need to check upstairs first before the ambulance arrives, and I've just had the bright idea of calling Kate's mobile to find where it is in the house. Guy's number will be on that.

And that's when time speeds up.

I'm in Kate's en suite, calling her mobile from mine, but there's no ringing sound coming from anywhere in the house. I'm scouting around, going as fast as I can, because I know the ambulance will be here soon and I need to hurry.

I open the bathroom cabinet and get an instant uncomfortable insight into their lives. As well as the antidepressants, Kate is also stockpiling Canesten Duo for thrush, glycerine suppositories – something I had to give Sam once when he was really backed up – and three bottles of Regaine hair restorer.

Guiltily, I poke between the bottles to see if there's anything else hidden, all the while perplexed by the Regaine, because Guy's hair is not thinning in the least. He's got that thick, floppy, luxurious hair and can often be seen tossing it back from his face in one movement. Like Michael Heseltine used to do back in his prime.

It's a strange thing to see these people's lives displayed in this way, a hidden insight into the real workings of the family, but I suppose that's what happens after a catastrophic event such as a child going missing. Or an overdose. The layers of respectability and properness are removed and, in an attempt to get to the truth, the family is stripped bare. Left exposed for all to see.

I pick up a bottle from the bottom shelf, something for nits that I've used on the kids in the past, something that doesn't work one bit and—

All at once I shiver; my body goes numb.

Fergus.

Kate's son, Fergus. Where is he?

How could I have forgotten about him? Christ, what if he's here and wakes up and wanders downstairs, only to see his mother in the state she's in?

On finding Kate, I'd clean forgotten about Fergus being in the house. *Please let him be with his Aunt Alexa*, I'm praying as I move along the hallway towards his room. Please let him be with his daddy. Please—

I flick off the light in the hallway so as not to send a sharp shaft in there and startle him, and I open the door to his bedroom as quietly as I can. My hand is shaking. I pause for just a moment and sigh out, trying to steel myself.

Then I push the door slowly.

He's there, asleep on his bed. His duvet has managed to rearrange itself horizontally across the single mattress so that his feet are poking out the end. It's so warm in here, though, that he's unaware. I loiter in the doorway, unsure what to do. I could go in and wake him, try to keep him here and protect him from the scene downstairs. Or I could close the door again and hope he remains asleep until they've taken her away.

I don't know what to do.

Fergus moans gently and turns on to his side, facing away from me.

I need to make a decision.

Short of a better plan, I take the key out of the lock from the inside of the door and lock it from the outside. This is not ideal, I know. If Fergus wakes in the next ten minutes, he'll panic when he can't open the door, and I hate the thought of this quiet, thoughtful child panicking.

Suddenly I'm filled with rage at Kate for putting me in this situation. Couldn't she have killed herself when Fergus was at school?

Then I stop, telling myself that she wouldn't have been thinking at all. To get to the stage of suicide, I imagine she wasn't really in a place for rational thought.

But still . . .

Kate, what the fuck were you *thinking*?

Blue lights are now bouncing off the wall opposite and I walk over to the window. Kate has this area dressed with a window seat, like a lovely reading corner. There's an overstuffed, striped chair angled tastefully in the corner and a bookcase to the side. Someone – must be Fergus – is reading *Swallows and Amazons* by Arthur Ransome; it's been left open and placed downwards to keep the page. I tried to get James to read that one, but he gave up two pages in and went back to his collection of Wimpy Kids. I'd consoled myself at the time with the notion that boys don't really like classic books, but it seems as though I was wrong.

I watch from above as a paramedic makes her way along the front path. I need to hurry.

I'm at the top of the stairs as she comes through the front door. She looks up. She has a lovely face and, fleetingly, I think about how many people must have looked into that face when they were scared, or perhaps dying, and gained some comfort.

'She's in there,' I tell her, gesturing towards the kitchen.

'Nice house,' she remarks absently, and I agree. 'It is, isn't it?' I say.

There's something about the presence of paramedics that makes a frantic situation almost normal. They go about their business in such a controlled manner that, for a time, you forget you're dealing with life and death.

I follow her into the kitchen and stand back so as not to get in the way. The man on the floor with Kate greets the pretty paramedic, saying, 'Roads a bit tricky, eh, Megan?'

'Just a bit. How's she doin'?'

He brings her up to speed as another paramedic comes in carrying a stretcher. 'Not safe for a trolley,' he remarks to no one in particular.

'I'm her friend,' I tell him, and he nods grimly.

'Have you checked the house for anything else she could've taken?' he asks, and I tell him yes, I've found nothing. I'm about to tell him I can't be entirely sure, though, because there wasn't time to do a thorough check, when we hear urgent banging coming from upstairs.

I close my eyes.

When I open them they are all looking to me for direction. 'It's her son,' I whisper sadly. 'Any chance you can get her out of here quick?'

By the time I get to the top of the stairs, Fergus's desperate hammering has turned into more of a bored, methodical tap.

I hate the idea of Kate travelling to hospital on her own, without someone she knows, but that's the way it has to be. I don't know Alexa's number off the top of my head, and since I don't know how to get hold of Guy—

I unlock Fergus's door and plaster a smile across my face, a smile my own children would be instantly suspicious of, but it will have to do.

I decide to go for the half-truth option. I haven't got it in me to concoct some sort of elaborate lie to spare this poor child any further trauma, so I simply say: 'Fergus, I know you weren't expecting to find me here this morning,' and I give a nervous kind of laugh, 'but your mummy has become unwell – in fact, she's had to go to hospital . . . She asked me to look after you for a bit. Is that okay? How about we go and get you some breakfast?' His eye has flared up again. His left one. It's bloodshot in the corner and the lid is swollen. I'll have to apply the drops Kate uses.

At times, I find Fergus odd. Strange. And I'm used to boys. With two of my own, there have been loads of boys round at our house over the years. I'm used to the hyper ones who can't sit still and wreck your bathroom if you don't keep an eye on them. I'm used to the ones who won't eat anything except hot dogs or cream crackers or sour Haribos. I'm used to the ones who don't speak at all, the ones who if you put them in front of a DVD go into a trance and don't come out of it again until the credits run. I'm even used to the ones who say 'fuck' and 'shit' and 'crap' and 'bastard'. For some reason, hearing a seven-year-old use the word 'bastard' has always been particularly amusing to me.

But, as I said, Fergus, I find odd. I don't know what to do with him.

I can't find a way in. It's as if the more I try to connect with the child, the more he stares back at me blankly, as if I'm getting it all wrong. So I've kind of stopped bothering. Sam and Fergus have only ever been friends probably under duress, I see now, because Kate and I are friends. It's suited us for the two of them to play together. But now that they've reached seven, the differences in the two boys have become more pronounced and – well, I can kind of see why Sam was charging Fergus a higher rate to play with him. Because he's what you'd call hard work.

When I tell him Kate's in hospital he doesn't say a word. Nothing. Just follows me out of the room and down the stairs. I walk into the kitchen and realize it still smells a bit sour from where Kate was sick . . . and there's the unpleasant, foul odour from the other thing . . . but Fergus doesn't comment. He sits himself at the kitchen island, looks straight ahead and waits for me to put something down in front of him.

'What do you usually have?' I ask pleasantly. 'Weetabix? Rice Krispies?'

'Porridge.'

I frown. 'Every day?'

He nods, without emotion.

'Porridge it is then.'

I'm opening and closing cupboards. Kate's kitchen has around four times the storage space of mine. Each cupboard is beautifully organized and spotlessly clean inside. It takes me some time to find both the porridge (I'm looking for a blue box – Quaker Oats or Scott's – but instead I discover it's in a brown-paper bag, an organic, steel-cut variety I've never heard of) and then I have to deal with the baffling choice of pans.

'How much sugar do you like?' I ask Fergus while I'm stirring the stuff, which seems to be taking far longer than it should.

'Mummy sweetens it with honey and blueberries.'

I smile at Fergus, because, of course she does.

'Would you like to get those out, and you can put them on yourself?'

He jumps off the stool, looking so small in this huge space. I glance over as he stands in front of the fridge and – you know when you hear those stories of children getting locked in freezers and ovens, and you think, Is that even possible? Looking at Fergus now, I can see how it is. He's such a tiny, skinny thing he could easily climb inside and go unnoticed. His brown hair is sticking up vertically on his crown after his sleep. It's accentuating the flatness of the back of his skull, giving him an elfin, almost pointed head from this angle.

'Fergus,' I say carefully, 'has your daddy gone away somewhere?'

He shrugs. 'I don't know.'

'Was he here last night . . . when you went to bed?'

'Uh-huh.'

'You saw him, then?'

'Yes.'

I pause, deciding whether to push this further, whether it's right to question a seven-year-old this way. 'Fergus . . . did your mummy and daddy have an argument last night?'

He bites his lip, reaches inside the fridge for the blueberries, then casts me an uneasy look.

I make my voice soft, sympathetic-sounding, and go back to stirring so I don't appear confrontational. 'Did you hear them shouting?' I ask him.

'A bit,' he says, reluctantly.

I smile and roll my eyes, make a gentle smacking sound with my lips, as if to say, *Grown-ups, eh?*

After a moment I nudge a little further. 'Sorry to be nosey, Fergus . . . it's just we could really do with finding your daddy . . . and I'm not sure where he is. Did he tell you if he was going out? Did he mention anywhere he had to be last night?'

He closes the fridge and says, 'No,' firmly.

As well as the honey and the blueberries, Fergus is surreptitiously carrying a small packet of Cadbury's Buttons – which I'm guessing are usually off limits at breakfast time. He puts them on the table and guiltily covers them with his hand when he sees me eyeing them.

I spoon the porridge into a bowl and carry it over.

'It's a bit hot,' I say gently, and lean over to blow on it a couple of times.

Fergus looks up at me. 'Daddy never tells us when he's going for a sleepover,' he says. 'That's why Mummy gets upset.'

I take a step back, conscious that my face is registering shock, that my mouth has gaped open. I can't think quite what to say.

I whisper: 'Do you know where he goes, Fergus? Does he ever tell you where he goes?'

And Fergus opens his eyes wide before going to speak. Then

the front door slams and we hear footsteps. Instinctively, I put my arm around Fergus's shoulders, just as Guy appears in the doorway. He's unshaven and his eyes appear sunken and blood-shot. He tosses his hair out of his eyes rather dramatically and fixes me with a chilling stare.

'What are you doing here?' he asks. 'And where the hell is Kate?'

29

'DO YOU HAVE ANY idea why your wife would have taken an overdose, Mr Riverty?'

Joanne has been at the house for less than a minute but she can see all is not as she'd expected to find it. First off, why is Guy Riverty not at his wife's bedside? Second, why is Lisa Kallisto here at this hour, washing a pan of porridge as if her life depends upon it?

Guy Riverty sits at the kitchen table, his head in his hands. He looks like he's still in yesterday's clothes and as if he's not slept for over a week. He rubs his face, exhales long and hard and answers Joanne's question with: 'She thinks our daughter's dead. She's not in the best of spirits. How would you be?'

Lisa moves from the sink and dries her hands on a tea towel. Then she begins wringing it in her fingers. Joanne looks to her. 'You found her?'

She nods. She's uncomfortable. As if she's embarrassed to be here. Her mouth is set in a thin line of tension.

'Can we continue with the questions once I've got Fergus out of the way? He doesn't know yet. He doesn't know what his mother has done.'

Joanne asks, 'Is there anyone who can run him to school—'

'I will,' Lisa jumps in quickly.

'Anyone else?' Joanne could do with keeping Lisa here for the time being. The woman is skittish in the extreme, and Joanne senses it's not just about the overdose. She takes out her notepad.

Guy looks to Lisa. 'Have you rung Kate's sister yet?'

Lisa gives her head a quick shake. 'I didn't know the number.'

'It's 35648. Can you call her? Ask her to come here right away?' Lisa doesn't answer, just marches out quickly.

'So, Mr Riverty,' Joanne begins.

'"Guy" is fine.'

'Guy, then.' She pauses briefly. 'Been somewhere, have you?'

He doesn't answer.

'Where were you last night?'

'I was here.'

'What about three thirty yesterday afternoon? Where were you then?'

'I've already given a statement about this,' he says irritably, and Joanne keeps her face blank as if she's unaware of his point. 'If you're asking me where I was when that other girl went missing, I was here. With Kate. She's told the police. She's said that I was here with her.'

'Anyone else see you?'

'Yes – no – maybe. There are people coming and going from here all the time. If you hadn't noticed, our daughter is missing.'

'Perhaps you can have a think for me, see if you can't come up with another person – *other than your wife*, that is – who saw you here.'

Joanne jots down today's date in her notepad.

'Am I being accused of something?'

She looks up at him, smiles. 'Not yet,' she says.

'So why are you asking me the same questions I was asked yesterday?'

'Because the person who provided your alibi, Mr Riverty, has just tried to take her own life.' She tilts her head to one side.

'Perhaps she might not make the same statement when she recovers?'

'I was here,' he says firmly.

'Mind if I have a look around?'

'Help yourself – just don't get Fergus worked up. He's in his bedroom and, like I said, he doesn't know about his mother. He thinks she's unwell.' He rubs his face again with his hands, muttering, 'Fuck,' emphatically under his breath.

'I'll be discreet,' Joanne whispers.

She enters the hallway and finds Lisa Kallisto standing staring at the telephone as if she's not quite with it.

'You okay?' Joanne asks.

'Bit shaken,' she replies. 'That wasn't an easy call to make . . . to Kate's sister.'

Joanne nods sympathetically. 'I bet not. She's on her way, is she?'

'Yeah. God, poor family, they must wonder whatever's coming next.'

'How was it that you came to find her? I got your message by the way, about the dog—'

'Sorry?' she says, and stares at Joanne blankly. Then it dawns on her. 'Oh, yes, Bluey. Christ, I'd forgotten all about that. That's what I'd come round here for – to speak to Kate to see if she knew the bloke who'd taken him. You know, to see if it rang any bells with her. I thought . . . maybe . . . I just thought that he could be—' She exhales. 'I don't know what I thought,' she admits. 'I certainly didn't think I'd find what I did, that's for sure.'

'Why do you think she did it?'

'Kate?'

'Mmm.'

She shrugs. 'All got too much for her. That would be my guess. I mean, *how do* you cope when something like this happens? I suppose the answer is you don't.'

'She took antidepressants, right?'

'Yes.'

'Did she seem depressed to you?'

'Never. But don't read too much into that. Seems everyone's on them nowadays. Well, everyone except me. When I told my doctor I thought I might be depressed, he told me I was just pissed off . . . there's a difference, apparently.'

Joanne smiles. 'Sounds like we've got the same GP. Maybe you should tell me about the man and the dog?'

'Seems a bit daft now, after this—' Lisa sweeps her arm out wide and gestures towards Kate Riverty's kitchen.

'Tell me anyway.'

She describes the circumstances of the missing Bedlington Terrier to Joanne and how desperate she was to rehome him, and how she thought her prayers had been answered by the guy in the pinstripe trousers and—

Joanne stops taking notes and looks up. 'Pinstripes, you say?'

'Yes, he was very smart. Expensive. Not my usual kind of customer.'

'How old?'

'Mid-thirties.'

'Good-looking?'

Lisa blows out her breath. 'And *then some*.'

'You get his name?'

'Charles Lafferty.'

'I don't suppose you got an address? Phone number?'

Lisa drops her head slightly. 'I was going to do all that when he brought Bluey back. I know it's probably coincidental and it's really no use to you . . . but I thought if I could tell Kate about him she might recognize him from the description or something. Too late now.'

'It's not useless. Everything helps.'

Joanne flips her notepad shut and leans in close towards Lisa.

Nodding her head in the direction of Guy Riverty in the kitchen, she whispers, 'Has he told you where he was last night?'

'I didn't ask.'

'What do you think he's up to?'

'No idea.'

Joanne heads upstairs to talk to the boy.

DS Ron Quigley meets Joanne at the hospital. Kate Riverty's not conscious yet, but she's alive.

Ron hands Joanne a strong tea in a polystyrene cup from the WRVS shop. Joanne senses Ron's been entertaining the two old dears behind the desk with tales of macho policing, as they seem quite giggly and flushed when she arrives. They are both easily in their eighties, and one is wearing a wig pulled a little too low on her forehead. The other has one of those swollen, soft lady-bellies which jiggles under her velour dress as she speaks.

'Thank you, girls,' Ron says, smiling, charming them. 'Keep up the good work now.'

'We will, Detective!' they chorus.

Ron and Joanne move into the main foyer area. It's hot, stifling, as hospitals are, and Joanne removes her parka and slings it over her elbow. She's conscious of her blouse gaping and tries to draw her cardigan closed, even though she feels heady from the heat.

'What's your best guess, then?' Ron asks her, meaning what does she make of Kate Riverty's suicide attempt?

Joanne goes to speak but spies a reporter she's seen knocking around outside the Riverty house. The woman gets up on seeing Joanne, one of her high heels scraping across the floor as she does so, and rushes towards her. Joanne's dealt with the reporter before. She's a pushy, awkward type, who misquoted Joanne about an arson attack once, and Joanne has no interest in talking to her now.

Joanne signals to Ron with her eyes and they move quickly away, along the hallway, down towards the X-ray room before she answers his question.

'I think she lied for him, gave him the alibi, then couldn't cope with knowing he was involved. He didn't find her after she took the pills; the friend did. And he didn't come home last night . . . so where was he? He didn't want to tell me, got pretty defensive actually.'

'So you want to bring him in?'

'I think we should.'

'On what basis? There's nothing to charge him with. There's no evidence of him kidnapping his own kid, even if he is a shifty bastard—'

'I don't know, Ron. Something stinks.'

They hear a noise like a power tool starting up and pause, glancing into the plaster room to their right. A kid is having the cast taken off his leg and looks like he's about to pass out with fear. The technician is trying to get him to understand that the plaster saw does not cut through skin, but the child is not convinced. Neither is his mother.

'You've spoke to the medics?' Joanne asks Ron as they move on down the hallway.

'Yeah, reckon she's going to be fine. Pills weren't in her system long enough to do any real damage.'

'When can we talk to her?'

'Soon as she's awake. That could be this afternoon, though. Might be best to head back, bring Guy Riverty in now, and speak to his missus later. Probably more time-effective that way.'

Joanne drains the rest of her tea and looks back and forth along the corridor, trying to locate a bin. 'Do you think she really meant to die, Ron, or are we looking at a cry for help here?'

Ron shrugs. 'I always think it's a cry for help unless they

manage to pull it off. You want to do it, you do it. The people that really want to go through with it, they make sure it's going to work and hang themselves.'

'Hanging's too violent for women to contemplate, Ron.'

'Effective, though.'

Joanne shakes her head. 'Remind me never to come to you when I'm feeling depressed.'

'What?' Ron says, pretending to look hurt. 'I've been told I'm a very good listener.'

30

I'M AT HOME, in the shower, washing my body after leaving Kate's. My clothes are in the washer on a hot cycle and Joe is sat on the toilet (fully clothed, seat down), speculating on Kate's state of mind.

I'm still shaky and jittery and can't quite trust my limbs to do what they're supposed to do. When I bend over to soap my lower legs I almost slip and fall.

Our shower is an over-the-bath type, which, although useful for cleaning off the dogs when they've been rolling in fox shit, means we don't have those non-slip ridges you get in a shower cubicle. And right now I could really do with some. I ditched the bath mat last month when I noticed the underside was starting to look like a biology experiment.

'Did Fergus see Kate unconscious?' Joe asks me.

'I managed to keep him upstairs until the paramedics took her.'

'Poor kid. He'll grow up weirder than he is already.'

'*Joe!*' I admonish.

'What? You're the one's always saying he's strange.'

'Well, he is . . . but still.' I turn off the water. 'Pass me the towel, will you?'

Joe stands, moves his eyes up and down my naked body. 'Looking good, Lise,' he says quietly, and holds the towel out wide for me to step into. Then he wraps me up and kisses my wet forehead. 'Don't you ever go doing anything like that,' he says. 'I'd die without you, Lise. We all would.'

'Not planning on it,' I say, and I kiss him on the mouth. His body responds immediately – as it always does – and he whispers, unexpectedly, 'You up for some?'

'There's not time—'

'There is.'

'It'd feel wrong, me and you doing it in the bathroom while Kate's having her stomach pumped.'

'We don't need to tell Kate,' he says, his breath warm inside my mouth. 'Besides, you saved her life this morning. I'm sure she'd forgive us . . . Really, she owes you, if you think about it—'

He slides his fingers beneath the towel. They come to rest under the creases of my buttocks.

'But she wouldn't have *taken* the pills if Lucinda was still here, and Joe, that's all my fault, and—'

I'm becoming more breathless by the second, despite my protestations.

'I need this, baby,' he says, pulling me in hard towards him as the towel falls to the floor. He slips his tongue inside my lips. I'm pressing against him.

'Okay,' I say. 'Okay, but we need to be quick.'

'Quick,' he replies, undoing the belt to his jeans, 'I can do.'

He turns me around so I'm facing the bath. He lifts my right leg so my foot is balanced on the edge of the tub, and, because I know I'm not quite tall enough for this position, I lean my weight backwards. Then I wriggle my left foot up on to the top of his steel-toecapped boot.

I feel him inside me and exhale. Sigh out and almost collapse against him. The relief I feel is overwhelming, and I whimper as he holds me firm. Thank God he still wants me. Thank God he wants me after what I've done to him.

A few moments later, and it occurs to me that, from a certain angle I must resemble a child, a small child who's learning to dance by placing her feet on top of her parent's shoes.

Well, kind of like that, anyway.

I walk downstairs, thighs like jelly, as if I've done two hours on the leg-extension machine at the gym, and the phone is ringing. I pick up just as my voice kicks in on the answer machine . . . 'Hello we're not at home right now, if you'd like to—'

'Hello?' I say, out of breath, flustered. 'I'm here—'

'Lisa, I've just tried you at work, but they said you weren't in yet.'

My mother.

She won't ring my mobile because of the cost. She'd rather call everyone she knows trying to locate me than pay twenty pence a minute to BT.

'I'm late because—'

'Never mind,' she says, cutting me off. 'Did you hear? They've arrested Guy Riverty, and—'

'*What?*'

She enunciates slowly as if the line's bad. 'They . . . have . . . arrested . . .'

'Yes, yes, I heard you. Why? Why have they arrested him?'

She takes a deep drag on her cigarette. The first words of her sentence come out strained as she exhales and speaks at the same time. 'I don't know that part. Marjorie Clayton was delivering half a pig to the neighbours opposite and she saw him being taken in. If I had to guess, I'd say it's because they think he has something to do with his daughter's disappearance.'

'No, that can't be right, I—'

She interrupts again, just as I'm about to tell her about

finding Kate this morning. 'It's *always* the father,' she says, a triumphant tone to her voice. 'I don't know why the police didn't take him in to start with, instead of wasting time when they could've been getting on with—' Her voice trails off.

She's no idea what the police could have been getting on with, but that won't stop her having an opinion about it.

'Christ!' I say. Then I hear Joe coming down the stairs.

'What's happened?' he mouths, still doing up his trousers. His face has that dazed look of deep contentment that only comes from sex. I could probably ask him to do anything right now and he'd agree to it. I suppose he already has.

My mother is in mid-sentence, 'One second, Mum, Joe's here—' I cover over the mouthpiece with my hand. 'They've arrested Guy,' I tell him, and his eyebrows shoot up.

Meanwhile, my mother's saying: 'Joe? What's he doing at home? Why's he not at work?'

'He's just not,' I snap. 'What else did Marjorie say?'

Marjorie farms in Troutbeck. She's one of those people who is always complaining about how tough it is for farmers these days but manages to keep a brand-new seven-seater Land Rover Discovery on the road easily enough. It's an odd pairing – her and my mother. My mother truly *is* skint, but she believes Marjorie's claims of living in poverty without question.

My mother says, 'Marjorie said Guy Riverty looked mad about it.'

'He would . . . Christ!' I exhale, shaking my head.

'What?' mouths Joe.

I cover the mouthpiece again. 'He's cross,' I whisper, and Joe rolls his eyes like, *No shit, Lise.*

'So that wife of his is not going to be best pleased,' says my mother.

'She took an overdose this morning. I was the one who found her.'

My mother gasps. After a second she says, 'Well, it must be true, then.'

'What must be true?'

'That he's abducted his own daughter. Why else would she try and kill herself?'

'Perhaps because another girl went missing yesterday? Perhaps because she then thought her daughter would not be coming back?' My tone is abrasive. 'Don't be so quick to judge, Mum.'

'She wouldn't leave her son without a mother,' she replies tartly.

'How do you know what she'd do? How would any of us know?'

'She just wouldn't do it.'

'I know *I* wouldn't do it, but I don't know what *she'd* do, and neither do you. Quite honestly, you acting all gossipy is really the last thing I need to be listening to.'

'Why was it you who found her and not her husband?' she asks.

I pause. Reluctantly, I tell her, 'Because he wasn't there.'

'Where was he?'

'I don't know.'

My mother scoffs. 'Well, if you want my advice, I wouldn't be going anywhere near that house. And I *certainly* wouldn't be going around there alone. You don't know what they might be hiding.' When I don't comment, she adds, 'Anyway, Marjorie says that Guy Riverty is rude and arrogant.'

'Marjorie is rude and arrogant.'

'I'm going.'

She clicks off and I close my eyes. I can't seem to think properly, can't seem to organize my thoughts into separate, manageable portions. It barely seems possible.

Kate has overdosed.
Guy has been arrested.
Lucinda is still missing.

31

DC JOANNE ASPINALL takes a moment to get herself together. She enters the interview room, her face blank, her demeanour one of calm efficiency. DC Colin Cunningham's already in there with Guy Riverty, but it is she who will be leading the questioning.

She sits down opposite Guy and feels a pang of irritation as she has to adjust her left bra strap. It's beginning to chafe on an already broken bit of skin, and it's cutting in badly.

She feels she's breaking the professional air she's tried to cultivate – and she's right. Flicking her right index finger deep inside her blouse, she sees a shadow of distaste fall across Guy Riverty's face. He looks away.

Joanne is about to feel this insult viscerally but then reminds herself that *of course* Guy Riverty would be sickened by the sight of her. He likes his women thin. Thin and around thirteen years of age.

For the first time since this investigation started, Joanne wonders if it's a coincidence that his wife, Kate, is also incredibly skinny, with the body of a child.

Joanne lays her notes down in front of her and has to suppress a smile. She's remembering a wickedly cruel joke she heard about Victoria Beckham the other day, along the lines of 'Victoria is so thin she can't have the bath water too hot or else she turns into stock.'

Guy Riverty sits back in his chair, one foot crossed on to the opposite knee, trying his best to look bored and irritated.

His mane of hair is pushed back from his face, flopping over to one side. It's a pretty-boy hairdo that Guy's too old for but which Joanne imagines is still effective in pulling a certain kind of woman.

He's wearing the same clothes Joanne saw him in that morning: cream cords with a black, fine-knit turtleneck and black jodhpur boots. His jacket is slung over the back of his chair. The image would be bordering on Simon Templar if Guy weren't just a little bit scruffy around the edges. Joanne's gaze rests on something red and sticky on his right thigh, something she doesn't like the look of.

Guy's manner has totally changed since two days ago, when Joanne met him for the first time. Then he was fidgety, jumpy, but absolutely quick to help out. Anything at all to find his daughter. Joanne had thought at the time that if she were to make a loud, sudden noise, Guy Riverty was liable to shoot three feet into the air like a startled cat. He was full of bristling energy.

Now, as she looks across the table to him, he's exuding a relaxed, cocky air, a manner that's atypical of a person about to be questioned. This unnerves Joanne slightly, puts her more on guard.

'So, Mr Riverty, hello.'

He lifts his palm in a sarcastic acknowledgement of her presence while at the same time keeping his face expressionless.

'You've had a drink, I trust?'

'A coffee,' he says, yawning. 'I've had a crappy cup of coffee.'

'You'll have to excuse us,' she says, 'we're all out of skinny lattes at the moment. Now, you are not under arrest, Mr Riverty, but you do understand that this interview is being recorded?'

He nods and shoots her a contemptuous look. 'Why am I here

wasting time with you when my wife is fighting for her life in hospital?'

Joanne takes the lid off her pen and leafs purposely through the pages in front of her. Without glancing up, she says, 'I believe you've been told that your wife – Mrs Riverty – is going to make a complete recovery, and is not *in fact* fighting for her life.' She looks up. 'I'm sure she'll be fine.' She smiles. 'Now, if we can start with—'

'What happens if I refuse to answer your questions?'

'Then we won't be able to eliminate you from this inquiry as quickly as you require in order for you to see your wife in hospital. Or for you to return home to take care of your son. It would be a shame if he were to be confused again by a change in arrangements, wouldn't you agree? He's been through a lot these past couple of days . . . A quiet lad, isn't he?'

Guy moves his eyes slowly up and down Joanne's body. 'Get on with it, then.'

Joanne smiles breezily. 'Do you have any objection to us taking your mobile phone from you?'

He reaches into his jacket pocket and slides it across the desk. 'For the purposes of the tape,' Joanne says, 'Mr Riverty is handing his phone to DC Aspinall.'

'And no objection to us searching your house?'

He shakes his head. 'No,' he says.

'Good. Right. Let's begin.'

Guy spreads his hands wide. 'Go ahead.'

Pen poised, Joanne asks, 'Would you say that you have a happy marriage, Mr Riverty?'

'What?'

'A happy marriage. You and Mrs Riverty?'

He stares at her. 'None of your fucking business.'

'Do you love your wife?'

'What's this got to do with anything?'

Joanne waits. Holds his stare.

'Yes, I love her,' he snaps. 'Of course I love her.'

'What reason can you give as to why your wife tried to commit suicide this morning?'

He pushes his chair back, makes to stand.

'I'm not answering this bullshit.'

Joanne is unrelenting. 'I wouldn't be wasting my time asking irrelevant questions, Mr Riverty. My time is as precious as yours. More so, in fact. Particularly when two girls' lives are at stake . . . Now, if you wouldn't mind—'

'What has this got to do with finding my daughter?'

Joanne arches an eyebrow at him. 'Answer the question, please.'

'I've no idea why she did it,' he says. 'She didn't leave a note. I think you need to ask *her* why she did it.'

'I intend to. But, first, I'd like your thoughts on the matter. Had you been arguing at all?'

'Yes, but that's not why she did it.'

'So you *do* know why she did it?'

'I didn't say that. I said it wasn't because we were arguing. We're married, we argue. Our daughter is gone. It's hell. We're out of our minds with worry. It would be weird if *we didn't* argue. Kate is a mess, she can't cope—' Then he shakes his head. 'What am I saying? Naturally, she can't cope – who would cope in this situation? Nobody.'

'Why do you think we brought you in for questioning?'

He shrugs. 'I have no idea what the police are thinking. But my best guess is that you have no fucking idea where my daughter is, nor where this other girl is, and you're desperate. You need to be seen to be doing something—'

Joanne flips two pages along in the notes. Tries to cover the fact that, yes, they are getting desperate. 'Your wife supplied your alibi for your whereabouts yesterday afternoon, yes?'

'You know she did. We've been through this – how many times is it? I've lost track.'

'Where were you last night?'

'At home.'

'You're sure?'

'Yes, I'm sure.'

'Where were you this morning when Mrs Kallisto found your wife unconscious?'

'I was out.'

'Where?'

'It's not relevant.'

Joanne tilts her head. 'I think it is.'

'Do I have to answer?'

'No, but—'

'Then I won't.'

'Mr Riverty. Let me explain again. At the moment, you are not under arrest. But that can change right this minute if you decide not to cooperate with this inquiry. It's up to you. Now, if it were me, I'd save myself a lot of trouble, not to mention bad press, by answering the questions I put to you.'

'To arrest me, you have to charge me. *With what* are you planning to charge me, Detective?'

'We can hold you here without charge. You are aware of that?'

He stares at her, unfazed. 'I am. And if that's the course of action you wish to take, then you had better make arrangements for my son. Because he'll be expecting someone to be there to pick him up from school.'

Joanne's face doesn't register his attempt to make things difficult for her. He's appealing to her maternal side, not a common tack taken by suspects, but one that's used all the same.

Most people become plain abusive when being questioned. Joanne's used to it. Expects it. She's been called all manner of things. The worst of it often coming from the mouths of women. Women you wouldn't think could generate such hatred towards another woman.

Nothing surprises Joanne any more. In this job, you deal with the dregs of society. Same families, same faces, same problems, again and again. None of it touches her. At least, that's what she tries to convey.

Joanne replaces the cap on her pen and straightens her spine. 'It remains your responsibility to make arrangements for your son to be collected from school, Mr Riverty. Would you like to take a moment to make a phone call?' She pauses, waits for an answer. When none is forthcoming, she adds, 'I could do with a coffee, actually, so perhaps now would be a good time to break.'

Still he doesn't speak, just narrows his eyes slightly in an attempt to mask his annoyance with her.

Joanne pushes the desk phone towards him and stands. 'Take as long as you need,' she says. 'No need to rush now that we've got plenty of time. I'll go and get myself a crappy coffee.' Spoken as if an afterthought, she says, 'Oh, you might want to contact your solicitor while you're at it – kill two birds with one stone—'

She gathers up the paperwork, exchanges glances with DC Cunningham and heads out into the corridor, almost walking slap bang into Cynthia Spence. Cynthia is a member of the civvie staff brought in to take the pressure off CID. She's ex-police and takes on some of the routine interviews for Cumbria Constabulary.

Joanne's worked with Cynthia on a number of occasions. She's good at what she does.

Cynthia asks, nodding her head towards Guy Riverty, 'He talking yet?'

Joanne steps away from the thin rectangle of fire-resistant glass in the door, out of Guy Riverty's line of sight. 'Being cagey,' she says. 'Refusing to tell me everything.'

'Are you leaving him to stew for a bit?'

'Learned my best tricks from you, Cynth.'

Cynthia takes a quick look at Guy. 'Give him at least half an hour in there on his own.'

'That long?'

'He's twitching madly already. I'm guessing he's not the type who's used to waiting. He's *certainly* not the type to put his head down on the desk and pretend to sleep – I've had a run of those lately. Let him wait for long enough and he'll give you what you're after.'

There's a burst of laughter from the end of the hallway, and Joanne and Cynthia turn to see two young women from admin draping tinsel around the door frame to their office. One is halfway up a stepladder, laughing so hard she has her hand lodged between her legs. The other is twirling Christmas baubles around as if they're attached to her nipples. Cynthia shakes her head at them good-naturedly and tells Joanne they'll catch up later.

After grabbing a coffee, Joanne takes a minute to stop by Ron Quigley's desk, just to check if there have been any developments in her absence.

Ron's on the phone, looking harried. He holds his palm up so Joanne doesn't interrupt him but motions for her to stay where she is. Something's happened. Something big. Ron's taking down an address and nodding as he receives instructions.

'So what time was it?' he's asking. 'Yeah, yeah . . . I understand. I'll get round there now, straight away.'

He makes a circling action with his index finger, signalling that he's almost finished with the call. Ron Quigley does not get this animated easily and Joanne feels a flutter of excitement mixed with an impending dread. Developments at this stage are rarely good. She's hoping another child hasn't vanished, one, because, obviously, that would be shit. But two, she'd have no choice but to let Guy Riverty go, because this time his alibi was definitely watertight: he was being interviewed by her.

Ron ends the call and tears off the piece of paper on which he was writing from the pad.

He takes a long inhalation before speaking. 'Girl number three's turned up. Same deal. Dumped in Bowness, no idea where she is, thinks she's been raped. Probably more than once. She's not in a good way.' His jaw is tight as he speaks. Spitting the last words out is difficult for him.

'So what's happened to girl number two?' Joanne asks. 'What about Lucinda Riverty? If girls one and three are back, then where is *she*?'

'Big fat mystery, that,' Ron says grimly. 'There's a meeting with the DI in five minutes, might shed some light on it.'

'And, in the meantime, what do I do with Guy Riverty?'

'Is he still in the interview room?'

Joanne nods.

'What's he said about where he was this morning?'

'Told me it wasn't relevant to our investigation.'

'Not relevant?' Ron angles his head slightly to the side. 'Make the fucker wait, then.'

32

I PARK IN THE PUBLIC Pay & Display.

Opposite, they're unloading a stretcher from the air ambulance. I stay in the car for a moment.

When patient and crew are safely inside, I make my way towards the hospital building, wondering whether Kate has regained consciousness, wondering whether she can even recollect taking the pills. I've heard stories of people unable to remember, people who wake and are genuinely shocked to learn they tried to take their own life. Will that be the case with Kate?

The sun has melted the ice in patches. It's now possible to walk in some places without breaking your neck. Or perhaps not, I think, reflecting on the stretcher taken from the air ambulance.

I decide against fully trusting the ground and take tiny, even steps, my arms stuck out to the side, ready for a fall. The car park's been gritted but it's a haphazard attempt. There are great, bare sections devoid of grip, sections where you have to hope for the best.

I heard on the radio on my way to the infirmary that the emergency services are stretched to the limit after the freezing rain of yesterday. I consoled myself with the knowledge that, had I found Kate any later, the paramedics might not have got to her in time.

Although I suppose if I'd found her any later, she'd be dead regardless.

I'm outside the main doors, and there's a throng of people. Some are in dressing gowns and slippers, having a smoke. There's a teenager on crutches craning his neck in the direction of the main gates, perhaps waiting for a lift.

Some poor sod in his early fifties is conducting a survey. With his clipboard raised, he's trying to put a brave face on things, but looks as if he's losing the will. He has the haunted appearance of the newly unemployed.

The automatic double doors open as I approach, and I head over to the main reception desk. A plump lady glances up from her work. 'Yes, love?' she says pleasantly. She has thick darts-player forearms and steel-grey, curly hair that's been cropped close to her head.

'I'm looking for Mrs Kate Riverty. She was brought in this morning.'

The receptionist begins typing and turns her head to view the screen, which is placed at an angle. 'Ah, yes, she's just been moved to a general ward.'

'Is that a good thing?' I ask, nervously. Scared that Kate's condition has deteriorated.

'Usually means they're on the mend,' she says matter-of-factly, before pointing over my shoulder. 'You want to go back out through those doors, the way you came in, cross the car park . . . try not to break any bones . . . and go on over to that brown building. You want ward four. It's on the second floor.'

'Thanks,' I tell her, and head over there.

Ward four has six beds. All occupied.

I see Alexa sitting by the side of Kate's bed at the far end of the room and my stomach lurches. I shiver, and a cold sweat springs up in my armpits. Alexa looks at me as I enter but doesn't alter her expression. Her face is set.

Kate is sleeping – or else still unconscious. She has a drip in her right wrist and she's dressed in a white hospital gown. It gives her the look of a psychiatric patient. Or maybe that's just because everyone else on the ward is dressed in their own night-clothes, and she's a little out of place.

'How's she doing?' I whisper, and Alexa looks away. She's not yet decided whether she's going to speak to me or not.

Then she hisses, 'Did you have to come?', and I say, yes, of course I had to come. I found her.

This seems to soften her a bit. I can see her thawing marginally as she thinks through the situation – *what if she hadn't found her . . .*

She speaks without looking at me. 'Physically,' she says, 'they say she should recover quite quickly. The pills weren't in her system long enough to do any real damage. As for psychologically, well, obviously, we'll have to wait and see about that.'

Alexa's tone is as cold as it's possible for a person to be. She's spitting out her words and it's clear that, even without the added complication of me having slept with her husband, because of Lucinda's disappearance, she's holding me fully responsible for what Kate's done to herself. If I hadn't actually found Kate, saved her, Alexa would throw me out of here right this second.

I fetch a chair from the stack over in the corner and sit down next to Alexa. She shuffles over, put out. I sense she doesn't want to talk about what's happened, so I turn my attention to Kate.

Her wispy blonde hair is fanning out on the pillow, giving her an ethereal quality, the skin on her forehead is a milky-blue, as if she's been smeared with an emollient. I find it hard to look at her. Dropping my gaze slightly, I notice her lips. They're thin. They seem not to be her own. There's a trace of black charcoal in the corner creases, which has the effect of turning her mouth downwards.

'Has she spoken yet?'

Alexa shakes her head. 'Opened her eyes a couple of times, but that's it. They've told me she's going to be sleepy for a good while, so not to panic if she doesn't communicate.'

'Poor Kate,' I say, and all at once feel unbearably sad about the whole thing. I'd driven here on automatic pilot. Too dazed about the news of Guy's arrest really to plan what I'd say to Kate even if she was awake. I say a silent prayer and give thanks for small mercies, grateful she's still out of it.

Alexa folds shut the magazine she's been reading – *Vanity Fair* – then takes a hanky from her handbag and dabs underneath her lower lashes. Her mascara is as neat as when first applied, not like last night.

'When did you last talk to her?' Alexa asks me.

'I spoke to Guy last night, but I'm not sure when I—' I pause. When *did* I last talk to Kate? Suddenly I can't even remember what day it is.

'What day is it?' I ask Alexa, and she looks at me as if I'm losing my mind. 'I've lost track,' I explain. 'A lot's happened.'

'Thursday,' she mutters.

'Sorry, everything's just got a bit jumbled.'

We sit in silence for a few minutes, Alexa stroking Kate's hand a couple of times. Then I lean in towards Alexa, dropping my voice. 'Are you going to tell her about Guy when she wakes, or do you think it would be best not to mention it right now?'

She gives me a sharp look. 'What about Guy? I tried ringing him, but he's not picking up.'

My eyes widen involuntarily. 'He's been arrested,' I mouth. I sit back and bite my lip, not quite sure what to think. Why hasn't he rung her? Why hasn't he at least let someone know where he is?

Alexa turns in her seat. 'Dear God,' she says. 'Arrested for what?'

I shrug, embarrassed. 'I'm not really sure.'

She stares straight ahead, but I can see her mind is electric. The pulse in her temple is racing and that vein on her forehead has risen up; it's like an earthworm beneath her skin. After an awkward silence she pushes her chair back and stands.

'I have to make a telephone call. Will you stay with Kate?'

I nod.

'Don't leave her,' she warns.

''Course not.'

Visibly shaken, Alexa grabs her handbag. 'I'll try not to be long,' she says, striding away. Her heels click across hard resin flooring, her flat, shapeless Mum-bum barely swaying in her designer jeans. When she disappears through the ward entrance I exhale.

What a mess.

I can't imagine what Alexa must be feeling.

Your sister takes an overdose, naturally you are frantic with worry but at the same time relieved beyond measure that she didn't actually succeed. You're also filled with questions as to her motivation.

I imagine Alexa had concluded – as had I, at first – that Kate couldn't cope with the news of the third girl gone missing. Her disappearance brought with it the near-certainty that Lucinda was not coming back. People have killed themselves for a lot less.

Now she has to process the news that Kate had possibly tried killing herself because she'd stumbled upon something that links Guy to the missing girls.

I cast my eyes around the ward for the first time since arriving.

It's been painted in an ugly salmon-pink, the colour of Germolene. Striped turquoise curtains hang by the side of each bed, ready to be pulled around when privacy is needed. It's an old bloke's idea of what women like. Reminds me of the decor of a bad wedding-reception venue.

The visitors at the next bed begin saying their goodbyes, telling the lady they'll be back tomorrow, with more magazines, more Lucozade. For a moment I'm nostalgic for the Lucozade of old, when it used to come wrapped in that special netting that told the world you were *really* poorly.

Short of somewhere to focus my eyes – that's not on Kate, or on the rest of the patients in the ward – I pick up Alexa's copy of *Vanity Fair*. It's not my usual choice of reading but my mind is racing and I need something to do with my hands. After a quick flick through, I decide *Vanity Fair* is rubbish. There's far too much text. I'd rather read *Now* or *OK!*

I begin reading an article on a posh celebrity who lives in Bermuda. She's someone I've never heard of who's loosely connected to the Royal Family. She's all blonde hair and legs, late thirties, and has just had her first baby. 'It's amazing,' she beams. 'It's *the most* incredible thing. It's so beautiful, it's astonishing. There's *so* much love.'

I shut the magazine with disgust, mentally dusting my hands.

Just once – *once* – I'd like to come across a new mother in a magazine who says, 'I'm finding this really hard. It's not at all like I thought it would be. I don't think I'll be having another . . . And' – she says this next part sniffling into a hanky – 'my husband's been next to useless. I thought he'd make a wonderful father, but, well, he's leaving it all to me. He's being a complete dick, actually.'

I glance towards Kate distractedly and immediately jolt backwards, almost falling off my chair.

Her eyes are open and she's watching me.

'How are you feeling?' I ask her quickly, trying to gather myself. My voice comes out strangled-sounding and desperate.

Her eyes are rheumy, the linings raw. She tries to smile. 'What are you doing here?' she asks.

'Came to see you.'

'Thank you.'

'Oh, that's all right,' I ramble. 'Alexa's here too, but she just had to nip out to make a call. She'll be back in a minute.' Kate closes her eyes and I reach for her hand, giving it a gentle squeeze. 'We're glad you made it, Kate.'

I look to the ward entrance, willing Alexa to return, willing her to hurry. I feel a little out of my depth here and I'm not sure I'll handle this properly.

No sign.

With her eyes still closed, Kate whispers, 'Where am I?', and this shocks me.

I'd assumed, moments earlier, that she was lucid. That she knew what happened and was not mentioning the pills, in the first instance, because she was embarrassed. Or perhaps because I was not the right person to talk to.

Suddenly I feel woefully inept, like I am *absolutely not* the best person she should be talking to about it. Even if I did find her.

'You're at the hospital,' I say tentatively. 'Lancaster Infirmary.'

'Oh.'

'Do you know why you're here?'

'Not really.'

'That's okay . . . just rest for now,' I say, and her eyelids flicker open a little. She looks like one of those cruel pictures you see of celebrities exiting the clubs in the early hours. The ones with their eyes half closed, looking like they're totally plastered.

'Lisa,' she asks me, 'is Guy here?'

'Not yet.'

'Is he coming?'

Uneasily, I say, 'I expect so,' because I can't come up with anything better to say to her when put on the spot.

Is he coming?

Not likely.

He's in a police cell, or else he's being interrogated about your missing daughter.

As I think about this, it crosses my mind that Kate has not yet asked about Lucinda. *Has she come back? Is there any more news?* You would expect at least that . . . wouldn't you?

This conspicuous lack of enquiry further cements in my mind the certainty that Kate suspects Guy is responsible. I know it would be the first thing out of my mouth, doped or otherwise: *Where is my child?* I'd be shouting on waking, *Where is my—*

All at once, and as if from nowhere, Kate gives a violent, involuntary shudder. I jump up towards her. 'Kate? Kate? Are you okay?'

She nods, seemingly unable to speak, and I'm not sure what to do. Do I press the emergency call button? Do I run and get the nurse?

I'm about to alert the staff when I see a tear course down Kate's cheek. She opens her mouth, but no words come out. And it's only then that I realize she's too distressed to communicate. The huge shudder she gave was the precursor to this, her now-anguished sobbing.

'Oh, Kate,' I say, and try to put my arms around her. Again I notice how thin she is. I can feel the ribs in her back. It's as if they're sitting directly beneath the fabric of the gown, no flesh at all in between.

My face is next to hers, and I kiss her hair softly. It smells faintly of sour vomit but it's not totally unpleasant, more like the acid smell of a well-used Thermos flask. I don't pull away. Somewhere in the distance I hear the fast, hard clicking of Alexa's boots, but I don't register her presence until she speaks.

'Have you told her?' she demands from the foot of the bed. 'Have you told her about Guy?'

I turn around quickly. '*No*,' I mouth, my eyes wide.

Kate must have an inkling, though, surely. If Kate suspects her husband of foul play, she must know it won't be long before the police cotton on to it.

'Told me what about Guy?' Kate asks, stumbling on her words. 'Is he . . . is he injured?'

Alexa fixes Kate with a steady look. 'He's been arrested.'

Instinctively Kate moves her hand to her mouth in dismay, but gets a stab of pain from the drip cannula. She whimpers softly. Her whole face is contorted and I am now more confused than ever. Again she goes to speak, but cannot. She looks to me, whispering, 'Why?', and I'm thinking, *I thought you knew why.*

I thought you'd discovered Guy has been lying to you, and that's why you tried to kill yourself. If it wasn't for that reason, then . . . what is it?

I stop with the speculation when I notice Kate's pleading eyes are still upon me. 'Why?' she says again, silently, but I have no answer.

I mean, what on earth am I supposed to say?

33

I'VE HAD MY PHONE switched off inside the hospital. There are signs all over the place saying mobiles interfere with the defibrillators or ventilators . . . or something, which I'm sure is probably bollocks, but can understand all the same. The last thing you'd want lying in a hospital bed is some loud-mouthed idiot telling the world how important he is.

When I reach my car I switch my phone back on and see I have a text. It's from Lorna, one of the kennel girls at the shelter. It says simply:

Bluey back.

I give out a small cry of relief and climb behind the wheel. I get the heat going and immediately ring Lorna. As soon as she answers, I say, 'Where was he?'

'Tied to the fence at the bottle bank by Booths,' she says breathlessly. She must be in the middle of mopping up. 'Mad Jackie Wagstaff found him at seven this morning, when she was recycling her empties. She dropped him off saying he must have been abandoned, because the car park's empty at that time. She sends her apologies for bringing you another dog, by the way, but said she couldn't just leave him there.'

'How long do you think he'd been there?' I ask.

'No idea. She said he was a sorry sight. Poor bugger had his head down as usual, waiting for someone to come and get him. Probably stand there all bloody week if he had to.'

I feel a sob building in my chest and have to take a couple of breaths to stifle it.

'Lisa,' Lorna asks, 'you still there?'

'Yes,' I sniff, 'just relieved he's all right . . . *is* he all right?'

'He seems okay. He's not eaten, but that's not unusual for him. I might mix a bit o' cat food in with it, see if he'll have it then. What d'you think that fella wanted with him, anyway? Why run off with him then go and dump him? . . . I said to Shelley, "What's the point in that?" '

'I've got a theory – I'll tell you about it when I get in. I shouldn't be too long, depends on how bad the roads are.'

'They're better than yesterday.' Then her tone changes: 'Lisa?'

'Yeah.'

'Joe told us about your friend in hospital. Is she going to be okay?'

I'd asked Joe to telephone work for me and let them know the score, told him to tell them about Kate so I could get straight to the hospital to see how she was doing.

'She'll recover,' I say to Lorna. 'I've just seen her, and she was sitting up and able to talk. Her sister's with her, I've let them have some time together.'

'Did she, like, have problems or something?'

'She's the one whose daughter's missing.'

'Oh,' she says emphatically. 'Oh, that's awful.'

'I know,' I say, and I tell her I'll be around in half an hour.

As I drive, my head is muddled with thoughts. I try listening to the radio but I can only get Radio 2 in this area, and I can't stand the string of moaners who ring in to Jeremy Vine at this hour, so I turn it off.

My exhaust is blowing worse than ever and as I press on the accelerator I frighten a young mother standing at the lights with a pram. I check my mirror and see she's shouting something angrily in my direction. I hope I've not woken her baby, I hope—

What the hell is Kate doing trying to kill herself?

That's what I can't get out of my head.

I wanted to shout it at her. I wanted to shake her senseless and make her tell me just what the bloody hell was going on.

Now I can't think straight. Now my head feels like someone's firing pellets at it from close range, and every time I try to think rationally, every time I try to go through something from start to finish, the thought is obliterated before I can come to any proper conclusions.

Why didn't she ask for Lucinda when she woke up?

Why did she fall apart so badly when she was told Guy had been arrested?

And this is a minor point, but I'm going to go ahead and voice it because it's pissing me off, why did neither Kate, Alexa nor, come to think of it, Guy, thank me for saving Kate's life?

I know they're all over the place presently, but I'd have thought one of them might at least have said, 'Thank God you came, Lisa.'

But no. Nothing.

My knuckles are a bloodless white on the steering wheel and I tell myself, *Okay, stop. For now, just stop thinking. Because Bluey's back.* It's the *one good* thing to come out of today.

Bluey's back and I've made the decision that tonight he's coming home to live with us.

34

Joanne's in the incident room along with four other detectives, waiting for the arrival of DI McAleese. It's a glass room, built last year after one of Cumbria's longest-serving detectives – DS Russ Holloway – died from pancreatic cancer.

A photo of Russ taken on his first day in uniform hangs in the corner; there's a small commemorative plaque beneath. Joanne gazes at it now and remembers stopping the car when Russ mentioned pain in his abdomen, pain he'd complained about for the third time that week. Joanne had refused to drive any further until he rang his GP for an appointment, but by then it was already too late. Incredibly, he passed away just three weeks later.

McAleese comes in and shuts the door behind him. He's wearing a deep-red shirt and contrasting tie; the shirt is dotted with patches of sweat, something Joanne has never seen on McAleese before. He's a meticulous man, educated to a higher level than most in the room. He studied to be an actuary, and when he joined the force he was fast-tracked. Made the grade of DI in record time.

McAleese is looking harried, which, as the Senior Investigating Officer, is natural, but it's not a natural state for him.

'So I'm assuming the news has travelled, and you're all aware that our third girl has turned up?' He does a quick survey of the faces in front of him; there's a quiet muttering of 'Sir.'

Confirmation that, yes, they all know. 'Francesca Clarke's back with her family, and we'll be conducting the questioning at her home shortly. She's in no state to be brought in. Doc's examined her, and he's got what we need.'

He clears his throat before continuing. Loosens his tie slightly.

'Our man's got more brutal this time.' He says this as if it was half expected. 'I'll spare you the nasties for now. Suffice to say, she won't be getting over this in a hurry. We've got a couple of FLOs with her, and a counsellor's on her way from Preston. Some psychologist woman who's had experience in dealing with violent rape.' He breathes out wearily and says, 'She's supposed to be very good—' But like the rest of us he's thinking it doesn't really matter how good she is. It's another life ruined.

McAleese chews at the end of his pen, everyone's quiet because he's mentally ticking things off a list in his head. He bites the side of his cheek and says, 'Francesca Clarke's father's going ape-shit, he's not happy with the handling of the case, etc., etc. . . . I need a volunteer for him . . . Anybody?'

Since no one's coming forward in a hurry for what's bound to be a shitty job, Joanne says she doesn't mind doing it. Sometimes she's better at diffusing situations than her male colleagues; she has a way of making the complainant feel as if the force is genuinely sorry for whatever it is they're being accused of . . . without it actually being accountable.

It's a skill she developed as a teenager, working in a couple of the Lakes' poshest hotels as a chambermaid. When outraged guests complained they'd found a hair between the bed sheets, or a rust-stained teapot, Joanne found it incredibly easy to apologize, going well over the top with how absolutely unsatisfactory the situation was. Because that's all the guests were really after: a 'sorry'. No one ever said you had to mean it. And yet, Joanne notices how often folk pull hard against saying it.

DI McAleese tells Joanne, Thanks, but no thanks. He wants her to stay on Guy Riverty for the time being. Drag out any information he has about anything. 'That bastard's wife didn't try to kill herself for nothing.'

Fine by her. She didn't want to abandon the interview anyway. She's got the feeling they'll only end up bringing him back in again, and she still wants to know where he was last night. Something's telling her that it's *unquestionably relevant* to this investigation, even if Guy Riverty says it's not.

McAleese continues with the meeting, designating the door-to-door, and there's some grainy CCTV footage that needs looking at. When they quickly fall into discussion about what form the press release should take, Joanne's phone vibrates twice in her pocket. She pulls it out and reads a message from Lisa Kallisto, saying:

Sorry for inconvenience. Missing dog back. Much ado about nothing!

Joanne reads the text again and interrupts her boss. 'Sir, does the public know that girl number three is back yet?'

'Not officially. It's not been released. Why?'

'Just got a text off the woman from the animal shelter – she rang me yesterday to say someone had stolen a dog. The old, grey one, remember?'

'Same as the dog spotted with the guy loitering round the school?'

Joanne nods. 'Well, the dog's back. A coincidence, you reckon?'

'Maybe,' he says, 'but worth a look into.'

She turns to Ron Quigley. 'We ever DNA'd a dog before, Ron?'

He smiles. 'Not as far as I remember.'

On her way back to the interview room, Joanne calls Lisa Kallisto.

Lisa answers, saying, 'Oh, God, sorry about all that. You must think I'm completely mad. Bluey's back, and he seems fine, so no harm done.'

'Are you with the dog now?'

'What? No. I'm in my office sorting through bloody bills, he's in a kennel.'

'Don't bath him. Or brush him. And keep him isolated until someone picks him up.'

Lisa gives out a small yelp. 'What has he done?'

'He's not done anything.' Joanne smiles to herself. 'It's more a case of where he might have *been*, we need to test him for—'

'Oh my God,' Lisa says. 'You're saying that Bluey is *evidence*.'

Joanne probably wouldn't have put it quite so dramatically but, 'Yes,' she answers. 'We need the dog for evidence.'

'What do I need to do?' asks Lisa.

'You don't need to do anything. Like I said, don't let anyone wash him or brush him. Might be best if you don't take him for a walk either.' Joanne says this as an afterthought, not really sure if it will make any difference or not. 'I'm going to contact Forensics, see if I can get someone out to you straight away. There might be a delay, though – what time are you there till?'

'Forensics?' Lisa gasps.

'Yes.'

'Oh, I'll wait for as long as it takes for them to get here. My husband's got the kids 'cause I need to catch up on things—'

'I'll contact you later if I need anything else, but that should be it for now.'

'Detective?'

'Hmm?'

'Have you got Guy Riverty there with you?'

Joanne's about to say, Yes, he's been detained in custody, but instead says, 'Why do you ask?'

'It's just that—' and Lisa pauses here, seemingly reluctant to continue. Finally, she says, 'Something's wrong.'

'With who?'

'With all of them,' she replies bluntly. 'Today I felt very uneasy. I just got the feeling they were hiding something. The whole lot – Kate, Guy, Kate's sister, Alexa. They acted strange, not as I would have expected under the circumstances.'

'In what way?'

'I can't really explain. But this morning Fergus told me something. He said his mum gets upset when his dad doesn't come home, and I got the impression it's not unusual for him to disappear like that. That it happens often. That's weird, isn't it?'

Joanne ends the call thinking, *Yes, that* is *weird.* She would knock her husband's head off if he disappeared overnight. But then, since she's not married, really, who knows what she'd do? Women put up with all sorts of things they never signed up for when they started out in their relationship. Why should she be any different?

Joanne pushes open the door to the interview room. She's already steeled herself for the stream of abuse she'll undoubtedly get from Guy Riverty. He's been in here stewing for over an hour and must be ready for a proper row.

But as she walks in she stops, startled for a second by the scene in front of her.

Guy is slumped over the desk. He has the posture of a man who's already broken. Joanne clears her throat to speak and he lifts his head. There's a mixture of snot and spit running down his chin.

Guy is weeping like a child. Shameless emotion too raw to hide. He looks at her sadly and says, 'I have a wife.'

'I know,' replies Joanne uneasily. 'But she'll be okay, Mr Riverty. Your wife *will be* okay.'

And he shakes his head. Wipes his nose on his jumper, leaving a silvery mucus slug trail on his expensive black turtleneck.

'I have *another* wife,' he says, and keeps his gaze steady on Joanne. 'Another wife . . . and a son. A baby boy.'

Joanne's eyes widen involuntarily. If she's being honest with herself, it's not really what she was expecting him to say.

35

'DOES MRS RIVERTY know?' Then she adds quickly, 'Mrs Kate Riverty, I mean.'

'Yes.'

'That must be tricky.'

He sighs.

'What makes her stay with you?' An unprofessional question that has nothing to do with what Joanne really needs to know about the situation, but one any woman would be bursting to ask all the same.

'I wish I knew. I wish she'd agree to a split, but she won't. I've tried many times to convince her that it would be better for everyone, but she won't agree to a divorce.'

Joanne is perplexed by this.

'So she'd rather share you?' Her tone is more incredulous than she means it to be, her words coming out not so much confused by the fact that Kate Riverty is willing to share a husband, but rather that she is willing to share a husband like *him*. As if Guy Riverty were some kind of prize catch that Joanne is not aware of.

The rebuff registers on Guy's face.

He says, 'It's a lot more complicated than it might appear,' and Joanne, noticing that she's still standing, pulls the chair from beneath the table and sits down.

Without meaning to, she's surveying Guy Riverty, trying to

work out what would make a sensible woman compromise herself and her family in that way.

Why not just tell him to fuck off to his new wife?

Why not do what any normal woman would do? Why not chuck him out, why not *chuck his clothes out*, bad-mouth him to every person she comes across, then have her hair done, buy a ton of new underwear, sleep with someone better-looking and get on with life? That's what Joanne would do.

She smiles sympathetically at Guy. 'She must really love you.'

'That's the thing,' he says, sighing. 'She doesn't.'

'So why does she want you?'

'Your guess is as good as mine,' he says. Then: 'No, actually, that's unfair. I know the reason. Kate has very clear-cut feelings on marriage and family. If you do it, you do it for life, and you don't put your children through a separation for the sake of whim, or just because the love isn't as strong as it used to be. The children come first.'

Joanne looks past Guy, turning the situation over in her mind a couple of times. After a moment, she says, 'So why don't *you* leave? Why not move in with your other wife?' He's about to answer when another thought occurs to her. 'You're a bigamist in the true sense of the word, then? You are actually married to two women?'

He nods. 'I married Nino—'

'Nino?'

'My Georgian wife. I married her in Georgia when—'

'Hang on. I don't understand—'

'Nino came over here for work. I employed her to clean the holiday cottages and, without really meaning to, I found myself in her company more and more. I realized it was turning into something special . . . and before I went ahead and, you know—'

'Slept with her?'

'Yes, before I took the relationship further, I told Kate that I wanted a divorce. I told her I wanted to move out and start a life with Nino . . . Are you going to arrest me for being a bigamist?'

'Eventually, but not right now. Explain to me why you haven't left Kate.'

'Because she's always threatened suicide.'

'I see. So how did you find yourself married to the two of them?'

He exhales. 'My relationship with Nino developed over the next few months . . . Even though I tried my best to keep my distance I found that I simply couldn't, and the whole thing really took its toll on Kate. More than I thought possible.'

'So you found yourself between a rock and a hard place.'

Guy looks at her dolefully. 'Let's say life didn't quite work out the way I'd hoped it would,' and Joanne thinks, *Mister, join the club.*

'Nino became pregnant – unexpectedly. Again I begged Kate for a divorce, again she insisted that she'd kill herself before she'd ever let that happen. And I believed her. I can't stress how much I believed her. I never would have gone through with this if I hadn't. But now we were faced with the problem of Nino being an unmarried mother and being cut off by her own family if she remained as such. And I felt that, as understanding as she'd been about the situation with Kate, she really didn't deserve that. She didn't deserve to have *nothing*. Nino was petrified I'd stay with Kate and she would be left here in the UK with no guarantee, no evidence of our relationship. So I took the easy way out and married her in Georgia. In front of her family and friends.'

'Who else knows about this?'

'The children know there's a problem, but not the full extent of it. Kate's sister, Alexa, knows about Nino.'

'Then last night you were with—?'

'Nino – yes,' he replies. 'We have an apartment at Helm Priory in Bowness. It's in a good spot. Nino doesn't drive, so it's handy for the village. She can pick up what she needs without being totally reliant on me.'

'And that's why Lisa Kallisto discovered your wife this morning. You were staying there.'

He nods.

Joanne remembers how she followed Guy Riverty two nights ago. How on leaving the doctor's surgery he'd swung a left up Brantfell Road instead of going home.

Brantfell Road loops round into Helm Road. The prescription he'd picked up must have been for his son. Nino's son.

Joanne's thoughts then return to Kate. 'Why choose now to commit suicide . . . when this has been going on for – how long?'

'I've been with Nino for four years.'

'So why choose now?'

Reluctantly, he says, 'Because she couldn't cope with my leaving her alone, with Lucinda missing.'

Joanne sucks in her breath. That really is shitty.

Guy says, 'I know what you're thinking,' and Joanne tilts her head. 'You're wondering what type of man could do something like that to another person.'

Joanne's actually thinking that, if this was a TV crime drama, the detective would answer: 'Doesn't matter what I think. My job is to try to make sense of the disappearance of your daughter and bring whoever's responsible to justice.' But because this is real life, Joanne says, 'What a total-bastard thing to do. Who taught you how to treat women like that?'

He looks at her levelly. 'You don't understand. Kate has . . . Kate has issues. Complicated problems.' And Joanne gives him a look as if to say, *Yes, you, you bastard. You are her problem.*

'Let me guess,' she says, sitting back in her chair, 'your Russian wife understands you much better.'

'Georgian,' he corrects.

'My mistake.'

Guy takes a long, deep breath.

'Kate has been seeing a psychotherapist for a number of years now at the Bupa hospital. When I first told her about Nino, she took it hard. Threw herself into being a doting mother.'

Joanne nods, signalling for Guy to go on, but for now he can't. It's as if what he's about to reveal is too painful, and it takes him a moment to summon the strength to continue.

'Around that time, Fergus developed a problem with his eye. We tried everything,' he says. 'Took him everywhere. The eye would get dreadfully swollen and crusty-looking, and there was always a low-lying infection we could never quite seem to get rid of. At one point we thought he might lose the sight in it altogether. Kate was really good, taking him down to London to the eye hospital time and time again, but they couldn't identify the cause. Until' – Guy pauses here, folds his lips inwards and blows up his cheeks in an expression of sad resignation – 'until a new Canadian doctor thought he found the answer.'

Joanne looks at Guy expectantly.

'He contacted me, me alone, to say that they'd found a number of fibres on the cornea.'

Joanne shakes her head. 'What fibres? How'd they get there?'

'Kate put them there.'

Joanne's mouth drops open.

'Kate had been rubbing Fergus's eye with the corner of her pashmina shawl.'

'Why?'

'Good question. I knew she was taking my relationship with Nino hard but I was truly bewildered by this. Shortly afterwards she was diagnosed with Munchausen syndrome by proxy. We discovered she'd also been using a pipette to drop bleach into the eye as well. Though not routinely, she said. Only when she felt her life was getting completely out of control.'

'Bleach? Jesus!' Joanne says, thinking she needs to run a check on this as soon as possible.

'So is she cured?' Joanne asks.

'Evidently not,' Guy says sadly, 'or I don't suppose she'd be in hospital.'

He makes his way back, congratulating himself on a job well done. He's getting better at this, getting better every day at covering his tracks, at being invisible.

He drives through Windermere and thinks about making a quick stop at Windermere Academy. He could take another look at the girl he has lined up next. Perhaps he might even get to talk to her today. He knows she's seen him. She likes him. He's watched her watching.

Eventually he decides that two in one day is probably pushing things, even for him. So he drives on towards home. He needs to keep a lid on this thing if he's to keep it fresh. If he's to keep on doing it. He can always come back in the morning, he decides. See if he can't catch her attention when she steps off the minibus.

He visualizes her walking towards his car and his skin prickles with anticipation. Her dark skin, dark hair, chocolate-brown eyes . . .

DAY FOUR

Friday

36

IT'S MORNING. Thirty-six hours have passed since Alexa was round here calling me a whore, and Joe is up first. He's naturally quiet and wounded around me, like there's been a death, and I'm just praying to God he doesn't have a change of heart and decide to give up on me.

The weather is on the change. Last night the forecast was for thick cloud and grey skies for the North-West. The high pressure responsible for the plummeting temperatures and all that dry, cold air from the north is on its way out. We're in for a milder spell. Perhaps we won't have a white Christmas after all.

I can hear Joe opening and closing cupboards in the kitchen.

'Lise?'

He's shouting from the bottom of the stairs, and I mutter something – not a proper word, more of a low moan – to let him know I'm awake and can hear him. 'One of the dogs has puked up a load of yellow shit,' he says.

Wearily, I call out, 'I'll sort it,' and put my head back beneath the duvet.

This isn't Joe doing tit for tat. It's not 'You slept with someone else so you have to do all the crappy jobs from here on in. Joe's not like that. No, he just knows I'd prefer to do it myself, because anything Joe uses to clean up, i.e. cloth, mop, Scotch-brite scourers from the side of the kitchen sink, ends up destroyed in the process.

Kitchen cloths turn brown and get covered in grass (golf-shoe cleaning), the mop goes black and beyond rescue (cleaning of taxi roof), and so on and so forth.

I turn over and try to organize my thoughts for the day ahead. Kate is looming heavily, but just now, it's Bluey who's at the forefront.

Yesterday evening a young woman arrived at work in an unmarked white van, ready to collect Bluey. Before her arrival I'd got a little giddy about him being taken away for forensic analysis. The idea of Bluey being the missing link, the missing piece of the jigsaw in the hunt for the abductor of the three girls – well, needless to say, I got a bit excited about it.

But when she actually turned up with the bare cage in the back of the van I was seized by a wild panic that they were going to experiment on him. This was for no good reason whatsoever, and the young forensics assistant didn't know what to do when I started shouting. When I realized I was making her frightened, I stopped. Sheepishly, I handed her the lead and told her it had been a difficult week and I was very sorry for my outburst. 'I'm not normally hysterical,' I said to her, and she left, quick as she could. Poor thing.

I wonder now how Bluey is. I wonder if he's okay. She assured me he would be well looked after and would probably go home with her for the night. 'Probably?' I'd said accusingly, and she'd said, '*No, definitely*.'

I hope to God he comes back. I don't think I could cope if something happened to him, on top of everything else, little old bag of bones that he is. I wouldn't forgive myself.

Joe shouts again that I need to come down and deal with the mess right now before the other dogs start lapping it up. So I swing my legs over the side of the bed, slide my feet into my slippers, and by the time I get down to the kitchen Joe has the coffee made and has filled the mop bucket with steaming water.

'You put some bleach in this?' I ask him, lifting the bucket out of the sink, and he says, 'Yeah, just a bit.'

He's already dressed in his work gear: clean jeans, a white shirt beneath a cotton or woollen jumper and polished boots. 'You look handsome,' I tell him, but there's something in his face that makes me look at him twice. 'Are you all right?' I ask, and he says, 'Yeah,' but there's something odd. 'Your face is different,' I say, and he shrugs. It's as if his lines are not quite in the same places as they were last night. Like when the crevices bracketing a person's mouth get filled with Restylane and they look sort of strange.

'You're sure?' I ask him, and see a momentary flash of annoyance.

'I'm not exactly gonna be shit-hot right now, Lise, am I?'

'Suppose not. Sorry. I love you,' I say, yawning. 'Do I look like crap?'

'You're beautiful,' he answers, coming over and kissing me on the mouth, 'but your breath's rank.'

I watch him as he's shrugging on his jacket, his hair slightly damp – just a little too long – and curling on to his collar.

'What do you fancy for tea?' he asks, and I tell him I'll pick up some steak.

'It's Friday,' I say. 'Let's watch a film, get pissed and have sex when the kids have gone to bed. Try to pretend this week never happened.'

'Paradise,' he says, and kisses me, on the forehead this time. Then he picks up his keys and he's gone.

I clean up the mess in the utility room. It's impossible to tell which dog was ill, since they all gobble down their food with equal gusto, so I quit stressing about the things I can't do anything about and sit down at the table with my coffee. Since yesterday I've adopted the mindset that there's always a reason for everything, and even though I know that's really a load of crap, I'd say it's helping.

I sip my coffee. David Bowie and Bing are singing 'Little Drummer Boy' softly from the radio over in the corner, and I decide I'd better get the Christmas tree up this weekend or else the kids will be on at me non-stop.

I hear them upstairs now. Alarms have gone off, and there's a thump, followed by fast-moving footsteps. Ever since Sam could walk, which he did at nine months, he runs to wherever he's going.

I hear the bathroom light going on, then off, then a quick run back in there because he's forgotten to flush, then he's down the stairs in less than ten seconds and sitting across from me.

'Morning, Mum,' he says, upbeat. I smile, cheered by his morning enthusiasm, knowing that within a couple of years it will wane to the series of grunts and complaints I get from the other two.

'Did you have a good sleep, Sam?'

'I had an extra-bad dream,' he says dramatically. 'I dreamt Mario and Luigi were on, this, like, really big rollercoaster and—'

I'm nodding vaguely, pulling a scared face when required, looking worried for the Super Mario Brothers as the dream is relayed (or rather, made up on the spot).

Mario and Luigi have featured heavily in our lives for a couple of years. Sam has, as well as every single game available, soft-toy versions of the two main characters which he plays with all the time. Last week I overheard Luigi say to Mario, 'I'm gonna go take a crap,' and wondered momentarily if Barbie ever found herself saying that to Ken.

I pour the milk over Sam's cereal and place it in front of him. As he eats, he's still talking. The Christmas fair is on Monday after school and I was supposed to send in raffle prizes. He's been told to ask me if I could serve tea or run one of the stalls.

I nod to him on autopilot, tell him I'll talk to the teacher, because I've zoned out. Sam is fiddling with his eye, getting rid of the sleep that's stuck to his lashes, and suddenly there's this itch at the back of my brain that I can't quite get to.

It's an itch that's been there since yesterday evening, tickling away at the edges of my dreams, giving me the sense that if I could just reach a little further, if I could just *think* a little harder, I would learn what I needed to know.

But it's no use. The more I try, the further it moves from my grasp. So, for now, I forget it.

37

IT'S 8.30 A.M. and Joanne's taking notes as DI McAleese brings them up to speed.

He tells the team that Forensics have lifted a reasonable sample from beneath the fingernails of Francesca Clarke, the third victim. Although they're not expecting to find the perpetrator's skin under there – he's been far too meticulous, far too careful for that. It's canine DNA they're after – skin cells from the Bedlington Terrier.

If they can place the dog with Francesca Clarke, *then* get a positive ID from Lisa Kallisto for Charles Lafferty – the scrote who took the dog – they'll have enough to tie him to the girl. And possibly enough for a conviction.

They just need to find him.

But there's nothing to go on except the name Charles Lafferty, and the only thing flagging up on that is a brutal assault made on a forty-year-old estate agent in Windermere. Other than that there's no record of employment, and nothing turning up on the ViSOR database.

McAleese doesn't want this to turn into a waiting game. He doesn't want to sit around counting down the hours till the abductor strikes again. They need a sighting, a number plate . . . anything.

So they're back on door-to-door, and back to wading through hours of CCTV that's been gathered from within a two-mile radius of every school in South Lakeland. They know they're looking for a good-looking, well-dressed guy in his mid-thirties. 'Shouldn't be too hard to find him,' McAleese says, and they all groan. 'TIE anyone cropping up twice,' he instructs, and winds up the meeting.

Ron Quigley turns to Joanne. 'Going to be a long, long day,' he says, and she agrees, though she's still thinking about Guy Riverty – released without charge yesterday afternoon.

In the end they had nothing to keep him in on and, after being almost certain he had something to do with his daughter's disappearance, Joanne actually ended up feeling sorry for the poor bugger.

Two hours, four cups of tea and half a packet of custard creams later, Joanne's found nothing on the CCTV – save for a couple of sightings of Joe le Taxi and a white 4x4 which she's thinking about following up on when there's a knock at the door. It's the desk sergeant from downstairs. 'Sorry to bother you, Joanne, but there's a woman asking to speak to someone working on the kidnapped girls' case. Says she wants to speak to a lady officer. You okay to come down?'

'Have you checked her out? Not just a paranoid timewaster, is she, 'cause I've spoken to enough of them already. I'm right in the middle of this.'

He opens the door a little wider. 'She's adamant. Says she's got some information. She seems legit.'

'Fine. Be right there.'

Joanne approaches the woman, who's sitting on one of the plastic chairs over by the windows. The woman is looking at her feet, avoiding eye contact with anybody else in the room. A length of Christmas paper-chains, done for the station by the nearby primary school, has come loose from the ceiling. It's dangling a couple of feet from the woman's head.

'You wanted to speak to a police officer?' Joanne asks as the woman lifts her head. 'I'm Detective Constable Aspinall. I'm working on the case.'

She's a mousy little thing. Fortyish, dark-blonde hair, small frame. She's wearing a mumsy outfit of jogging pants, trainers and a pale-blue Regatta jacket.

'Can we talk somewhere more private?' the woman asks, and Joanne says, 'Okay. Just give me a minute to find a free room.'

Five minutes later, and the mousy woman tells Joanne her name is 'Teresa Peterson.'

'And what did you want to talk to me about?'

'The girls.'

Joanne waits for her to continue but, for now, that's all Teresa Peterson seems able to say.

'You have some information about the girls who were abducted, is that it?'

Teresa blinks hard, stares downwards. 'Yes,' she says.

Joanne takes a couple of breaths, thinking, *This is not going anywhere.* Again, she waits. But when she suspects the woman might just stay like this for the rest of the day, she says, gently: 'What's upsetting you, Miss Peterson? What is it about this that's making you distressed?'

'Mrs,' she says, then: 'Mrs Peterson. Look, I'm not from around here. I've not been here long and so I'm not sure, I'm not completely sure—'

Joanne's thinking she should have got Cynthia Spence to deal with this. 'Whatever you tell me is held in complete confidence. Are you worried that you might get into trouble for speaking up?'

'What if I'm wrong?'

'What if you give me the wrong information?'

'What if I give you the wrong *person*?'

Joanne relaxes her shoulders. She explains, 'We have somebody who can positively identify the suspect once we locate him. If the person you name is not the suspect, we'll know immediately.'

Joanne reaches forward and touches Teresa Peterson's wrist, just briefly. 'You have nothing to be fearful of. Really, nobody is going to be charged with something they didn't do. Why don't you begin by telling me what leads you to suspect this person.'

Teresa Peterson reaches into the pocket of her waterproof jacket and withdraws a tatty piece of tissue. She blows her nose then closes her eyes. Her lips begin moving but no sound escapes. Joanne realizes she's either praying or saying some sort of mantra, trying to ready herself.

Then her eyes flicker open. 'I needed a photograph,' she whispers, 'a photograph of my shoes. They're Kurt Geigers and they're too tall for me . . . I'm not really the type who can carry off stilettos. I look silly. Shouldn't have bought them, but I got them in a flight of fancy, and, well, they're just sitting in the wardrobe, doing nothing.'

She looks at Joanne as if to say, *Do I go on?* And Joanne says yes.

'When I found the camera it wasn't where it should be, not where we usually keep it.'

She's wringing her hands in a mad way now, and Joanne glances at her watch.

'Anyway, that didn't matter,' she says. 'I found it. But when I went to take the picture – oh, sorry, I forgot to say I was putting them on eBay, that's why I needed the photo—'

'I kind of assumed—'

'When I went to take the picture, it wouldn't work. The memory card was gone and I thought, *That's strange.* There was no reason for it. And that's when it hit me.'

'That's when what hit you?'

'That it's my husband. It's my husband who has been taking those young girls.'

Joanne smiles at the woman in front of her and sighs.

'Mrs Peterson, I think you may have jumped the gun a bit here.'

She shakes her head. 'No. I found the memory card in the inside pocket of his coat.'

Joanne raises her eyebrows.

'That's why we moved to this area,' Teresa Peterson says quickly. 'We had to leave our home because he'd done it before. It was never proven, but Merv says mud sticks and so we came north when we saw the advert for a married couple to run the hotel.'

'Which hotel?'

'The George at Grasmere.'

'Where are you from, Mrs Peterson?'

'Ipswich. Suffolk.'

'And your husband's name is Merv?'

'Mervyn Peterson. If you check, you'll see he was taken in for questioning when a friend of our daughter's claimed he photographed her.'

'How old was she?'

'Twelve.'

Joanne strains to keep her face blank.

'He denied it, promised me it wasn't true, and I believed him. But now I've found this.' She removes a Sandisk 4GB digital card from her handbag and passes it to Joanne.

Joanne looks at her levelly. 'What's on this, Mrs Peterson?'

The woman starts to shake. 'Pictures. Pictures of girls . . . it's got sexual images of adolescent girls on it . . . and there's a few of his mother. She was seventy last month, so we went down for a family get-together.'

'The images on here, you're quite sure that they're not of your daughter? Not personal photographs that she could have taken herself and didn't mean for you to see?'

Teresa shakes her head. 'It's not her,' she replies. 'I'm certain.'

38

I DROP SAM AT SCHOOL, speak to Mrs Corrie, his teacher, about the Christmas fair, and agree to make a few batches of just about the only thing I'm any good at – courgette cake. I'm no cook, we know that. However, it's basically the same recipe as banana cake but, for some reason, people are way more impressed by it.

Sam's teacher mouths, tactfully, 'How is Kate doing?', to which I mouth back, 'Okay.'

I rang the hospital last night and was told that, all being well, Kate would be home some time today. When I voiced my concerns about her state of mind I was told that she'd been evaluated and a community psychiatric nurse would stay with her on her return.

Mrs Corrie asks when I think Kate will be *back on her feet again*, the subtext being: Will she be in to help with the Christmas fair? Which is a ridiculous thing to suggest with Lucinda gone, and the state Kate's in at the moment. But I know she's only asking because they are going to be totally sunk without her.

Kate is the spine of school fundraisers, from which everything else hangs. Without her, the Christmas fair will be a disaster. No one will do as they promised. No one will bring in the prizes, the wine, the cakes, the games. Nothing will get done without gentle reminders from Kate. As it stands now, it will probably end up costing the school money even to throw the party.

The day is as grey as was promised. And as mild. There's a noticeable rise in temperature and I have no need for my gloves, my hat. The exhaust on the car is still blowing, but I ignore it. It'll have to wait.

When I get into work Lorna tells me she's updated the website and that there's a message on the answer machine to say Bluey will be returned some time later this morning. They have managed to collect the samples they needed. And there's another message. A mad message from a frantic woman (who sounds drunk) in Grasmere. She needs us to collect a dog, urgently, because of a change in her circumstances, and she can't get the dog to us herself because her car has been towed away. The dog is a Doberman.

'Have you rung her back?' I ask Lorna.

'There's no answer. She's probably passed out. She left an address, though. Are you going to go up there?'

'I'll see how the morning goes.'

'You look tired, if you don't mind me saying.'

'It's not been the best week of my life.'

'Want me to go?' Lorna asks.

'It's okay,' I say, and smile. 'I'd rather be driving than cleaning out kennels . . . sorry.'

'Worth a shot.'

Lorna's done her hair with henna again and the dye has stained the skin behind her ears and at the nape of her neck. I don't say anything. Her fingernails are brown as well.

'How's your friend?' Lorna asks. 'They found her daughter yet?', and I shake my head. 'Must be awful,' she adds, and I feel something stirring softly inside.

I'm gazing over at the door deep in thought, Lorna saying, 'Lisa, are you okay?' a sympathetic tone to her voice.

'What? Yes,' I reply quickly. 'Just need to get busy. How are those kittens doing?'

'Only one left. I've christened him Buster.'

'Buster's good,' I tell her, and go through to the back room to get started. See if I can syringe some food into him.

When I walk in I see Lorna has bagged up the last two kittens that didn't make it through the night ready for collection, and hear the tiny mewling sound of Buster.

I reach down into the cage and pick him up. He's jet black on his back, with a white chest and white undercarriage and a small, black, triangular patch of fur under his chin. It's as if he's wearing a dinner suit, like a tiny James Bond. He purrs as I lift him. I begin checking him for fleas and find two straight away. I grab the comb to get rid of them before starting on with the syringe. He'll make it, I decide.

I check his gums – they're a good, healthy pink – and his eyes are bright. 'Make sure you live,' I say to him, and he stares back at me wide-eyed and mischievous.

Then my mobile beeps in my pocket and I check the screen. My heart skips when I see it's from Kate.

Thank you. You're a life-saver! reads the text, simply.

And I reply, *Any time*, and sigh.

She must be on her way home.

39

THREE SQUAD CARS are on their way to the George Hotel at Grasmere to pick up Mervyn Peterson. Joanne is in one of them, and, at the moment, as they wind their way along the eastern edge of Lake Windermere, she's stuck behind a fifteen-year-old Escort with a fish sign in the rear window. 'Bad case of Christian driving,' she says to Ron, and taps her fingers on the steering wheel.

This is the bit she lives for. The bit when she gets to string this fucker up by his testicles and deliver him to the courts for the abduction and repeated rape of three young girls.

She knows it's him. She can feel it's him. Teresa Peterson detailed the previous allegations against him as well as saying he went AWOL on Wednesday night – when Francesca Clarke was abducted. There's little doubt in Joanne's mind. She can't wait to get him in the interview room.

Ron Quigley's at the side of her, swallowing Rennies like Smarties, his right knee jumping and bouncing in anticipation.

'What you thinking?' he asks her.

'I'm imagining slapping the cuffs on and holding the bastard down with my knee.'

A fine drizzle has begun to fall as Joanne glances across to the lake. Beyond, the Langdale Pikes are obscured by cloud and the lake itself is granite-grey. Still plenty of snow around on the banks for now, but it'll all be melted soon enough. The whole place is in monochrome.

'Be good to get a conviction before Christmas,' Ron muses, and Joanne agrees.

She asked Teresa Peterson about the thing that'd been baffling her most about this case. 'Where could he have taken the girls? Where could he have taken them without being seen?'

Teresa had shrugged. Said she had no idea. So Joanne told her about Molly Rigg. 'Molly said she could smell laundered sheets and the room was painted cream. She said it was bare.'

And Teresa Peterson had blanched white before answering, 'The hotel has a couple of cottages on the grounds. They've not been rented out for a while, we only open them up when we're busy.'

'Can you see them from the hotel?' Joanne asked, and Teresa had shaken her head.

'Not really. They're off to the side of the main building. No one's got any reason to go near them when they're not being used.'

Joanne had reported her findings to DI McAleese and the scene-of-crime boys were on their way.

They drive through Ambleside and Joanne tries flashing her lights at the Escort in front to signal for it to pull over – it's doing less than twenty miles an hour – but the woman driving is oblivious.

She presses hard on the horn while Ron waves his arms around in the passenger seat and finally the woman pulls off to the right towards Rydal Mount – Wordsworth's house when he wrote 'Daffodils'. At last Joanne's able to put her foot down.

Ten minutes later and there's the sound of gravel crunching and pinging in the wheel arches of the Mondeo as it pulls up outside the George Hotel, followed by the two other squad cars. 'Let's hope the lovely Mervyn is at home,' Ron says, climbing out.

They herd into reception. It's a huge, oak-panelled space, a stag's head on the far wall, big oak staircase.

Joanne approaches the young skinny girl with blue-black hair who is behind the desk. Warrant cards are flashed, voices are kept hushed and the girl informs them in a Spanish accent that Mr Peterson is currently with the fire officer up on the third floor. 'You like, I call him for you,' she says flatly, and Joanne says, No – thanks, but they'll go up and find him for themselves.

DI McAleese leads and Joanne follows closely, with Ron and a couple of uniforms behind her. The hotel is overheated and the air is thick with the smells of newly laid carpet and furniture polish. The stairs turn at a right angle and a balding guy carrying a briefcase pauses to let them pass. 'Something happened?' he asks McAleese, who's about to continue on but then changes his mind.

'You a guest?' McAleese asks him.

The guy says, No, he's the fire officer.

'Have you just been with Mervyn Peterson?'

He nods. 'I'm on my way to inspect the pool area. Peterson's finishing taking some notes in room eleven. Top of the stairs, turn right, end of the hallway.'

McAleese sprints up the stairs two at a time. Adrenalin floods through Joanne's blood as she does the same. They are so close now. She can hear the rush of bodies behind her as she moves. At the top she begins breathing hard. She thinks about whipping her parka off but there's no time. McAleese is striding ahead of her.

Room eleven. The door is closed. McAleese puts his ear to it, pulls a face to signal there's no sound from within, and bangs on the wood. 'Police. Mr Peterson, open the door.'

Nothing.

'Get ready,' McAleese whispers.

Joanne's heart is beating in her throat.

McAleese gestures for Joanne to push down on the handle. Silently, he counts with his fingers: one, two, three.

They burst in, McAleese into the bedroom, Joanne heading straight for the bathroom. Then the wardrobe.

'It's empty, boss,' she says.

'Next room.'

Ron is sent to check the fire escape while one of the uniforms radios to the officers left downstairs to cover the exits. Strange, Joanne hadn't expected Mervyn to run. She'd formed a picture of him in her mind as the type of cocky bastard who would stand his ground, try and bullshit his way out. She hadn't had him down as a runner.

She knocks on the door of room nine. 'Police!' she shouts; doesn't wait for an answer.

The first thing she sees is a pair of calf skin loafers hanging off the end of the bed.

Joanne takes four paces forward and sees his face for the first time. 'Mervyn Peterson?'

Instantly it's clear to Joanne how he managed to get those girls into his car. He has a most beautiful face, but her eyes don't stay on it for long.

He smiles at her, sitting up, 'You've caught me red-handed,' he says, yawning. 'I was just about to have a sneaky . . . nap.'

'Boss, he's in here!' Joanne shouts towards the door. 'Room nine.'

She hears the pounding of feet, and Mervyn looks taken aback.

'Heck,' he says emphatically, 'whatever is the matter? Has something terrible happened?' His eyes are shining and he's smirking like he's Terry-Thomas caught in a sticky situation with the law.

'Save it,' Joanne says, and DI McAleese is at the side of her.

He casts his eyes over Mervyn and his expression falters.

Mervyn's trousers are bunched around his ankles and his semi-erect penis lies flat across his stomach. He coughs and watches Joanne's reaction as his dick twitches twice. Bouncing playfully on his flat, taut stomach.

'Mervyn Peterson, I am arresting you on suspicion of—'

Seconds later, Joanne tells Mervyn Peterson to put it away and to get dressed. So that she can cuff him. She fixes the cuffs tighter than she ought to and leads Mervyn out of the room by his elbow.

As they make their way along the corridor towards the stairs, covered in front and behind by her fellow officers, Mervyn leans in close.

'I saw you looking,' he whispers in Joanne's ear, his voice singing with delight. 'I saw your face when you found me.'

And Joanne replies, deadpan, 'Did you.'

40

'NO COMMENT,' REPLIES Mervyn smugly. He glances at his solicitor, who nods once in response. Mervyn is wearing a clean, thick-cotton Italian shirt, which he insisted on bringing along with him to the station, as well as clean socks and underwear. 'In case I get searched,' he said.

Joanne shifts in her seat.

She'd begged McAleese for this opportunity, for this interview. She needs to get something out of him. But they've been at this for more than twenty minutes now, and Merv the Perv isn't talking.

Joanne decides to break from the questions and just sit. She could do with running another tissue under her armpits, beneath the underwired section of her bra. It won't be long before the sweat seeps through her shirt. The room is painfully hot.

Mervyn's smirking at her.

'What?' he says, in reaction to her silence. 'Are we going to have a staring competition now, Detective? Have you run out of things to ask me?'

'Your wife made a statement alleging you took photographs of adolescent girls, Mervyn. You don't want to answer my questions, I can understand that. You think you're just going to land yourself in more trouble by talking, so I can see you want to keep quiet. I'd most likely do the same in your shoes.'

'My wife is delusional.'

'Seemed pretty together to me. She came across as a sensible, clear-headed type of woman.'

He scoffs. 'No comment.'

'Though I have to say, I wouldn't have automatically put the two of you together.'

He raises his eyebrows at Joanne.

'You're an odd pairing,' she explains.

'If you say so,' he replies.

'How did you meet?'

'No comment.'

'What about your daughter? How old is she, eleven?'

'Twelve.'

'Only a year away from your favourite age, Mervyn. Where are you hiding Lucinda?'

He leans forward in his seat and fixes her with a chilling stare. 'I did not take those girls. I am a father. I am a husband. I am not a paedophile, as you are suggesting. You have no evidence, Detective, to prove I am involved in any of this, and if you're hoping for some kind of weepy confession from me, then you will be waiting for a very long time. I've told you. I did not do it.'

'What does the name Charles Lafferty mean to you?'

He shrugs. 'Never met him.'

'I think you have.'

Mervyn rolls his eyes.

'It's a name you use, isn't it, Mervyn?'

'You're ridiculous.'

'It's an alias you use when you're pretending to be someone else.'

'Why would I want to be someone else?'

'Perhaps you're embarrassed of who you are,' Joanne replies.

Mervyn laughs contemptuously. 'I am not at all embarrassed

by who I am, Detective,' he says, correcting her grammar. 'Perhaps you mean yourself. Maybe it's *you* who's embarrassed by who *you* are.' He pauses and gives her the once-over. 'Not married, are you?'

Joanne meets his stare. She doesn't answer.

'And why is that?' he asks.

'Good men are thin on the ground, wouldn't you say?'

'Perhaps it's more a case of butch women getting left on the shelf.'

Joanne leans towards him. In a low voice, she says, 'We know it's you, Mervyn. We've got DNA.'

He doesn't speak, but she sees his expression quaver, just fleetingly.

She continues, 'Why don't you help yourself and tell us why it is you do what you do. It can help your defence. If you keep on saying "No comment", we've got nowhere to go. No one's going to sympathize with a guy like you who won't admit to what he's done. Especially not inside. You start telling me what drives you, we might be required to get a psychiatric evaluation. I've heard they can be really useful when the time for sentencing comes around.'

'What DNA?' he asks.

'Oh, Mervyn. I can't go telling you all my secrets, can I?'

'You're bluffing.'

'I'm not allowed to bluff.'

He sits back in his chair. Takes one breath in and sighs it out heavily.

'I don't believe you,' he says.

'I'm not lying, Mervyn. We can place you with one of the victims. And now that we've got you here, I expect a line-up will be next on the agenda. There's always a good chance one of them will pick you once they set eyes on you.'

Mervyn looks to his solicitor. Joanne watches. The solicitor's face is impassive. He drops his gaze and shakes his head to the side.

'No comment,' Mervyn says firmly.

Joanne moves her hand across the desk as if she's reaching out to him. 'Mervyn,' she says softly, almost sadly, 'we've got the dog. That dog you used to lure away your last victim? We found him. And guess what? He turned out to be a lovely old bundle of evidence.'

Joanne runs her hands under the cold-water tap and rinses her face. Her cheeks are flushed crimson and her shirt is sticking to her. She grabs some paper towel from the dispenser and wets it before wiping it over the skin of her back and midriff. Nearly there, she tells herself. Almost there.

McAleese, who'd been watching on a monitor next to the interview room, authorized the break. Mervyn had requested some time alone with his solicitor and McAleese granted it. He had a hunch that Mervyn would return to questioning singing a different tune, but Joanne wasn't so sure. She got the impression Mervyn would keep this charade up till the death. He was a born liar. Joanne reckons she's never met one quite so brilliant before. As if he himself believes every word to come out of his mouth. He'd be one of those people you hear about who can throw a polygraph.

The team regroups in the briefing room before Joanne and McAleese make their way down to the cells to collect Mervyn for round two.

The duty sergeant opens the door and the first thing Joanne sees are the pinstripes. And Mervyn's bare torso. His ashen face stares at her as he hangs by his shirt from the iron bars of the cell window.

Joanne runs forward.

He's already turning blue when she grabs him – grabs him around the hips, lifts his weight up in her arms.

'Fuck,' she hears someone say, but she's not sure who, because she has everything focused on keeping this bastard up as high as she can.

Joanne's not going to let him die. She has Molly Rigg's desolate face in her head as she summons strength in her arms. She won't let him die.

His weight has pulled the knot taut. The body is jerking as McAleese hacks through the cotton, trying to free him. Joanne feels another set of arms around Mervyn Peterson's girth, halving her load.

Then his body bends at the waist as the shirt is cut from the steel bar.

His upper half flops forward and Joanne staggers, along with the duty sergeant, to lower Peterson to the floor without dropping him. 'Get an ambulance,' McAleese shouts to a figure in the doorway.

Joanne kneels down and puts her fingers to his neck. 'Weak pulse, we need to get this off.' The remaining shirtsleeve is continuing to cut into his throat. It too has been pulled taut with the weight of him. Joanne tries to slip her fingers underneath, but she can manage only one.

'Jesus!' says McAleese. 'We're going to lose the cunt. Joanne, breathe some air into him.'

She fires a look at McAleese, hesitates, then does as she's asked. There's no time to get the resuscitation shield. All the while, McAleese is cutting at the shirt with the blade of his Swiss Army knife.

Joanne feels sick to her stomach as she holds Peterson's nose and covers his lips over with hers. He tastes of coffee. Sweet. The images from the memory card his wife brought in are coming thick and fast.

Breathe in. Blow out. Naked girls' bodies. Breathe in. Blow out.

Christ, she could stick her fingers to the back of his eye sockets and drag out his fucking brain rather than do this.

Breathe in. Blow out.

Breathe in.

McAleese has cut through the cotton and tells Joanne to stop. Says Peterson's colour is returning.

'Let's see if the fucker can breathe,' McAleese says, and they watch as his chest begins to rise.

Seconds later, his eyelids flicker.

McAleese shoots Joanne a look to keep on her guard lest this wacko goes for her.

McAleese says, 'Thought we'd lost you for a second there, Peterson.'

Mervyn's eyes open wide. He's disorientated. Perhaps he thinks this is heaven, Joanne thinks fleetingly.

'Can't let you go popping off like that when you've raped three little girls, now, can we?' McAleese says.

Mervyn looks at them, confused. 'Three?' he asks.

41

I'M STANDING ON the doorstep of a picture-postcard cottage on the outskirts of Grasmere village, thinking about puppies. Why do so many people choose a puppy rather than an adult dog? Why, when they are so ill-equipped to deal with them?

I've rung the doorbell, but the front curtains are drawn. There's no movement from inside. The Doberman must be round the back. If it was in there I'd have heard it barking by now.

Puppies are hard work. They crap, they chew, they cost money. The adult dogs we rehome come neutered, vaccinated and chipped. That's around a hundred and sixty quid saved right there. But everyone wants a puppy. Because *how do you know you're not taking on someone else's problem dog?*

They fail to realize that it is they who will be producing another problem dog.

I glance around me while I wait. The cottage is one in a run of four. They are nicely set; far enough back from the road. It's a good spot. Clematis is growing around each door, brown and ugly right now but I imagine it looks lovely in the summer. There's no activity at the other cottages save for an electrician's Transit parked in front of the house next door. Each has that tidy soullessness of a holiday home.

I ring again and a figure appears behind the frosted glass. The door swings open and, instinctively, I take a step back, because the sight before me is rather alarming. It's around 1.15 p.m. and the woman I'm looking at is wearing a dressing gown. Her yellow hair is everywhere, and she has lipstick smeared across her cheek, almost all the way to her left ear. I'd put her at mid-forties. Attractive, but haggard.

'I've come to collect the dog. The Doberman?'

'Come in.'

There's no hallway; we're straight into the living room. 'Have you been burgled?' I ask, because there is stuff strewn everywhere.

'What?' she says, giving the room a brief scan. 'Oh, no . . . I've just not had time to tidy up.'

There's an ashtray piled high with fag ends on the floor next to the sofa. Grey stains on the carpet nearby, where she's kicked it over a few times. The coffee table is covered with discarded clothes, mugs, paper documents, wine bottles, DVDs, underwear.

Loose Women is on the TV, but it's been muted. I think she may have been asleep on the sofa when I knocked, because there's a duvet hanging half on, half off.

'Sorry about the mess,' she says, shifting some clothes off the other sofa so I can sit down. 'I've had a bit of a bad week.'

'Is the dog outside?'

'In the shed.'

'I'll need some details before I can take him . . . her?'

'Him. Diesel,' she replies.

'Is he your dog to give away?' I ask.

'No he's my husband's . . . shortly to be *ex*-husband.'

I give her a weak smile.

'I'll need your husband's consent, then,' I say, and she drops her head back against the sofa as if it's going to be a problem.

I decide to fill out what I can for now and worry about that part later. She tells me her name is Mel Frain. Her husband's name is Dominic.

'Has the dog been neutered?'

'No.'

'How old is he?'

'Eighteen months. He was good at first, then he got to tearing up the house, so recently we've had to keep him out there.' She motions with her hand towards the back of the house.

'Any health problems?'

'No. Listen,' she says standing up, her dressing gown gaping open, 'I need a drink, you want one?'

'Tea, please.'

'I meant a proper drink. I'm having wine.'

'Bit early for me.'

'Okay. Well, excuse me, will you, while I get myself one.'

She goes out, I hear the fridge opening and she returns with a supersized bottle of Pinot Grigio and two glasses with lipstick marks around the rims, fingerprints on the stems.

'Brought you a glass in case you change your mind. I've got no tea.' She bends forwards to pour. Distracted, I see she has a pair of fake boobs that are strangely buoyant even though she's without a bra, and I wonder if she's one of those poor women who unwittingly got the industrial-grade silicon implants. She'll probably need to have them whipped out after Christmas.

Mel Frain takes a huge gulp of wine, sighs and sits back. 'Sorry about that. I'm finding it hard to get through the day at the moment.'

I nod, not really wanting the adultery story that's clearly heading my way.

'I came home last week,' she says without emotion. 'Found my husband in bed . . . with my dad.'

'Oh dear,' I say. 'What did you do?'

'Threw up.'

'Understandable.'

She nods.

'So where are they now?' I ask.

'Fucked off to Sitges on the Costa Dorada for Christmas.'

'What about your mum?'

'She's pretending it's not happened.'

I blow out my breath in a whistle.

'Sorry I can't keep the dog,' she says, 'but I work all day. And he needs walking, and I haven't got the energy – the state of things as they are.'

'We'll find him a good home,' I reply, thinking there's no use in trying to contact her husband to authorize Diesel's removal. 'Okay,' I say, handing her the form. 'Just sign at the bottom there and I'll go and meet him.'

We get Diesel into the cage in the back of my car. His nails could do with a trim but other than that he's in good health. Handsome-looking dog with a lovely shiny coat. I've got high hopes.

As I'm shutting the boot, the electrician's van in front pulls away and I see another car is now parked further along outside the other cottage next door. I turn to Mel Frain. She's crying a little after saying goodbye to Diesel.

'See that car?' I say. 'Have you seen it here before?'

'Comes and goes,' she replies. 'It's a holiday home. I think that's the owner's car.'

'When did you last see it?'

'Couple o' days ago, maybe.'

There's that itch again, the one at the back of my brain. Difference is, now I can reach it.

I look at the registration.

Kate's car.

42

I'M NOT SURE HOW long I've been standing here for. It can only be minutes, but it feels longer. Mel Frain has disappeared inside to get back to her wine, and the rear windows of my car are beginning to steam up from Diesel's panting breath. I open the driver's door, put the key in the ignition and lower the back windows down an inch. Dogs die in hot cars is what I must be thinking.

But my eyes are on that house. The end one in the line of four.

Why is Kate's car here? She's only just got out of hospital.

I walk over and stand outside the front door. It's an odd feeling. Like the calm before the storm. I could turn around now and not face this. I could get in the car, drive back to the shelter and pretend like I never saw. And maybe the person I used to be would do exactly that. Because she avoided confrontation, she didn't challenge authority.

I go to knock but, at the last second, I stop. Instead I move a couple of steps to my right and peer in through the window. I see Kate and Lucinda on the floor with a big cardboard box. They're unpacking decorations for the Christmas tree. For a moment I think that Kate and Guy must have a Christmas booking – people don't like arriving with the place not looking festive.

And then relief floods through me, almost knocking me

sideways. Lucinda is here. Alive. I stifle a sob as I watch her. She's safe. Thank God she's safe.

Then my eyes move to Kate and my blood runs cold.

I move away from the window and back to the door. Silently, I try the handle.

It's locked.

My breath's coming out in raggedy gasps. I try to calm myself but, as I rummage through my memory of the last four days, the anger's building. I feel like the fool I've been taken for, and I now know I have to stop thinking and *do* something.

I walk around the side of the house and try the back gate. It's open. Gently, and without sound, I push against it.

I'm in the garden. It's been paved for easy maintenance with the odd pot here and there. In the corner is a barbecue covered up for the winter, and a picnic bench painted in a stupid duck-egg colour that's classic Kate. It's her trademark. She'd paint everything in that colour if she could.

The back door is a split stable door. It's unlocked, so I slowly go in and look around the kitchen, stunned. There's a freshly bought baguette out on the worktop. Kate must have picked it up from the bakery on her way over here. The smell of the bread fills the room. It's their lunch, to be eaten when they've finished the Christmas tree, and I can just picture them, mother and daughter – *best friends*, as Kate always told me they were – eating happily.

I hear voices. I can't make out the actual words, but the tone is light, happy, normal. The hatred I'm feeling now is almost paralysing.

Next to the baguette is a bread knife. I pick it up. It feels light in my hand. It's cheap. The type you'd buy from Poundstretcher or B&M Bargains because you begrudge spending on an expensive item if it's not going to be for you. I waggle it around in the air. For a moment I'm the mad woman. The woman who's come to take revenge.

I close my eyes for a second, steadying myself, then I hear movement from behind the door to the front room. Stepping forward, I open it fast.

Kate is on the other side. She doesn't speak when she sees me, just stares.

She's no longer the haunted vision of the past few days. Now, she seems healthy, robust, and I wonder how that's even possible: how could you fake that kind of grief?

Her eyes move to the knife at my side and she blinks rapidly.

Lucinda is still unaware. She's got her back to us and is threading baubles on the branches of the tree, chatting to her mother. Her movements are slower than they ought to be though, her speech dragging somewhat.

She's dressed in a hoodie and pink sweatpants. Her neatly bobbed hair swings forwards as she bends.

Kate speaks without turning around to her daughter. She doesn't want to take her eyes off the knife. 'Lucinda, sit down on the sofa, sweetpea.'

Lucinda turns and gapes when she sees me standing in the doorway.

I glare at her.

'Did your mother tell you it was *me* they blamed for your disappearance?'

Lucinda doesn't answer, looks to her mum for guidance.

'Did she?' I demand.

Lucinda nods. Her face registers fear, but her eyes are glassy; she's not quite with it.

Kate tries to take a step towards me, but I raise the knife. 'Don't,' I warn her, and she retreats.

I'm shaking. I know I'm shaking, but this is what I have to do. I've been seized by the certainty that if I don't stop this woman, she'll go on to destroy others. I hold the knife out in front of me, brandishing it like a machete.

'Lisa,' Kate says, 'what are you *doing*?'

And I laugh.

'Why me?' I ask her. 'Why did you think you could do it to me?'

She stays silent. Still staring at the knife.

'Answer me!'

'Because I knew you would blame yourself. I knew you would blame yourself and I—' She stops, smiles lightly in my direction.

'And?'

'Anyone else would have fought it,' she explains. 'They would have picked holes in it, but I knew you wouldn't. I knew you'd blame yourself without question . . . and you were always so pushed for time, you could never really attend to things the way you needed to.'

I look past her to Lucinda, who's rolling the hem of her hoodie between her fingers. 'You know your mother is fucking deranged, don't you?'

'*Lisa!*' Kate admonishes sternly. 'Language, please.'

'You know she's mad?'

Lucinda won't look at me.

'Who the fuck kidnaps their own kid?' I shout at them both.

Kate spreads her hands wide. 'Someone who's desperate to save her marriage,' she replies earnestly.

'And you went along with this?' I snap at Lucinda. 'You just went along with it?'

'I thought it would make Daddy come home.'

'From where?'

'Daddy has another family,' Lucinda says. 'It makes us all so sad. We thought that if we could make him see, then he would stop.'

'What family?' I ask, thrown. 'What other family?'

Neither of them answers so I turn back to Kate. 'This is fucking child abuse. Look at what you've done to her. She thinks this is normal. She thinks this is—'

'She wants her daddy back – what's so wrong with that?'

'*What's wrong* is that they'll put you away for this, so she won't have a mother *or* a father. And why's she speaking like that? All slurry? Have you drugged her or something?'

'Lisa, calm down. I can see you're angry. I understand that, I would be angry in your shoes. But we really didn't have a choice. We tried to get him to stay with us, and he wouldn't.'

I can't take in what she's saying. I can't believe she's actually done this on purpose.

'How could you?' I say, confounded. 'How could you stand there crying when I begged for your forgiveness, knowing what you were doing to me?'

She shrugs as if to say there was no other option. She did what she had to do.

'But we were friends,' I say to her, and she turns away.

I think about how broken Sally became over this, blaming herself for Lucinda's disappearance.

I think about how guilt-ridden both of us were at what transpired from our mistake. A mistake we never actually made. Both of us feeling like failures – me as a mother, Sally as a friend.

Suddenly I can see myself clearly. I see how easy it must have been for Kate to pin this on me. Because she's right. *Of course* I wouldn't question it. Of course it would be *all my fault.* The woman who spreads herself too thinly, the woman who doesn't feel good enough, who acts *less than.* She will always be an easy target.

I look at Kate now and I'm embittered that I allowed this to happen to my family. Then a thought occurs: 'How were you going to bring her back home?' I ask. 'There are two police forces out looking for Lucinda. What were you going to do, smuggle her back in and pretend that it never happened?'

'Lisa, why don't you put the knife down so we can talk properly?'

'Fuck off.'

Lucinda speaks up from the sofa. 'I was going to say I'd run away.'

'To where?'

'Here,' says Kate. 'Lucinda knows this house. She comes along with me and Guy when we're checking the properties. She could hop on a bus outside school and get here unnoticed – if she knew where the keys were kept. Which she does. On the hooks in Guy's office. We have over ten empty properties at the moment; because of the time of year, Guy wouldn't notice if one set of keys wasn't where it should be.'

'Would probably have his mind on other things,' I say sarcastically, 'what with his daughter missing, and his wife—' I don't finish the sentence.

Studying Kate's face, I say, 'What about the overdose? Why would you do that? What mother would leave her children alone . . . regardless of whether she has a marriage or not—'

'I knew you'd find me.'

'What?'

'I knew you'd find me,' she repeats, and my mouth drops open.

'How?'

'You sent me a text,' she says simply. 'You sent a text saying you were on your way over. And I thought it's either now or never . . . I didn't take as many pills as you thought. It wasn't as risky as they made it out to be—'

'You did that to get Guy back?'

I'm dumbfounded as she nods her head as if to say *It's what anyone would have done, Lisa. Really, it is.*

'You're insane.'

'We all have secrets, Lisa.'

I swallow.

'Every one of us is hiding something we don't want the world to know about. Remember? We all want everyone to think our family's perfect, that we got it right. Well, I *did* get it right. I did everything right. And it still went wrong. And I'm sorry, Lisa, but I just wasn't willing to accept that. I fought for my family. I did what I needed to do.'

'You need locking up.'

'Is that what you really think?'

''Course it's what I think – do you think this is *normal*?'

She sighs out as if she can't believe I'm finding this so difficult to comprehend.

'Why didn't you tell Joe about the affair you had?' she asks.

'What's that got to do with anything?'

She repeats: 'Why didn't you?'

'Because, in so many words, you told me not to.'

'I'm not your mother. I'm not your conscience. You didn't tell him because you looked at what you've got and you knew that, even though it was wrong, you'd do what you needed to do to keep your family together.'

'Yes, well, it's not a secret any more, so—'

'Yes,' says Kate gravely. 'Sorry about that.'

'About what?'

'I had to give Adam the nudge he needed. I told him to tell Alexa, or else I would. How did Joe take it, by the way? I felt bad about that. I've always liked Joe.'

'You did that?'

She sighs. 'I needed something to take your minds off Lucinda for a while, something to buy me some time.'

I stand there, stunned. I go to speak but find I can't.

And it's then that she goes for the knife. She reaches out so fast that her hand is on the blade in a second.

I pull back and feel the resistance on the serrated edge. It's cutting her. It's cutting through the flesh on her hand, but she keeps with it.

'Kate, stop!' I say, mortified at what is happening. But she doesn't.

I jerk, hoping to get the knife away from her in one quick movement, but still she holds on.

'Jesus, Kate!'

I'm staring at her, not believing she's doing this, but she stares right back at me. Her eyes are white and bulging.

'I won't let you take her,' she screams at me. 'I won't let you take Lucinda.'

'I'm not going to take her, you mad bitch! Let go of the knife!'

She must be bleeding. She has to be bleeding.

'Mummy!' Lucinda's shouting, crying. 'Mummy, stop, you're getting hurt. Please—'

Kate, keeping her eyes on me, shouts, 'Mummy has to do this. Just give Mummy a minute.'

She's strong. So strong. Where has she got this strength from?

Incensed, I scream at her, pulling at the knife wildly, 'Why do you always do that? Why do you refer to yourself in the third person? She's thirteen, Kate. She's not a baby! Stop treating her like a bloody baby, it won't make her *love* you any more!'

And I can't say what this triggers, but all at once her eyes well up with tears and I feel her grip slacken. It's as if, just for a second, she doubts herself. It's as if she can see who she is from the outside and her strength withers.

So I kick her. I kick her hard in the shin.

I've got my boots on and I kick her viciously, like I really mean it. And she yelps.

She stumbles backwards and falls. She starts scrabbling away, blood pouring from her hand, and I'm transported back to that winter when I was eight. My father's wife slicing at her wrists. The irony isn't lost on me. A second family. Another second family that's screwed a woman up to the point of madness.

Kate is staring up at me, anticipating another kick. Lucinda is taking off her hoodie so she can wrap it around her mother's hand. And that's when my phone rings.

Each of us stares at one another, unsure of what to do.

'Don't move,' I warn them. 'Move, and I'll stab you.'

I pull the mobile out of my back pocket and take a step away.

'Mrs Kallisto?'

'Yes.'

'Cumbria Police,' the voice says. 'I'm afraid there's been an accident—'

Christmas Eve

43

THE SNOW IS BACK, bang on time. Windermere village is bustling with people as Joanne makes her way to the butcher's to pick up the turkey.

Jackie's at work this morning, but because of the way Christmas has fallen this year – on a Sunday – Joanne has the day off. And suddenly she's feeling all Christmassy. This year it's not just going to be *another day*. This year she's looking forward to sharing a proper Christmas dinner with Jackie, all the trimmings, the two of them falling asleep on the settee after the Queen's speech, bellies full of chocolate Brazil nuts.

She picks up a couple of parsnips from the florist's – they do a sideline in root vegetables this time of year – and nips into Boots for some last-minute bits and bobs.

Neither of them gets much in the way of presents. Jackie's son hasn't sent anything for the past couple of years, so they've taken to spoiling each other a little. Joanne puts some overpriced body butter in her basket and, as an afterthought, a Scholl foot spa.

She studies the box and gets a vision of Jackie sitting in her carer's uniform, half a pint of Baileys in her hand, steam rising up around her ankles. And Joanne decides that, yes, this is exactly the right gift.

The clouds are low and brooding as Joanne leaves the shop. They're in for another covering of snowfall this afternoon, so there's a frisson of excitement in the village, of wanting to get home, to close the door and shut the world out. Wait for Christmas to arrive.

A tuba-, trombone- and trumpet-player are tucked into a sheltered spot just by the Abbey Bank; the last few bars of 'Joy to the World' are audible as Joanne approaches the butcher's.

There's a queue inside, but it moves quickly. Everyone's already pre-ordered and paid for their birds, so it's just a case of picking them up. Joanne wanted to go for a turkey crown – what with there being only the two of them – but Jackie would hear none of it. 'Brown meat's the best bit,' she said.

Joanne is about to cross the street and head home when she sees someone reverse into one of the spaces right in front of her. She stops, recognizing the driver. She can't see inside the car too well – the windows are obscured by steam as the car is filled with bodies – but she knows who it is.

Joanne approaches and taps on the window. Lisa Kallisto cuts the engine and opens the driver's side door. Joanne leans in and sees Lisa's three kids in the back, squashed together, the excitement of Christmas clear in their faces.

Joe's in the front passenger seat, the Bedlington Terrier that Forensics used sitting in the footwell between his knees. Both of Joe's lower legs are in plaster.

'Hi, Lisa,' Joanne says. 'How you doing?'

'Good. You?'

'Fine, thanks.' Joanne looks past Lisa to Joe. 'They let you out of hospital for Christmas, then?'

Joanne heard on the grapevine that Joe's taxi left the motorway and ended up in a ditch. He survived but fractured both his feet.

'Came out on Wednesday,' Joe says. 'I've got a wheelchair to get about with,' and he gestures behind him to the boot of the car.

Joanne smiles. 'They any idea what caused your blackout, yet?'

Joe looks shiftily from side to side.

When he doesn't answer, Lisa rolls her eyes, leans sideways towards Joanne and lowers her voice away from the kids. 'He'd been having TIAs – transient ischaemic attacks – mini-strokes.' She glances at Joe. 'And for reasons best known to himself he decided to keep that little piece of information from me and the kids.'

Joanne raises her eyebrows.

'He thought it was better if I didn't know about it,' Lisa says, and Joe looks rueful.

'You know why,' he says quietly.

Lisa gives him a soft dig in the ribs. 'Daft sod thought I'd leave him if I found out . . . Anyway, they've put him on Warfarin, so he should be okay.' She reaches behind Joe's seat for her handbag. 'What's the word on Kate? You got any more news?'

'She's been charged.'

'What with?'

'Kidnapping, false imprisonment and perverting the course of justice.'

Lisa takes a long breath in. 'Shit,' she says. 'Shit, that's worse than I thought.'

'You did the right thing, Lisa.'

'Did I?'

'You didn't have any choice. She was hurting her children – you couldn't let that continue, you know that.'

Lisa swings her legs around, makes to climb out of the car. 'If I did the right thing, why do I feel so lousy about it? . . . Do you think she'll lose the kids?'

'A prison sentence is more than likely.'

Lisa digests this and sighs out sadly.

'Will she not try and plead . . . will she not plead mentally unfit – or whatever it's called?'

'She might, but then there's less chance of her keeping the

children in the long term, if that's the way they decide to play it. Have to wait and see.'

'What a mess,' Lisa says, standing and closing the car door.

She looks past Joanne's shoulder at the Christmas lights slung low across the street. Joanne watches as Lisa tries to shrug off what she's just been told. It's Christmas Eve, Joanne can feel her thinking, it's all about the kids now.

Lisa turns to Joanne. 'You got your man, though, didn't you?' she asks, brighter now. 'You got the man who took the other girls?'

'We did.'

'That's good. *Was* it that same guy who'd been talking to Lucinda after school? Was it him?'

'He's not admitted it, but yes, we're pretty sure. From what we gather, Lucinda came home and told her mother about him, and Kate hatched the fake-abduction plan . . . Then she was just waiting for the right opportunity—'

'Waiting for me,' Lisa cuts in resignedly. 'Kate was waiting for me to screw up so she could pretend Lucinda was gone.'

Joanne can sense the hurt still fresh in Lisa.

After a moment Lisa asks, 'Are her children all right? I know I should probably get in touch, but I can't seem to bring myself to do it.'

'They're with their dad.' Joanne touches Lisa's elbow briefly. 'They're going to be okay . . . don't be too hard on yourself, eh, Lisa? With Kate's state of mind the way it is, who knows what she might have done next?'

44

I WISH DC ASPINALL A merry Christmas and leave Joe, the kids and Bluey inside the car while I nip to the butcher's. This is our last call of the morning. Once I've got the turkey we can go home, get the fire going and curl up and watch a daft film. Wait for Christmas to come to Troutbeck.

The butcher's window is filled with good stuff. Pheasants, guinea fowl and some ready-stuffed partridges sit on the left side of the display; a stack of game pies, terrines and pâtés are on the right.

I loiter for a moment before going in.

The news about Kate has hit me harder than I thought it would. And, yes, I know she'd completely lost it. And, yes, I know someone that deranged cannot keep their family. And don't get me wrong, I am still angry. There's this hot ball of fury I've been carrying inside my stomach since last week, I am so fucking mad about it all. But then I'm also saddened for her.

I'm heartbroken by the fact that she pushed so hard to keep her family together she ended up losing all of them. She's lost everything.

I look back to the car. My whole life is inside that car. And I couldn't imagine losing any of it. Not one bit.

I push open the door to the butcher's and take my place in the queue. The line is winding its way along the back wall. I glance at the people waiting to be served, and it's then that I see Alexa.

She stands second from the front. Her back is to me, but I know it's her.

I close my eyes. I let my weight fall against the cold, tiled wall. For a second I think about ducking out to avoid her, but then what's the use? This is a small place. I'm going to run into her sooner or later.

The butcher's son is serving today. He's fifteen, a quiet lad. You tell him your name and he retrieves the turkeys from the cold store at the back.

He hands over a small package in wax paper to an elderly lady at the front and she passes him back a bottle of Johnnie Walker Black Label. 'For yer dad,' she says, and the boy takes it shyly. Tells her 'Thanks.'

Alexa moves up and clears her throat. 'Mrs Willard,' she tells him officiously. 'I've ordered a large, free-range Bronze.'

The lad blanches and averts his eyes. After what seems like an eternity, he stammers out, 'I'm sorry, but we don't have a turkey for you, Mrs Willard.'

'What do you mean?' she laughs. 'I ordered it in November. Of course you have it.'

He shakes his head. 'I've been told to tell you we don't have one.'

His distress is visible. He moves from one foot to the other. The shop goes deadly quiet as everyone watches. I straighten my spine. I can almost feel the rage building inside Alexa from here.

'Get me your father,' she snaps. 'I'm not accepting this.'

He nods, swallows and steps away. Seconds later, his mother, Kath, appears. She's a buxom woman with thick arms, a bloodied apron and a no-nonsense look on her face. She was in the year above me at school. We played senior hockey together. Me as right back, her as goalie.

'Mrs Willard,' she acknowledges without emotion.

'What's going on here?' Alexa demands. 'Your son tells me you've forgotten to place my order.'

'Not forgotten. Cancelled.'

'Cancelled? Why? I didn't authorize any cancellation.'

'No. I did.'

I shift over slightly so I can get a good look at Alexa in the mirror that runs behind the counter.

Her mouth is gaping open. 'I don't understand,' she says.

'Nothing *to* understand. I just cancelled it.'

'Because of what?'

'I'll explain,' the butcher's wife says, matter-of-fact, 'but, to be honest, I think you've got a bloody cheek coming in here. Showing your face after what you and that crackpot sister o' yours done to this community . . . Our husbands put their lives at risk searching for that young girl, out in that snow and ice. These shops lost *business* on account o' you – no folk wanting to come here and spend – and what when we're already struggling for trade. If I were you I'd think long and hard about moving. No one round here's going to want much to do with you—'

'But that wasn't me!' Alexa exclaims. 'I didn't have anything to do with what my sister did, I didn't know—'

'The word is *you did know*.'

'I didn't—' Alexa says. 'Honestly, I really didn't.'

Alexa looks around the shop helplessly, perhaps hoping someone will speak up at this injustice, but everyone looks away.

The butcher's wife wipes her hands on the dishcloth she has threaded through the belt of her apron. 'You'll have to excuse me,' she says, 'but I need to crack on. A lot to get through today.' But she stays standing right where she is.

Alexa turns on her heel, and we come face to face.

She glares at me for an extended moment and I watch as she thinks about yelling some abuse my way. But the eyes of the shop are upon her. She realizes this, and struts out.

When she's gone, the butcher's wife catches my attention. One quick nod in my direction and she returns to the back of the shop.

Five minutes later and I get out to the car, slinging the turkey into Joe's lap. 'Hang on to this,' I tell him, and turn around to look at the kids. Sam's in the middle, cheeks red and scaly from the cold; Sally's on one side; James is on the other. They're almost bursting they're so excited to get home.

'I just saw Alexa,' Joe says. 'She didn't look too happy.'

'She wouldn't,' I tell him, putting on my seat belt. 'They said they're not serving her. Told her to go and shop elsewhere.'

Joe is tickled pink by this.

'What?' I say to him.

'Nothing,' he replies, but he's smiling broadly.

As I put the car into gear he reaches forward and gives the curls on top of Bluey's head a quick ruffle. They've become almost inseparable since Joe came out of hospital on Wednesday.

I check my mirror and pull away, head off towards home just as the snow begins to fall again.

I glance at Joe.

You watch, he'll have the bloody dog sleeping on the end of our bed before the week's out.

Acknowledgements

I would like to thank the following:

My sister, Debbie Leatherbarrow, and friend, Zoë Lea, for their unwavering support, help and encouragement, right from the start. Thanks for *everything*.

My marvellous agent, Jane Gregory, and the team at Gregory and Co. – Claire Morris, Stephanie Glencross and Linden Sherriff.

My wonderfully skilled editor, Rachel Rayner, as well as Corinna Barsan, Nita Pronovost, Jenny Parrott, Kate Samano and Sarah Day.

Alison Barrow, Claire Ward and everyone at Transworld. Ste Lea, Katharine Langley-Hamel, Dr Jacqueline Christodoulou, D. Anderson, Tony and Babs Daly, Christine Long, Amanda Gregson, Jackie and Iain Garside, Paula Hemmings and Adrian Stewart. Everyone at We Should Be Writing and YouWriteOn. And all the lovely ladies at Windermere Library.

Above all, love and thanks to James, Grace, Harvey and Patrick. I am so lucky.

Acknowledgments